MURDER AT SPOUTERS POINT

A MIRANDA LEWIS MYSTERY

MURDER AT SPOUTERS POINT

LESLIE WHEELER

FIVE STAR
A part of Gale, Cengage Learning

Detroit • New York • San Francisco • New Haven, Conn • Waterville, Maine • London

GALE
CENGAGE Learning

LIBRARY OF CONGRESS CATALOGING-IN-PUBLICATION DATA

Wheeler, Leslie, 1945–
    Murder at Spouters Point : a Miranda Lewis mystery / Leslie
Wheeler. — 1st ed.
      p. cm.
    ISBN-13: 978-1-59414-886-6 (alk. paper)
    ISBN-10: 1-59414-886-4 (alk. paper)
    1. Women historians—Fiction. 2. Murder—Investigation—
Fiction. 3. Rhode Island—Fiction. I. Title.
PS3623.H44M88 2010
813'.6—dc22   2010025170

First Edition. First Printing: October 2010.
Published in 2010 in conjunction with Tekno Books and Ed Gorman.

Printed in the United States of America
1 2 3 4 5 6 7 14 13 12 11 10

ADDITIONAL COPYRIGHT INFORMATION

In memory of my husband, Robert A. Stein

ACKNOWLEDGMENTS

I wish to thank Nancy Spence, Bill Littell, and Toby Peltz for answering this landlubber's many questions about sailing; Nancy for helping me choreograph certain scenes, Bill for taking me out on his sailboat, and Toby for helping me fine-tune the final chapters that are set on board. Any mistakes are my own. I also want to thank Richard Laurino for sharing his knowledge of casino gambling with me, including the practice of back-betting.

Further thanks go to David Coffin, folk musician extraordinaire, for introducing me to the fascinating and tuneful world of sea music, and to Rick Spencer and other Mystic Seaport chanteymen for the same.

Once again, the members of my writers' critique group— Mark Ammons, Kathy Fast, Virginia Mackey, Cheryl Marceau, Andrea Peterson, and Barbara Ross—provided the suggestions and encouragement that helped make this a better book. I would also like to thank my editor, Alice Duncan, for her careful reading of the manuscript.

Last but not least, many thanks go to my late husband, Robert A. Stein, and our son, Nicholas L. Stein, for patiently accompanying me on my various research trips to maritime and other museums and to a Native American powwow. Without their love and support, this book might not have been written.

CHAPTER 1

". . . Pequod, you will no doubt remember, was the name of a celebrated tribe of Massachusetts Indians, now extinct as the ancient Medes."

—Moby-Dick

"Sure you don't want to part with your hard-earned change, Miranda?" Nate asked, as the Clambanks casino complex came into view. White, multistoried with turreted gold roofs, it rose out of the surrounding woods like a fairytale castle, beckoning with the promise of instant wealth. Nate glanced at me from behind his trademark reflector sunglasses, which he wore even though it was starting to get dark.

When I'd first met him, nearly a year ago, those glasses had made him appear sinister. Not anymore. I knew Nate wore them to protect eyes he'd damaged with chemicals to avoid the draft during the Vietnam War. I also knew the tenderness that could be in his brown-black gaze when he removed them.

"Not tonight." I laughed, half wishing I hadn't told him about my long-standing abhorrence of gambling. This abhorrence— probably the result of my Puritan ancestry—made me save the nickels our father had given my brother and me to play the slots on family trips through Nevada.

"Last chance," Nate said as we approached the entrance to Clambanks. We stopped at a light while departing traffic flowed past.

"If there were a race track nearby I might be tempted."

The light changed and Nate stepped on the gas. So did the driver of an exiting white stretch limo. The limo ran the red and hung a left in front of us. Nate slammed on the Jeep's brakes and wrenched the steering wheel to the right, just missing the limo. Nate's curse was lost in the blare of the Jeep's horn, but not the threat that followed: "Teach the bastard a lesson!"

The Jeep rocketed after the speeding limo. I gripped the door handle, stomach knotting as the speedometer shot upward. "Don't!"

This time Nate listened. He slowed and pulled to the side of the road while he cooled off.

"Thanks." I stroked his arm, feeling the tension in his muscles. A volatile man, given to sudden bursts of anger, Nate didn't suffer fools or reckless drivers gladly. His confrontational style had gotten him into trouble in the past. In his work with the American Indian Movement, he'd earned the dubious distinction of being "first to be arrested and last to be released." But lately, in response to my complaints about his road rage and abrasiveness in other situations, he'd been trying hard to curb his temper.

I was trying hard, too. This meant controlling my workaholism—the thing that bugged Nate most about me. He groused that whenever I had a deadline looming, I cut short our time together or canceled outright. Now, although I was behind on the chapter I was writing for the textbook, *America: The Republic's Glory and Greatness* (*ARGG* when I was annoyed or frustrated), I'd agreed to make this weekend trip with him. At the thought of my unfinished chapter, I felt a guilty twinge. Maybe we were trying *too* hard to make our relationship work.

"How much farther to Jimmy's?" I asked.

Nate's old friend, Jimmy Swift, was the main reason we'd come to this part of coastal Rhode Island. A member of the Dottaguck Nation, Jimmy worked in grounds maintenance at

Clambanks. In his other life, he was a champion fancy dancer. He was competing in this weekend's powwow, Seguan, the Dottaguck-sponsored late summer festival of song and dance.

"It's just up the road." Nate's scowl changed to a grin. "What's this about you and the race track?"

When we arrived at the modest, one-story house, the front- and backyards were filled with people come for the "feed" Jimmy and his family were hosting after the evening's events. Like Nate and me, many of the guests were dressed for the muggy late August weather in shorts and t-shirts. Others still wore their powwow outfits. They presented a colorful array of beadwork, feathers, and fringe. I hesitated before leaving the car.

With my fair skin and curly red hair, I felt out of place in this almost exclusively Native gathering. That wasn't the only reason for my bout of butterflies. I was meeting Jimmy and his family for the first time. I wanted things to go well—unlike get-togethers with some of Nate's other friends, especially the activist ones. Then, I felt like The Other, and sometimes even The Oppressor. I glanced at Nate, hoping for a few reassuring words. He frowned at two Indians in powwow outfits who stood on the edge of the crowd, having a heated exchange.

Nate left the car and hurried over to them. I trailed uncertainly after him. By the time I got there, one of the Indians had stalked off. Nate spoke with the Indian who remained, a lean, wiry man of medium height, wearing a beaded headband with dangling eagle feathers, a shell necklace over his bare chest, and a buckskin loincloth over leggings and moccasins. The man's shaved head threw into sharp relief well-formed features that, like his body, seemed in constant motion. His eyes darted here and there, his forehead furrowed and smoothed, as he gestured excitedly at the other man's departing figure.

"Said I couldn't keep the beat tonight, that I'm gonna lose

points. Even had the nerve to suggest I'd be better off in the Golden Age category. Just because I can't afford to travel the circuit like him."

"Calm down, bro," Nate said. "You know Russell's a jerk, so don't let him get to you."

"I'll show him I can still turn on the moves."

" 'Course you will. Hell, if I were a betting man, I'd put good money on your winning."

"Too bad you're not," the other man muttered, " 'cuz—" Noticing me, he broke off and said, "Oh, hi. You're . . . ?"

"Jimmy, this is Miranda," Nate introduced us. " 'Member I said I was bringing someone?"

"Right. So you're Nate's girlfriend. Pleased to meet you." We shook hands, then he looked around. "Where's Sammy?"

"It's his weekend with his mother," Nate fibbed. In fact, I'd asked him to switch weekends with his ex-wife so we could have some time alone.

"Too bad. We were all looking forward to seeing him again," Jimmy said. As the person responsible for Sam's absence, I felt a prick of guilt. "Reba! Patty!" Jimmy yelled. "C'mon over and say hello to Nate and his girlfriend. Bring Kyle, too."

A teenage girl, wearing a dress covered with what looked like silver bells, left a long table piled with food and walked toward us. She was joined by an older woman pushing a wheelchair that contained a boy's twisted figure. The boy wore an outfit like his father's, but his head was tipped oddly to one side, his shoulders hunched almost to his ears, and his spindly legs turned in the opposite direction from his head. He peered at us through thick glasses.

Nate had prepared me for the fact that Kyle suffered from multiple disabilities—he couldn't walk or talk. Still, I was taken aback by the sight of the boy, the contrast between him and his athletic father was so marked. I worried my dismay showed on my face—that I was staring too much. Nate had advised me to look at Kyle directly and, above all, not avert my eyes.

As they approached, Kyle made short, barking noises, and held out spidery arms. Nate bent and gave him a big hug. "This is Miranda, Kyle," Nate said when the boy finally let go. Kyle made more noises and fastened his arms around my neck. He clung to me until I began to feel uncomfortable.

Finally, his mother said, "That's enough, sweetie. Hi, I'm Reba." A big woman with a friendly smile, Reba had darker skin and broader features than her husband. A fringe of black, curly hair broke like a wave over her forehead, extending almost to the rim of her black-framed glasses. After we shook hands, she asked the same question as her husband: "Where's Sammy?"

"With his mother," Jimmy answered for Nate.

Reba looked disappointed, and I felt another prick of guilt. "Well, it's good you two could make it," she said. "Is this your first powwow, Miranda?"

"I went to one in Harvard Yard a while ago."

"They have powwows at Harvard?" Jimmy sounded skeptical.

"It was very small."

"Seguan's big," Reba said. "It's one of the largest powwows east of the Mississippi."

"One of the richest, too, with over a million in prize money," Jimmy added proudly, "thanks to the new buffalo."

I knew he meant casino gambling. I glanced at Nate, wondering if he envied the Dottagucks their success after all the years his tribe, the Wampanoags, had tried unsuccessfully to get their own casino. But his expression remained unchanged.

"We've been fortunate," Reba said.

"You and the Assawogs," I remarked. "I saw signs for their casino as we were driving here."

Nate's cough and the strained silence that followed told me I'd committed a blunder. "Did I say something wrong?" I asked when nobody volunteered to enlighten me.

"The Dottagucks and the Assawogs aren't exactly friends," Nate said.

"Friends!" Jimmy roared. "After what they did to us, they're among our worst enemies."

"What did they do?" I thought he must be referring to some recent trouble.

"Oh, nothing much. Just burned down our stronghold at Mawnaucoi and massacred five hundred innocent women, children and old people. Then they hunted down the survivors and either killed them or sold them into slavery. With a lot of help from the English, of course."

I felt the jab at my ancestors, but my historian's curiosity made me press for details. "When did this happen?"

"Almost four hundred years ago. 1643, to be exact," Reba said. "There's much more about our history at the Dottaguck Museum of History and Culture. I work there, and I'd be happy to give you a private tour."

"I'd love that," I gushed, eager to make amends for both the atrocity my ancestors had committed and my ignorance of it. "But I won't have time this trip between the powwow, visiting my friends at the Spouters Point Maritime Museum, and—" I stopped at a cautionary signal from Nate. I was explaining too much. The Swifts didn't need to know our entire weekend itinerary. And why had I said *my* friends, as if Nate's friends and mine were mutually exclusive, though, in truth, they were.

"Another time," Reba replied.

"Yes." I'd struck out with Jimmy and Reba. In desperation, I turned to Patty. "That's an interesting dress you're wearing with all those silver bells."

"We call them jingles, and they're made out of old tin cans instead of silver," Patty said. "But thanks, anyway."

Another gaffe. I should've realized silver would've been much too expensive. "They're lovely. And so is the beadwork on your dress, especially those white flowers with red centers. What kind of flowers are they?"

"Rhododendrons."

"Really? I've never seen rhododendrons like that."

Patty exchanged glances with her mother and father. "The wild rhododendrons in Big Otter Swamp look this way. During the Dottaguck War my dad was telling you about, the swamp was a place of refuge for our people. The flowers' centers turned red with their blood."

"Oh . . . I see." And I did. I saw that for them the landscape was covered with blood, that even these beautiful beaded flowers served as a grim reminder of their past. I'd entered a world where I needed to tread carefully. Otherwise, I risked reopening old wounds and further alienating Nate's friends. As I cast about for a safe topic, I felt something brush against the back of my bare arm.

Looking over my shoulder, I gasped. The Indian who'd been arguing with Jimmy earlier stood directly behind me. Seen from a distance, he'd cut an exotic figure with his painted face and powwow regalia. Up close, though, he was terrifying. His forehead, nose, and part of his cheeks and chin were painted a stark white, while his mouth and the rest of his face were a dark red. Black rectangles outlined his eyes, adding to his menacing appearance.

"What's up now, Russell?" Jimmy demanded.

"Just wanted to say hello to Nate." Russell stepped out from behind me.

"Hello, Russell," Nate said tightly.

"She with you?" Russell jerked his head in my direction.

"That's right. Miranda, this is Russell Long Knife."

Russell's red lips curled upward in a nasty smile. "Well, well. Never thought I'd see the day when a top activist would shack up with a white woman. But things change, I guess."

My face went hot with anger and embarrassment. Nate squared his chest and rocked forward on the balls of his feet. "Get lost, Russell."

"I'm going." Russell waved a feathered stick at Nate. "But first a final word of advice for your friend." He jabbed the stick at Jimmy. "You want that prize money bad, don't you? Need it, too." He stared pointedly at Kyle, who shrank deeper into his wheelchair. "So wise up and switch to the Golden Age category. Or compete in traditional instead of fancy dance. 'Cuz you haven't got a prayer in hell of beating me." He whirled around, executed a fast split, and disappeared into the crowd.

"Asshole!" Jimmy spun around and aimed a kick in Russell's direction.

Reba and I exchanged glances. She heaved a sigh. *Men and their macho posturing,* she seemed to say. Aloud she said, "Now that's over, maybe you and Nate would like something to eat?"

"Yes, yes," Jimmy cried, grabbing Nate and me by the arm. "C'mon over to the food table and help yourselves. We've got burgers, fried chicken, green salad, potato salad, corn on the cob, beans, fry bread, berry soup, and plenty of cold beer."

The food and beer helped relieve the awkwardness of that first meeting with the Swifts. Still, as Nate and I drove toward the Native-owned inn where we were spending the night, I was glad I'd be with my friends for part of the weekend.

Erin Meloy and I had met several years ago at the Northeast Regional Social Studies Convention, where she was staffing the booth of the Spouters Point Maritime Museum, which was laid out in the form of a nineteenth-century seaport village, complete with wharves, replica ships, and various buildings. We'd quickly become fast friends, and I'd been embraced by her close-knit family: two brothers and their wives and kids. In their company

I could relax and be myself without having to think twice before I opened my mouth.

An ambulance shrieked toward us, jolting me from these musings. Nate pulled over to let it pass. In the flashing red light, he looked different—not terrifying like Russell Long Knife with his war paint—but alien all the same.

CHAPTER 2

*". . . whenever I find myself involuntarily pausing before coffin
warehouses, and bringing up the rear of every funeral I meet . . .
then, I account it high time to get to sea as soon as I can."*
—Moby-Dick

Erin Meloy was demonstrating how to harpoon a whale when I
arrived at the Spouters Point Maritime Museum the next morning. I joined a small knot of visitors on the wharf to watch. Erin
stood in the bow of a whaleboat, brandishing a long, narrow
piece of iron with a wicked-looking point at the end. Behind her
loomed the *Susan Kilrain,* a replica wooden whaling ship. With
her short, blunt-cut light brown hair and slim hips, Erin could
have passed for one of the teenage boys who'd signed on as seamen on nineteenth-century whaling ships. Only her clothes
didn't fit the part: the khaki shorts and sea-green, short-sleeved
polo shirt that were the warm weather uniform of the Spouters
Point Museum staff.

"Yankee whale men didn't board the whale like Native
Americans did," Erin said. "They just tried to get the boat as
close as possible—no mean feat. Whales have poor vision, but
their hearing is acute. They learned to associate the creak of
oars in the locks with trouble.

"The whale felt the harpoon like a bee sting in its side, but
that was enough to get it going on the so-called Nantucket
Sleigh Ride. This chase could last as long as two hours with the

20

whale pulling the boat at speeds up to twenty miles an hour. Or the whale might dive below the surface. If it came up underneath the boat—as whales had a nasty habit of doing—the boat was destroyed and the men thrown—"

The whaleboat rocked as her oldest brother, Luke, standing in the rear, began to move forward. Tall, with the lean, muscular build of an athlete, Luke had the same light brown hair, blue eyes, and regular features as his sister.

"Into the sea," Erin finished, frowning at the disturbance. She turned and made her way to the back. As she passed Luke, their arms brushed. Erin gave him a little shove. He glared at her and seemed about to shove back. Instead, he continued to the bow.

The jostling surprised me. Ordinarily, brother and sister got along well. Something must be up.

"The harpooner didn't kill the whale," Luke explained. "When the moment arrived, he switched places with the officer on board, who seized the killing lance." He held up a second piece of iron. "As you can see, the killing lance has a longer shaft than the harpoon. But it still couldn't reach the whale's brain. So the mate aimed for the whale's lungs. If he hit the mark, the whale's frothy spout changed from white to pink to the red of 'a chimney on fire,' as whale men called it."

Luke went on to describe the whale's agony—how it thrashed wildly, blood spurting over the men in the boat, until it turned upside down and lay still. This was the signal it was dead and could be towed back to the ship. "But just to be sure," Luke said, "the mate probed the whale's eyeball with the killing lance." He gave the lance a sharp twist in the air.

"Ugh," a woman standing next to me said. I agreed. Although I'd seen this demonstration many times before, I was still repelled by the imagined gore.

The presentation over, Erin, Luke and the four other

members of the squad rowed back to the *Susan Kilrain.* Minutes later, Erin joined me on the wharf. "It's great to see you, Miranda," she said as she hugged me.

"You, too."

"How's the powwow?" Erin asked on the way to the Quarterdeck Cafe.

"I haven't been yet. We arrived too late last night, and The Grand Entry doesn't start till noon today. I feel a bit awkward around Nate's friends, so I'm glad for the break. Will your new boyfriend be joining us?"

Erin shook her head. "George needed to take care of something. You'll meet him tomorrow evening."

"I'm looking forward to it. He sounds like a terrific guy from everything you've told me."

"He is," Erin said eagerly. Her expression changed, and she sighed. "I just wish Luke thought so."

"Luke doesn't care for him?"

"No."

"Why?"

"I'll explain over lunch."

We went into the Quarterdeck Cafe, ordered seafood wraps and fresh-squeezed lemonade, and brought our meals to a picnic table outside. After we'd taken a few bites, Erin said, "Luke thinks George is too old for me, and he doesn't like it that George has been married before."

If Erin had been in her teens instead of her mid-thirties, Luke's objections might have made sense. "That's all?"

Erin nodded. "Frankly, I don't think Luke would approve of anyone I fell for."

"Still playing the overly protective older brother?"

"That's right. He wishes I still lived with him and his family instead of having my own apartment."

I shook my head sympathetically. Over-protectiveness on the

part of parents or older siblings was a problem in my own family. It was one of the things Erin and I had in common. In Erin's case, however, her brother's hyper-concern seemed more justified, given the losses she'd suffered. Her parents had been killed in a car crash when she was eleven, and several years later, someone else close to her had died.

"I also think Luke would rather I continue to mourn Tom, and not hook up with anybody else," Erin said.

Tom had been Luke's best friend in high school, Erin's boyfriend, and the man she might have eventually married if he hadn't died from a pulmonary embolism on the football field.

"And that's probably what I'd do if I hadn't met George."

"Give Luke time. He'll come round. How long since you and George started seeing each other?"

"A little less than a month." Erin's face assumed the dreamy expression of the newly smitten. "Thank heaven Quint was sick that day," she murmured.

"Who?"

"Remember I told you George and I met at the Melville Marathon?" The Melville Marathon was an annual event at the Spouters Point Museum. Every year, on July 29, the anniversary of Melville's birthday, the museum organized a reading of the entire novel. The event began at noon when an actor dressed up as Melville read the first chapter. It continued until noon the following day with different volunteers reading sections of the book.

"Quint Doolin's the actor who plays Melville," Erin explained. "If he hadn't gotten sick at the last minute, George and I might've never met. I know the first chapter by heart, so I was going to fill in for Quint, but then this man in the audience came forward and recited the opening lines: 'Call me Ishmael. . . .' George made a much better Melville than me. Speaking of Melville, have you finished *Moby-Dick* yet?"

At Erin's urging, I'd tackled that behemoth of a book, but with little success. "It's been slow going. Maybe I should just come to next summer's marathon and hear it read."

"That's cheating," Erin protested.

I shrugged. "Seems like a painless way to get it done. About tomorrow night—anyone coming besides you, me, George, and Nate?"

"Flo and Vernon Higginbotham. They're a retired couple George is friendly with. Their sailboat is docked next to his at the wharf. And my brothers and their wives."

"You think that's a good idea, considering how Luke disapproves of George?"

"I'm hoping that if Luke sees that other people—you especially—appreciate George, he'll change his mind."

"You want me to be . . . a cheerleader for George?"

"If you don't mind."

"Not at all. I'll get out the pom-poms and brush up on my routines."

We both laughed. I wasn't the rah-rah type, and although I could walk and chew gum at the same time, coordinating leg and arm movements was another matter.

Erin's expression turned serious. She gave my arm an affectionate squeeze. "Thanks, Miranda." We chatted until it was time for her to go back to work. "See you tomorrow night," she called over her shoulder as she hurried in the direction of the *Susan Kilrain*.

Tomorrow night. Suddenly, the evening wasn't shaping up to be the relaxed get-together I'd expected. What if Luke's dislike of George boiled over into an ugly scene? What if I discovered I didn't care for him myself? I'd feel awkward pretending otherwise. As for Nate, he'd get along fine with unpretentious Erin and her brothers. But with the other couple and George, he'd be thrown into the world of wealthy yacht people, a world

I wasn't so comfortable with myself. If I felt ill at ease with them, Nate would feel even more of an outsider.

Mandolin music wafted across the village green from the bandstand. I recognized the rich baritone belonging to Erin's other brother, Mark. He was singing a song about a young maiden. I strolled over to say hello, and get his take on the situation with Erin, Luke, and George.

"Hey, Miranda." He put down his instrument.

"Hey, yourself."

Of Erin's two brothers, I'd always preferred Mark. Pudgy and pony-tailed, he was more laid-back musician than gung-ho sailor. And while I liked Luke, his take-charge attitude reminded me too much of my own bossy older brother at times.

"What's that song you were just singing?" I asked.

" 'The Maid on the Shore'."

"Nice."

"Thanks."

"So," I said after a moment, "things seem kind of tense between Erin and Luke right now."

"Luke's not thrilled with her new boyfriend."

"That's what she said. What do you think of him?"

Mark tugged on the albatross earring dangling from his left lobe. "He's okay. The main thing is that she's happy."

Go with the flow and don't look for trouble where it doesn't exist. That was Mark all over.

"Too bad Luke doesn't feel that way."

Mark shrugged. "He'll get over it." Mark's eyes were the pale blue of a summer pond, his gaze placid, except for every once in a while when something swam to the surface. As it did now. "What about you? Are you happy?" he asked suddenly.

"Why do you ask?" The question caught me off guard.

"You've got a new boyfriend, too."

"Of course. What a silly question." Even to my own ears, I

sounded defensive.

"That's good because she isn't."

"Who?"

"The maid in the song. Listen and you'll see what I mean." Mark played his mandolin and sang:

"There is a young maiden; she lives all alone. She lives all alone on the shore,-o
There's nothing she can find to comfort her mind, but to roam all alone on the shore, shore, shore. But to roam all alone on the shore."

He paused, taking a breath between stanzas. In the distance a dog yapped. "One of yours?" I teased.

Mark had a habit of feeding stray animals. Sometimes he even brought them home, much to the dismay of his wife, who complained that if she'd known she'd be running an animal shelter, she might not have married him. Mark did the same with stray people, with the difference that he gave them money and usually didn't try to bring them home.

"Nope," he said. "Belongs to a couple docked at the wharf. Spoiled brat poodles aren't my thing, anyway."

"Mine either." We talked a bit more; then it was time for me to leave. As I walked across the village green toward the museum entrance, Mark repeated the opening verse:

"There's nothing she can find to comfort her mind, but to roam. all alone on the shore, shore, shore. But to roam all alone on the shore."

There's nothing she can find to comfort her mind, but to roam all alone on the shore.

The plaintive, haunting lyrics echoed in my mind throughout the drive back until replaced by a different kind of music: the loud drumming and—to my unaccustomed ears—strange chanting of Native music.

CHAPTER 3

"I wished I had ten thousand pound,
I'd sail my ship for miles around."
—Lowlands Away, Sea Shanty

"Ready for a break?" Nate asked.

You bet I was. I'd arrived at the powwow in time to catch the tail end of the Golden Age category, in which senior men and women performed the various dances in separate contests. This was followed by the Junior category—boys and girls up to the age of twelve. I loved watching the kids. Some of them were so small they must've started dancing as soon as they learned to walk. Next came the teenagers, including the Swifts' daughter Patty, who competed in the jingle dress dance contest. The more I watched, the more I was able to distinguish the different styles of dancing, which ranged from slow and stately for traditional to frenetic for fancy dances.

Now, though, it was early evening, and hours of sitting on a hard metal grandstand had taken their toll. My rear end was sore, my legs were stiff, and my back ached from the lack of support. Even worse, the tented pavilion felt like a giant sweat lodge filled with steaming bodies. Around me, people fanned themselves with pieces of regalia, used small portable fans, and sprayed themselves with water from squirt bottles.

"Go ahead," urged Reba, seated on my other side along with Patty. "There's plenty of time before the men's fancy dance."

"Want us to bring you anything?" I said.

"We're good." Reba went back to crunching on an ice cube, her way of cooling off.

Outside, I noticed a booth selling Native beadwork. "Mind if I have a look here while you do the food stands?"

"Nope. What would you like?" Nate asked.

"A cold drink would be great."

"That's all?

I nodded.

"Back in five then." He headed off, a big, good-looking man wearing shorts, a Native Pride t-shirt, reflector sunglasses, and a backwards baseball hat. I felt a wave of fondness coupled with desire, remembering last night's lovemaking. I examined the beadwork. There were some attractive pieces but nothing as striking as the floral beadwork on Patty's jingle dress.

"You like Indian beadwork as well as Indian cock?"

I dropped the necklace I was holding and spun around. Russell Long Knife leered at me from behind red, yellow, and black face paint. Anger rose in my gorge. "Can't you open your mouth without being offensive?"

"Touchy, aren't you? Goes with the territory—the red hair, I mean."

"Get lost."

"Answer the question."

As I searched for a suitable retort, a barking noise caught my attention. It sounded like Kyle. I looked around, but saw no sign of him. "Figure it out for yourself," I snapped, brushing past Russell.

The cries continued. I followed them to the far end of the concession area. Kyle sat alone in his wheelchair, thin body twisted away from me like a plant straining toward the light. Despite the bright feathers of his powwow outfit, he looked rumpled and forlorn. I started toward him. Jimmy appeared out of nowhere. He ran over to Kyle and shook a scolding finger in the boy's face. "I told you not to—oh, hi, Miranda. I left something in the car and had to go back. Thought Kyle would be all right by himself. Where's Nate?"

"Getting a snack." Jimmy's outburst at his son surprised me, but I chalked it up to nervousness over the upcoming contest.

He shifted his weight from one moccasinned foot to the other. "I better get Kyle resettled with his mother and sister."

"Okay. Get a good rest?" Jimmy had taken Kyle back to the house in the late afternoon, so they could rest up for the evening contests.

"Yup, and now I'm raring to go again." Jimmy danced toward the pavilion, pushing Kyle ahead of him.

I returned to the beadwork booth, where Nate was waiting. He held a big cardboard tray of food and drink. There were two buffalo burgers, two orders of curly fries, and a couple of pieces of fry bread topped with strawberries and whipped cream.

"That's a lot of food," I commented as we sat at an outdoor table.

"I got extra in case you changed your mind," he replied sheepishly.

"Nate," I began, shaking my head.

"I know, I know. I heard those jokes, too."

During a lull in the afternoon contests, the master of ceremonies had amused the largely Native audience with weight-loss jokes: "It's time to lose weight when you can't see your moccasin strings," and "It's time to lose weight when you're sitting down, and then you stand up, and it looks like you're still sitting down." I'd also noticed that the Tribal Health Services had set up a booth, offering to do body fat analyses and check people's blood pressure.

"But a powwow wouldn't be a powwow without all this great food," Nate said. "I'll get back on the machines come Monday.

Have a strawberry." He held out a piece of red fruit with its white cap of cream.

It was sweet and juicy. I licked my lips and let Nate feed me another. And another. A slight breeze brought relief from the heat, which, even outdoors, was oppressive. Thunder rumbled in the distance. "Will they stop the powwow if there's a storm?"

"Probably not. They've covered the electrical cables going into the pavilion with dirt and wood chips. Besides, the thunderstorm may not even hit here. If it does, you stick close to me." He slipped an arm through mine.

It was nearly ten o'clock when they announced the last contest of the evening, the men's northern fancy dance. By then, the crowd had thinned somewhat, driven away by the heat and the threat of a thunderstorm, which, fortunately, bypassed us. When the dance was called, Jimmy rose abruptly, accidentally knocking over the drink I'd put down by my feet.

"Good luck, bro!" Nate reached across me to high-five Jimmy.

"Thanks." Jimmy smiled, but I could see the strain in his face. He'd acted tense during the preceding dances, jiggling a leg or tapping a foot, while his upper body bobbed up and down in time to the music—so much that the metal bench shook with his movements. Occasionally, I noticed him muttering to himself but couldn't make out what he was saying over the drumming and chanting. Just watching him put me on edge. I had to remind myself that I'd be nervous, too, if I had as much riding on tonight's contest as Russell Long Knife claimed Jimmy did.

Jimmy joined the other dancers in their colorful, heavily feathered regalia on the floor. Armed with clipboards, the judges took their places on either side of them, while the emcee issued final instructions. "Remember to judge by talent, ability, and style, rather than by name. And dancers, keep a distance from each other, so the judges can see you."

A pair of legs rubbed against my back, as someone took a seat behind me. I leaned forward with anticipation. Kyle cried out and gestured excitedly at his father. "Pipe down, kid," a man behind us grumbled. He rapped Kyle's shoulder with his rolled-up program.

"What the hell do you think you're doing?" Nate turned to glare at the man. I turned, too. He was dressed in suburban casual: pink polo shirt, white boat shoes, and navy pants with white poodles embroidered on them. I'd seen pants with whales and even hunting dogs on them, but never poodles. He must have special-ordered them. His face was deeply tanned, and his silver hair slicked back in a receding tide from his forehead. He didn't respond to Nate. Instead, his mouth remained compressed in a thin, cruel line. He held his rolled-up program in readiness for another strike.

"Hey! I asked you a question," Nate growled and stood.

"Nate." I placed a cautionary hand on his arm.

"The music's starting," Reba said.

Drumbeats filled the air, accompanied by "ya-yas," "hey-heys," and "lay-lays" of Indian singing. Nate sat down. I heaved a sigh of relief that he'd managed to control his temper. We trained our binoculars on the dance floor. I focused on Jimmy as he spun, pivoted, backpedaled and executed splits. I thought he looked terrific. But I wanted Nate's opinion. "How does Jimmy look to you?" I whispered.

"At the top of his form," Nate whispered back. "But so's Russell."

My gaze shifted to Russell Long Knife. He looked terrific also, I thought grudgingly. Remembering his crude remark to me earlier, I half wished he'd stumble and fall. A misstep now would serve him right.

Yet as the dance progressed, Russell's movements became

faster and even more spectacular, while Jimmy slowed and demonstrated less flair. "C'mon, man," Nate urged quietly.

Jimmy did his best, but neither he nor any of the other dancers was a match for Russell. The audience loved him, judging from the shouts and bursts of applause that greeted each feat of agility.

Around and around he went—a dizzying swirl of red-and-yellow with his head bobbing, feathered dance sticks shaking in his hands, feet barely touching the ground. I couldn't take my eyes off him. Whatever else I thought of Russell Long Knife, he was a superb dancer.

Faster, faster. The drumming reached a frenzied crescendo. Then abruptly it stopped.

Russell dropped to the ground in a perfectly timed split. He flung his arms outward. "Yeah!" The next instant, one of his feathered dance sticks flew through the air, landing in the dirt. Kyle made barking noises and pointed at the fallen stick. Around me, people gaped, muttered, and shook their heads, Nate included. The judges were shaking their heads, too.

"Ladies and gentlemen, let's give our northern fancy dancers a big hand," the emcee said after a beat. "And thanks to the Gray Wolf Singers for their wonderful music."

There was a scattering of applause, but mostly people went on muttering and shaking their heads in disbelief. Russell got up and began arguing with the judges.

"What's the matter?" I asked Nate.

"No part of a dancer's regalia is supposed to touch the ground. If it does, he or she's in trouble. Russell will lose points for sure, and might even be disqualified from this session."

"Really? Then maybe Jimmy—"

A rolled-up program exploded in my lap. The man behind us left the stands in a rage.

CHAPTER 4

"At sun-rise this man went from his hammock to his mast-head at the fore; and whether it was that he was not yet half waked . . . he had not been long at his perch, when a cry was heard—a cry and a rushing—and looking up, they saw a falling phantom in the air; and looking down, a little tossed heap of white bubbles in the blue of the sea."

—Moby-Dick

A late afternoon calm had settled over the Spouters Point Museum when I arrived the next day. On the village green, mute swans posed gracefully by the bandstand, which had earlier resounded with the lively music of sea shanties. Now it was quiet, the only sounds the occasional flap of canvas sails in the breeze, the clip-clop of hooves, and the jingle of bells, as a horse-drawn carriage made its last tour of the village.

The museum's peacefulness contrasted with the storm I'd just left—a storm that erupted following the announcement Jimmy had won the fancy dance contest. As Nate predicted, Russell had been disqualified the night before, and Jimmy's superior performance in the final session this morning earned him the necessary points. Russell angrily disputed Jimmy's victory: "Winner, my arse! Somebody messed with my dance stick. Put some stuff on it that made it burn in my hands until I couldn't stand it anymore, and I dropped the damn thing."

"You're crazy," Jimmy shot back. "I won fair and square.

You're just a sore loser."

"Liar and cheat!"

Amid a flurry of charges and counter-charges, I'd excused myself to help Erin prepare for tonight's dinner party. As I came out onto the wharf and the masts of the *Susan Kilrain* rose grandly above me, I tried to put the whole ugly scene out of my mind.

But what were those two young guys doing at the foot of a mast? Surely, they weren't going to climb it. My stomach flip-flopped as I realized this was precisely what they were attempting. At least one of them was. He moved nimbly up, while the other lagged behind, carefully testing each foothold before continuing. Terrified of heights myself, I could imagine his fear. Just watching was nerve-wracking.

"C'mon, Winston, you can do it!" Erin called from the deck, where she stood with a small group of young people. Winston, the laggard, kept at his painfully slow pace. His companion, meanwhile, had reached the first platform on the main mast. He swung dizzyingly outward with nothing to support his back, then brought himself in again to clear the platform. Refastening his safety line to the rigging, he climbed out onto a crosspiece of the mast. He straddled it, bent at the waist.

Spurred—or more likely, shamed—by his companion's success, Winston unfastened his safety line and extended a leg upward. A boat horn blasted in the harbor. Startled by the noise, Winston lost his foothold. His legs dangled helplessly in the air, while he clung to the rigging with one hand. I held my breath in anticipation of the sickening thud of his fall.

"Swing yourself back onto the rigging!" Erin cried.

Winston didn't move.

"Go for it!" Erin yelled.

Winston's body remained limp as a hanged man's.

"Hold on then, I'm coming up."

Erin scrambled up the rigging. She grabbed his feet and planted them on a rung. Winston hugged the rigging, face and body pressed so tightly into the rope it probably left marks on his skin. Finally, Erin coaxed him to lower one foot, then the other. The descent was even slower than the ascent. Winston stopped on each rung and had to be reassured by Erin, who stayed just a rung or two below him, before he would continue.

"Isn't she something?" said a man holding two large grocery bags who'd stopped to watch. "I certainly don't have the patience to coddle a scared college kid who—"

"College kid?" I said.

"He's a student from Gellis College who's doing an internship here. Big mistake, because he obviously isn't cut out to be a sailor." Shading his eyes against the sun, he squinted at me. "You wouldn't happen to be Miranda, would you?"

I nodded.

"George Kavanagh. Thought I recognized you from Erin's description. I'm pleased to meet you." He put down a grocery bag to shake hands.

So this was Kavanagh, the sailor and Melville enthusiast, who'd managed to sweep Erin off her feet in less than a month. He was a handsome man a bit past his prime. I noticed a thickening around his middle, traces of gray in his brown hair, and a spider web of lines fanning out from startlingly blue eyes. I could see why Erin was attracted to him, but also why Luke was wary. Kavanagh looked to be in his fifties, which made him at least fifteen years older than Erin.

He glanced around. "Erin said you were bringing your boyfriend."

"He'll be along in time for dinner."

"Great. The more the merrier. Now, if you'll excuse me, I better hustle over to the galley and don my chef's hat. Cocktails are at five, and don't be late!" He gave my hand a final pump, picked up the other shopping bag, and strode briskly toward the pier where his boat, a graceful, thirty-nine-foot sloop, was moored.

Minutes later, Erin and the group of students left the *Kilrain*. "Okay, guys, that's it for today. Good work on the mast, Rick," Erin told the student who'd made the climb successfully. "You, too, Winston. You'll make it up tomorrow."

Winston didn't reply. An Asian-American youth with skinny arms and legs and a flabby middle, he lacked an athlete's build. Still, he had nice features and would have been good-looking but for his sullen expression. While the other students scattered, he remained behind.

Sensing he needed cheering up, Erin said, "I mean it, Winston. You'll do fine. Should've seen me the first time I went aloft on the *Kilrain*. Nearly lost my lun—"

"Stop coddling me!" Winston broke in. "I'm not cut out to be a sailor and you know it!" His words echoed Kavanagh's so closely, I was almost sure Winston had overheard him.

"Winston." Erin held out a calming hand.

"Leave me alone!" He swatted her hand away and stormed off.

Erin turned to me and shook her head. "Poor kid. He's a misfit both here and at his school."

"How come?"

"I don't think he'd ever been on any kind of boat before he started this program. He's a city kid from Cambridge. His parents are recent Korean immigrants who run a restaurant there. So he's out of place at a small, rural college like Gellis."

"How did he wind up there in the first place?"

"Bad advice from his high school guidance counselor, who knew of a scholarship at Gellis Winston he would qualify for."

"I wonder why he chose maritime studies."

"Beats me, unless he read Conrad and Melville in high school."

"Speaking of Melville, I met George Kavanagh while you were busy with the students."

"You did!" Erin's eyes lit up. "What do you think? Isn't he just—?"

"We only spoke briefly, but he seemed very nice." I decided not to mention Kavanagh's putdown of Winston.

"I'm so glad you like him because—" She broke off as Luke strode toward us with a grim expression.

"Miranda." Luke greeted me curtly without his customary friendliness. Turning to Erin, he said, "I need to have a word with you—in private."

"But . . ." Erin glanced from Luke to me.

"I'll wait for you," I said.

"This won't take long," Luke assured us.

They went back onto the *Kilrain*, disappearing below deck. Five minutes passed. Glancing over at the sloop, I saw Kavanagh come out on deck with a tray. He deposited its contents on a long table with chairs that had been set up on the dock beside his boat, and went below again. More time passed. Kavanagh made several additional trips, but Erin and Luke didn't reappear.

I heard yapping sounds. A woman and a small white dog appeared on the deck of the sailboat moored next to Kavanagh's. The woman called out something to Kavanagh, who had come back on deck. I caught the words, "Onion dip . . . Happy . . . Erin?" Kavanagh glanced toward the *Kilrain*, saw me, and waved. I waved back. What to do? Explain that Erin was in a huddle with Luke, and we'd be along shortly? It was quarter past five. We were late, but then so were Erin's brothers and their families. Nate, too. The next moment, I saw him walking briskly toward the wharf.

"Sorry I'm late." He gave me a quick buss on the cheek, his expression glum.

"Is Russell still making trouble?" I asked.

Nate nodded. "He's holding fast to his story about the dance stick burning in his hand, and making him drop it. But with the stick gone missing—"

"What do you mean the stick's missing?"

"Someone must've made off with it after Russell dropped it, because they can't find it anywhere."

"Odd."

"Right, and without the stick there's no way to prove or disprove Russell's claim."

"Too bad. Something's going on here, too."

"What?"

"I'm not sure yet, but Luke and Erin went onto the *Kilrain* to talk privately a while ago, and they haven't come out yet."

"There's a guy on deck now," Nate said. "Is that Luke?"

It was Luke all right, looking even more grim than before. He left the boat and walked past without so much as a glance at us. He would have bypassed his brother and the two Meloy wives who were headed in our direction, the women carrying covered dishes, if Mark hadn't grabbed him by the arm and pulled him aside. They conferred briefly, then Luke continued on his way, and Mark returned to the women. They seemed uncertain whether to proceed, but finally they came over to us with Mark leading the way.

After I'd introduced Nate to them, Mark said, "Erin's still on board?"

"Yes. What's going on between her and Luke?"

Mark shook his head as if to say, "Not now."

"Do you think we should go over there?" Luke's wife, Maggie, motioned toward the dock where Kavanagh and the woman with the dog stood talking with drinks in hand.

"No, we'll wait for Erin," Mark said.

We waited and waited. Mark began to hum softly. From past experience I knew he did this in situations where he felt uncomfortable. Maggie and Mark's wife Jane both looked nervous. I felt awkward in the extreme. Erin was a no-show, and Kavanagh kept gazing in our direction, no doubt wondering what the reason for the delay was.

"I'll go see if I can get Erin to come out," I said.

I went on board and descended a narrow, winding staircase to the captain's quarters, the only place below deck where I could still stand upright. There was a table in the middle with bunks on either side. Not seeing Erin, I passed into the blubber room on the same level but with a lower ceiling, which meant that I had to stoop to keep from bumping my head. In the heyday of whaling ships like the *Kilrain,* this room would have been a beehive of activity, for here the whale fat was cut into large pieces, minced, then burned in tubs until it was rendered. Now, the blubber room was quiet and empty.

Reluctantly, I climbed down a steep ladder into the hold, where the barrels of precious oil had been stored. A wooden platform overlooked the stacks of bricks that had replaced the barrels. Above me, a piece of rope with a frayed end dangled in the breeze. I knew the rope had probably been used to lower barrels into the hold. Still, a tremor passed through me because of its resemblance to a hangman's rope. Erin wouldn't have . . . but where on earth was she? I scanned the vast, dimly lit space until I spotted her, crouched on the bricks in a shadowy corner. Lowering myself down, I walked carefully over to her. "What're you doing here? What's the matter?"

She turned a tear-stained face toward me. "Luke," she said between clenched teeth. "He's determined to wreck things between George and me. And this time, he's gone too far." She began to cry.

"Erin, I'm so sorry." I slipped an arm around her and she sobbed onto my shoulder. "Want to tell me what he said?" I asked after she'd calmed down a bit.

Erin hesitated. "It's too upsetting. A pack of lies also."

Naturally, this piqued my curiosity all the more. Did Kavanagh have a wife and family elsewhere? Was he a jailbird or a suspected killer? My hyperactive imagination was only too ready to fill in the blanks. "What do you want me to do? Mark, Jane and Maggie are here, and so's Nate. They don't want to go over to George's boat without you. Shall I tell them you're not feeling well and—"

"No! That's exactly what Luke hopes will happen. Why else would he badmouth George right before the party? I'm not going to let him ruin tonight. Have you got a tissue?"

I gave her one and she used it to wipe her face, then blow her nose. "Do I still look like I've been crying?"

"A little."

"Then please come with me to the bathroom while I wash up."

We left the *Kilrain,* explained to Mark and company that we were going to freshen up, and headed to the public restrooms. There, Erin doused her face with cold water, patting it dry with a paper towel. "How do I look now?"

"Better."

"Then I'm ready to face the world." She forced a smile.

Rejoining Mark, Jane, Maggie and Nate, we proceeded to Kavanagh's boat. As we came close, I noticed the name, *Sheila Anne,* painted on the stern. Erin had mentioned that Kavanagh had been married before. I wondered if the name belonged to his former wife. Or perhaps it harkened back to the wife or girlfriend of a previous owner. Kavanagh walked over to greet us. "Erin, my love, I was beginning to wonder." He kissed her on the cheek and shook hands with Nate, me and the others.

"This is my friend and neighbor, Flo Higginbotham." Kavanagh introduced us to his companion, a large woman with a helmet of bleached blond hair and a hard, heavily made-up face. She wore a sleeveless dress with a bold pink-and-orange tropical print.

"And this is Happy." Flo Higginbotham scooped up the white miniature poodle that cowered, yapping, at her feet. "Wuza matter, cutie-pie?" she crooned. "Is my little Hap feeling shy just now? These nice people aren't going to hurt you. I know they're dying to pet you." She kissed the top of the dog's head and held him out to Nate and me.

I extended a hand reluctantly. Happy bared his teeth and growled. I withdrew my hand.

"Now, now, Hap," Flo scolded.

"Where's Luke?" Kavanagh asked after the round of introductions was over.

"He . . . um . . . wasn't feeling well," Maggie explained. An attractive, dark-haired woman, she appeared flustered by having to cover for her husband.

"I'm sorry to hear that," Kavanagh replied smoothly.

"I'm worried about Vernon, too," Flo said. "He should've joined us by now. Why don't you go see if Daddy's all right?" She put down the poodle, who ran over to the Higginbothams' sailboat, jumped on board, and stood barking over the companionway.

"Coming, Hap!" a voice called. Moments later, a figure emerged. Even from a distance, I could see that Vernon Higginbotham was the man from the powwow who'd rapped Kyle with his program and almost come to blows with Nate.

CHAPTER 5

"I dreamed a dream the other night,
Lowlands, Lowlands, away, my John.
My love she came dressed all in white.
My Lowlands away."
—Lowlands Away, Sea Shanty

"Spouters Point in the fall, Palm Beach in the winter, Bermuda in the summer." Flo Higginbotham tapped a different finger for each place. "That's been our schedule since Vernon retired. But in all the years we've been coming here, this is the first time we've gotten to know people who actually *work* at the museum. First Erin, now you, Mark. It's so sweet you both do this."

"It's sweet all right," Mark quipped. "Gives me a chance to do my music and get paid for it."

"The museum's a very special place," Erin said quietly. "I can't imagine working anywhere else." Seated beside her, Kavanagh patted her shoulder fondly.

"But climbing up and down all those ropes—you've got to be a monkey or a circus performer," Flo babbled on.

"It's not so hard once you've done it a few times," Erin said.

"I wouldn't try it if you offered me a million dollars," Flo said.

"No one's offering," Vernon remarked sarcastically.

"Poor little Hap would have a heart attack if he saw his mommy way up high like that, wouldn't you, cutie-pie?"

"Cutie-pie" came running over when Flo held out a piece of salmon from her plate. Scarfing it down, the poodle got up on his hind legs to beg for more. Nate and I exchanged glances. *People and their dogs,* I thought. Happy must be the "spoiled brat poodle" Mark had mentioned.

"What line of work were you in?" Mark asked Vernon.

"Pet products," Vernon said. "Doggie deodorant, breath freshener, kitty litter. That sort of thing." He had a clipped way of speaking, which involved moving his lips as little as possible.

"Ah." Mark couldn't think of anything else to say.

"More wine, anyone?" Kavanagh removed a bottle from the ice bucket.

"I don't mind if I do." Flo extended her glass. "This is such good Chardonnay, it seems a shame to—"

"Riesling," Vernon corrected.

"Whatever. You always serve the best food and wine, George." Flo beamed at him as he filled her glass.

"Thank you. Your onion dip was excellent as always," Kavanagh replied graciously.

"It's just something I throw together with a package of onion soup mix and sour cream. But I do use real sour cream instead of that icky yogurt stuff. I know it's supposed to be healthier, but . . ." I stopped listening. Flo's words spilled into the evening like water from a faucet left running. She was right about the food, though. Served with fresh dill, lemon, and paper-thin slices of cucumber, the salmon was moist and flavorful; the Caesar salad, crisp and tangy; the cold rice salad, which Jane had brought, equally tasty. The fruity Riesling complemented everything superbly. The delicious meal, balmy air, and beautiful setting would have made for an enjoyable evening if there hadn't been so much tension.

Luke had obviously told Mark about the skeletons Kavanagh harbored in his closet, and he, in turn, had passed on the information to Jane and Maggie. This knowledge had cast a pall over them that their sporadic efforts to join in the conversation couldn't hide. Mark hummed and stared off into space, while the two women kept stealing surreptitious glances at their watches. Erin was trying hard to put a cheery face on things, but the strain was evident in her voice and manner.

Nate remained silent and inscrutable behind his reflector sunglasses, but I sensed his dislike of the Higginbothams. Flo struck me as a vain, foolish woman, and her husband had a definite mean streak. If Vernon remembered Nate and me from the powwow last night, he gave no sign. By tacit agreement, we pretended not to recognize him either. We couldn't very well come out and say, "We know you, you're the guy who hit the disabled kid you thought was making too much noise." Yet whenever Vernon opened his mouth, Nate's head turned sharply in his direction, and I felt him watching the man at other times as well. Watching and waiting for the moment when Higginbotham went too far?

I glanced at Higginbotham every now and then myself. In the world of wealthy yacht people, he fit in perfectly, which made me realize how incongruous his presence at the powwow had been. What had he been doing there? Slumming? If so, he hadn't liked what he'd seen because he'd left in disgust.

The only people who didn't seem uncomfortable were Flo and Kavanagh. Flo was probably too self-centered to notice that anything was wrong. If Kavanagh were aware of the eddies of unease swirling around him, he appeared to have made a conscious decision to ignore them. He was the perfect host, ever solicitous of his guests, whether it meant serving more food and wine, or filling in the conversational gaps that inevitably occur in any group of people who don't know each other well. Otherwise, he seemed content to let others—Flo especially—do the talking. I wondered a bit at this. Surely, he had interesting things to say. Erin had told me he'd sailed around the world. But tonight he didn't regale us with any stories of his adventures. "Why don't we move on to dessert?" he said now. He and Erin got up and began collecting plates. The rest of us helped except for Flo and Vernon. "If you need a hand, just holler," Flo yelled as we carried dishes back to Kavanagh's sloop. Vernon said nothing. Soon, all that remained was the salmon platter, which Flo had placed on the ground for Happy to lick. Nate bent to scoop it up. Happy growled and snapped at his fingers, but Nate was too fast for him. He started toward the sailboat with the platter. Happy went after him, sinking his teeth into Nate's pants leg. "Hey!" Nate shook off the poodle. Happy collapsed in a heap of white, whimpering fur. Flo gasped.

"How dare you!" Vernon waved a fist in Nate's face. Nate grabbed him by the wrist and jerked his arm down, nearly bringing Vernon to his knees. Flo screamed. "Nate!" I rushed to his side. He let go of Vernon.

"What's the matter?" Kavanagh and Erin returned from the sailboat.

"He kicked poor Hap!" Flo pointed accusingly at Nate. "Then he attacked Vernon."

I sprang to Nate's defense. "Your dog bit him, for heaven's sake. And if your husband hadn't—"

"Were you bitten?" Kavanagh asked Nate.

"Felt teeth in my ankle."

"He can't have broken the skin," Flo said defensively.

Kavanagh knelt and examined Nate's leg. "This wound needs attention. I've got a first-aid kit on the boat."

"I'll take care of it," Erin volunteered.

I went below with Erin and Nate. "I should've warned you about Happy." Erin applied antiseptic to Nate's ankle. "He nearly bit me once when I tried to take a plate away from him."

"Dog oughta be muzzled," Nate muttered. "His owners, too."

"Time to break out the champagne," Kavanagh declared with forced heartiness when we returned to the dock.

Champagne? What were we celebrating? The fact that round one between Higginbotham and Nate had ended without serious injury to either man? Perhaps bringing out the bubbly was Kavanagh's way of defusing more fireworks.

He uncorked the bottle with a flourish and began filling glasses. Jane put her hand over hers. "I really shouldn't with a baby on the way."

"One sip can't hurt," Kavanagh urged. "This is a special occasion."

"Oh?" Jane looked puzzled. Reluctantly she let him pour champagne into her glass.

Mark stopped humming to ask, "What exactly is the occasion?"

"You'll find out in a minute," Kavanagh said. He filled his own glass and put an arm around Erin. "We have some important news to share. I've asked Erin to marry me, and she's accepted. I don't mean to brag, but I consider myself one of the luckiest men alive to have the love of such a wonderful woman. I don't deserve it, but there it is, this amazing gift. Since Erin came into my life, I've felt blessed, truly blessed."

Tears glistened in Kavanagh's startlingly blue eyes, and for the first time that evening, Erin looked happy—radiant, in fact—as she smiled at him. He raised his glass. "To Erin, my lovely bride-to-be and the light of my life!"

So they were engaged. This was a surprise. I wished Erin had prepared me beforehand instead of keeping it a secret until the last minute. Then I might have done a better job of cheerleading. As it was, I raised my glass halfheartedly.

"To George and Erin!" Flo boomed.

"To Erin and George," I echoed faintly

There was no general rush to clink glasses. Nate and the

Meloys appeared as startled as I was by the announcement, so it took them a while to respond. The clinking that did occur was hesitant and intermittent like the scattered applause of an audience that isn't sure how to react to a controversial play. Higginbotham clinked selectively, with his wife and with Erin and George, but not with Nate and me or the Meloys. George kissed Erin. Happy barked.

"What's the matter, cutie-pie?" Flo crooned. "Do you feel left out of the lovey-dovey?" But the poodle's attention was trained elsewhere, on something he saw or heard, but we didn't.

Mark put down his half-full glass and rose. "Sorry to eat and run, but Jane's feeling kind of tired."

"I understand," Kavanagh replied evenly. "I'm glad you could join us tonight." He held out his hand. Mark shook it quickly. He and his wife and sister-in-law thanked Kavanagh, gave Erin hasty hugs, and they all left.

Flo stared wonderingly after them. "Why the rush? We haven't even had dessert yet."

"I think they'd had enough," her husband said pointedly.

I'd had enough myself—of the Higginbothams, that is. But out of loyalty to Erin, Nate and I stayed through dessert and even a little after. "I'm happy for you," I told Erin in parting, trying my best to sound sincere.

"Well, that was . . ." Nate commented, once we were out of earshot.

"Not my idea of a fun evening, either," I finished for him. "I feel bad for Erin. She wants so much for everyone to like George. Tonight was supposed to give us a chance to get to know him, and for her family to see him in a more favorable light. But that's not what happened."

"Did you know she and Kavanagh were going to announce their engagement?" Nate asked.

"No. She didn't mention it when I saw her yesterday, so either it was meant to be a surprise, or Kavanagh only just proposed."

"Isn't it kind of sudden? I mean, didn't you tell me they've only known each other a short time?"

"That's right. But she's convinced he's the man for her. What did you think of him, by the way?"

"He seemed okay. But if it's true about judging a person by the company he keeps, you gotta wonder. Flo Higginbotham's a piece of work, and her husband's a mean cuss if ever there was one."

"You can say that again. But it's not like Kavanagh and the Higginbothams are best friends. They probably only met because their sailboats are docked next to each other."

"Still . . ."

"I really hope things work out for Erin," I blurted.

"You care a lot about her, don't you?"

"She's like the younger sister I never had."

"I feel the same about Jimmy."

"You've known him a long time?"

"Yup. First met him when he was a kid, living on the street in Providence, strung out on drugs. I was on my way west on an assignment for AIM. He begged me to take him with me, and I did. While we were there, I took him to his first powwow, and it changed his life. He got clean and became a fancy dancer. That's why this business with Russell—" He broke off at a noise ahead. A figure crouched by a garbage dumpster at the rear of the Spouters Point Inne, a popular restaurant near the back entrance to the museum.

"What the . . . ?" Nate shone his pocket flashlight on the apparition.

The light revealed a woman with a face as brown and wrinkled as a walnut, surrounded by dirty, matted blond hair. Her pale blue eyes had a feral gleam. A catsup-coated French fry dangled from chapped lips like a bloody fang. She clutched a half-eaten hamburger against her chest. Nate stepped toward her. She shrank against the dumpster. "It's okay. We're not going to hurt you." He removed a bill from his wallet and held it out. "Take this and buy yourself a proper meal."

After a moment's hesitation, the woman leaped up and snatched the bill. I caught a glimpse of something white around her neck before she disappeared into the shadows.

"Poor woman," Nate murmured.

"Yes," I agreed, though the sight of her inspired more fear than pity.

We continued around to the front of the Spouters Point Inne. A couple was just leaving.

"Be a s-sport and take me home," a woman in a low-cut, lavender-flowered dress whined drunkenly. She lurched after her companion on three-inch stiletto heels.

"Sorry, sweetheart, but I got other plans," said a man wearing jeans and a gray t-shirt that matched his brush of gray hair. Unlike the woman, he sounded stone sober.

"Thought we wuz havin' a good time. Gotta bottle of your favorite single-malt whiskey at home," she wheedled.

"Not tonight." The man walked quickly across the street toward the parking lot.

"Who is she?" the woman yelled after him.

"Wouldn't you like to know?" he called back.

The woman cursed and gave him the finger, but he'd already disappeared into a minivan. She teetered back into the Spouters Point Inne.

Nate shook his head. "Two sheets to the wind. Hope somebody has the sense to give her a ride home."

By the light of a street lamp, I saw that Nate's mouth was set in a tight line. Drunkenness was a sore subject for him. His father had been an alcoholic who beat his wife and kids until he was finally killed in a drunken driving accident. We crossed the street and walked to the car. As we got in, I noticed the minivan was still parked in the lot. Apparently Mr. Single-Malt Whiskey wasn't in such a hurry after all.

CHAPTER 6

"I dreamed I saw my own true love,
His hair was wet, his eyes above.
I knew my love was drowned and dead,
He stood so still, no word he said."
—Lowlands Away, Sea Shanty

The phone wrenched me from sleep with the force of an alarm. I flung an arm outward, dislodging the handset and knocking over the glass of water I'd left on the bedside table the night before. A woman's distressed voice was calling my name. I found the handset and pressed it to my ear. "Hello?"

"It's me, Erin."

"What's the matter? You sound upset."

"George. He's gone." Her voice broke and she began to cry.

"Gone where?"

"I don't know. I . . . I think he went overboard."

"Overboard?"

"The police are sending a dive team."

"Omigod. We'll be there as soon as we can."

Nate yawned and stretched. "What's going on?"

"Erin can't find George. She thinks he might've fallen overboard."

Nate ground his knuckles into his eye sockets. "Huh? The boat was docked, for crying out loud, and it was a calm night."

"I know, but accidents can happen. We're wasting time

speculating. We need to get over there."

The divers were bringing Kavanagh out of the water when Nate and I arrived. We joined a crowd of police and civilians watching on the dock behind a police barrier. Erin stood next to Mark, Luke a little apart from them. I slipped in beside Erin, took her hand, and pressed it tightly. She gave me an anguished look before returning her attention to the divers. In their black wet suits and flippers, they reminded me of seals. Seals bearing a partially clothed body that only last night had been a living, breathing human being. They towed it facedown with its arms and legs trailing in the water, but when they brought the body to shore, they turned it over on its back.

"Jesus," Nate muttered. Erin gasped and crushed my fingers in hers. I gritted my teeth. A rusted piece of iron protruded from Kavanagh's chest. Above it, a series of red gashes formed a gruesome necklace around his throat. I wondered if the marks had been made by the iron, or if they were the work of fish. They looked hideous.

"That's . . . that's a killing lance in him!" Erin's voice rose in an agonized crescendo, putting into words what I'd just realized. She let go of my hand and lurched toward the body. I reached for her, but Mark got there first. He caught and held her, sobbing, in the protective cocoon of his arms. Luke looked away. Only two days ago, I'd watched him demonstrate the use of a similar lance.

"The thing they used on whales? This is terrible, just terrible, isn't it, cutie pie?" Flo Higginbotham said to the poodle snuggled against her. "Poor George! Who'd want to do that to him?"

"That's what we're going to find out, ma'am." As if on cue, a police officer joined the ones already there. He surveyed the corpse, then after conferring briefly with the other officers, he approached Erin and her brothers.

"Hello, Mike," Luke said.

The officer nodded in greeting. He was a stocky man with glasses and a thatch of dirty blond hair cut Buster Brown–style with bangs, which gave him a nonthreatening, boy-next-door appearance. "Your sister made the call?"

"Yes. He was a friend of hers."

"He was my fiancé, dammit!" Erin's blotchy face emerged from Mark's arms. "We announced our engagement last night at dinner. The dinner you boycotted!" She glared at Luke. He and the officer exchanged glances.

"I'm sorry for your loss, Miss Meloy," the officer said. "I'm Sergeant Michael Curtin. I don't know if you remember me, but I was friends with Luke in high school. Would you mind answering a few questions?"

"No, she's—" Luke began.

"Will you let me speak for myself?" Erin flared. To Curtin, she said, "What do you want to know?"

Curtin took out a notebook and held it open, pen poised. "Your fiancé's name?"

"George Kavanagh."

"When did you first realize he was missing?"

"I stopped by to say hello before work. He wasn't below, so I came back out. Vernon was on deck having his morning coffee." She indicated Higginbotham, who, tight-lipped as always, stood next to his wife. "He said he hadn't seen George since the night before. I figured George must've gone off somewhere. I was about to leave when I noticed blood on the deck, and that part of the railing was chipped." She began to cry again.

"Can't this wait until another time?" Luke intervened. "She's obviously very—"

"I said I'd speak for myself," Erin broke in. "What else do you want to know?"

Curtin flipped a page on his notebook. "When did you last see your fiancé?"

"Last night around eleven. We had a party on the dock so Miranda and Nate could meet George." She nodded at us. "And my family could get to know him better. Flo and Vernon Higginbotham were there, too. They all left before me."

Curtin adjusted his glasses and cleared his throat. "I know this is hard for you, Miss Meloy, but did your fiancé have any enemies you know of?"

"Not unless you count Luke. He didn't approve of George and tried to sabotage our relationship."

Luke recoiled as if struck. Curtin blinked with surprise. I was surprised myself. It wasn't like Erin to attack her brother in such a public way. I'd underestimated the depths of her anger against him. Mark stepped into the breach. "I'd like to take my sister home now," he said to Curtin.

"Okay, but don't leave the area. I'll want to talk more with both of you."

"You know where to find us," Mark said. "C'mon, Erin." He started to guide her away.

"But . . ." She stared bleakly at the body, now covered by a sheet. Underneath the cloth, the handle of the lance poked upward like a tent pole. "What will happen to him?"

Curtin spoke in a monotone, as if reading from a prepared script. "The body will go to the morgue. There'll be an autopsy. Then it will be released for burial or cremation. Do you happen to know if the deceased has any family in the area?"

"Family?" Erin repeated dumbly.

"Next of kin," Curtin said. "We need to notify them."

"He mentioned a son," Erin said slowly, "and there's the son's mother, his ex-wife. I think they live in Greenwich, but . . ." She seemed to be having trouble with the idea that others might have a stronger claim on Kavanagh than she did;

that, in death, her own hold on him was tenuous at best.

"Go with Mark," I urged.

Erin looked from the body to Mark and me and back again. "All right, but you come, too."

"Your friends will be along in a bit," Curtin said. "I want to ask them a few questions."

I nodded in agreement, as much for Erin's benefit as Curtin's. After a final glance at the shrouded corpse, she let Mark lead her toward the museum exit. Curtin signaled Nate and me to wait while he took Luke aside for questioning. I couldn't hear what they were saying, but I saw Luke shake his head several times in apparent denial of at least some of what Erin had said. When they were finished, Luke left and Curtin turned to us.

"You're friends of Miss Meloy's?" he asked after he'd gotten our names and contact information.

"I've known her for several years. Nate met her for the first time last night," I explained.

"Did her engagement to a man she'd known less than a month surprise you, Ms. Lewis?" Curtin asked.

Evidently, Luke had passed on this piece of information, probably in justification of his disapproval of the relationship. Aloud I said, "Yes, but I figured she knew what she was doing. They seemed very much in love."

"But Luke was against the relationship?"

"You heard what Erin said. He refused to come to the dinner last night, and beforehand he told her something about Kavanagh that really upset her."

"What was that?"

"She wouldn't tell me."

"How were things at dinner last night?"

"Tense. Erin was still upset by whatever Luke told her, and

Mark and his wife and Luke's wife appeared to know about it, too."

"What about Kavanagh himself?"

"If he sensed anything was wrong, he didn't let on."

"Do you have anything to add?" Curtin asked Nate.

Nate shook his head.

"That'll be all then." Curtin closed his notebook. "If you think of anything else, get in touch with me." He gave me his card.

As Nate and I headed toward the exit, I heard Flo giving Curtin her version of the evening: "Perfectly lovely. George is—oh dear, I guess I should say 'was'—a wonderful host. We were all enjoying ourselves tremendously until—well, I hate to say this, but that man who's just leaving has quite a temper and he obviously doesn't like dogs because . . ."

Nate quickened his pace. I didn't blame him. Why listen to a foolish woman falsely accuse him again of attacking both Happy and her husband? I started after Nate. Then, as if someone had abruptly switched channels, Flo's loud rant was replaced by a low, masculine murmur. I stopped and glanced over my shoulder. Higginbotham had gone into a huddle with Curtin while Flo pouted on the sidelines. Higginbotham's lips moved so rapidly that Curtin seemed to be having a hard time jotting down everything he said. Odd.

Although Erin had her own apartment, she still spent a lot of time at the family house and used her old room for storage. I figured Mark would take her there. When the rambling, white farmhouse with its green shuttered windows came into view, my spirits lifted slightly. I'd passed many happy hours here, hours of lively conversation over home-cooked meals. I hoped Erin would eventually draw comfort from these familiar surroundings, but at the moment her grief was too raw.

The sight of Luke's car parked in the driveway surprised me. He had every right to be here; it was his house, after all, but I had a hard time imagining Erin and him under the same roof just now. Apparently, Luke had similar qualms. As Nate and I walked past the car, we saw him sitting inside. He didn't turn to look at us but continued to stare stonily ahead.

Bypassing the rarely used front door, I led Nate around to the side. A breezeway, cluttered with children's toys and adult sports equipment, brought us into the large, homey kitchen. It was filled with the aroma of brewed coffee and freshly baked muffins. Erin sat at the round oak table, a coffee mug and a plate of muffins before her, both untouched. Her head swiveled around at our approach.

"Oh, it's you." She seemed relieved that it was us instead of Luke. She half rose and I bent over in an awkward embrace. Captain Ahab, a huge, ancient beast of indeterminate origins with matted black fur, a bushy tail, and one blind eye, limped over to Erin and me. He pushed his grizzled muzzle between us, eager to be included in the show of affection.

"Please sit down," Maggie urged.

"Have some coffee and muffins," Jane said.

"Do we get muffins, too?" asked a solemn-faced young boy with Maggie's dark hair and eyes.

"In a minute," his mother told him.

Nate and I took our places at the table while the two women bustled around us, pouring coffee and setting out extra plates and utensils. Captain Ahab buried his muzzle in Erin's lap. She stroked his head absently. Mark stood nearby, humming softly into his coffee.

The kitchen door opened, and Luke poked his head, turtle-like, into the room. "Erin, I—"

"That's it! I'm leaving." She rose abruptly, dislodging Captain Ahab's head from her lap.

"Won't you even . . . ?" Maggie pleaded.

"No. I'll just get some stuff from my room, then I'm out of here."

She clomped upstairs, Captain Ahab trailing after her. He placed a paw tentatively on the bottom stair, slipped, and would have fallen if Mark hadn't caught him by the haunches and eased him gently down. "It's okay, old boy. It's okay." Turning back to us, he opened his mouth then immediately closed it, perhaps because he couldn't find any similarly reassuring words for us. Jane scratched at an invisible speck of dirt on the counter. Nate shifted in his seat.

"Guess I shouldn't have told her about him," Luke said gloomily.

"Probably would've been best if you hadn't," Mark agreed.

"Damn straight you shouldn't have!" Maggie scowled at her husband. "Why couldn't you have kept your mouth shut, and let her find out for herself?"

Nate and I exchanged mystified glances. What did they know about Kavanagh that we didn't? "Find out what?" I asked.

Luke looked at his wife, as if seeking her approval before proceeding. She shook her head. "Let's just say she's better off without him," he said.

Thumps and bangs sounded overhead.

"What's Auntie Erin doing?" asked the boy who'd inquired about the muffins.

"I'm not sure, honey," Maggie said. "But I do know she's very, very sad."

CHAPTER 7

"All green and wet with weeds so cold,
Around his form green weeds had hold.
'I'm drowned in the Lowland Seas,' he said,
'Oh, you an' I will ne'er be wed.' "
—***Lowlands Away,*** **Sea Shanty**

"What now?" Nate asked in the car. Ten minutes earlier, Erin had left the family house, armed with a suitcase and a couple of bulging canvas tote bags. She looked like she'd cleared out her room except for the furniture.

"I want to look in on Erin."

I had Nate drive me to Erin's apartment in a low-rise building off Main Street in downtown Spouters Point. "Want me to wait in the car?" he asked.

"I may be a while. Why don't you go back to the inn? I'll call when I'm ready to leave."

Nate's fingers grazed my cheek. "Good luck."

Erin was huddled in a corner of the small, sparsely furnished apartment, surrounded by unpacked luggage. The bare walls and packing boxes dating back to her original move bore witness to how little time she'd spent here. Most likely, the place had served as a way station between the old life she'd lived with her family and the new one she hoped to share with Kavanagh. But now the bubble in which she'd floated blissfully for the past month had burst, leaving her marooned among the wreckage of those dreams. I knelt and put my arms around her.

"Thanks for coming," she murmured. "I couldn't stay in the house with Luke, but now that I'm here . . ." She gazed bleakly around the room. "God, I wish I'd spent last night with George. Then maybe he'd still be alive."

"Why didn't you? Were you too upset?"

Erin nodded. "After you left, George and I had a long talk. He wanted to know what was wrong. I told him what Luke said about him. He assured me it wasn't true. I believed him, but I still felt all wound up. I said I needed to be by myself a while. He said he understood. We agreed to meet for breakfast the next morning. That was the last I saw of him until they fished his body out of the water." She shut her eyes, as if to dispel the awful vision. Opening them again, she said, "I don't understand why anyone would want to kill him unless . . ." She let the sentence hang.

I knew she was thinking of Luke, wondering if her own brother could have resorted to murder to keep her from marrying Kavanagh. It was a horrible possibility, and one I didn't care to dwell on. But that didn't stop me from being curious about the skeletons from Kavanagh's past Luke had waved before her. "It's a mystery all right. Based on everything you told me, he seemed like a good person. But I only met him that once. I'm sure there are lots of things I don't know about him, and maybe you don't either." I hesitated before raising the question I knew would be painful for her. Then, as gently as possible, I said, "It might help if you told me what Luke said about him."

"Luke told lies," Erin snapped.

"Then tell me the lies."

I could see she was struggling with this, and half regretted asking. But I'm someone who likes to know the truth, however unpleasant.

"All right," Erin said finally. "But remember that the source

61

for this is far from objective."

"I'll bear that in mind."

"Luke claimed George was a regular at Clambanks, that he'd lost a small fortune gambling."

"Really? Did he appear to be having money problems?"

"Not exactly, but he was short on funds a while back. Like a lot of people lately, he'd taken a beating on the stock market. A company he'd invested heavily in went belly-up. So I . . ."

"You lent him money?"

"He couldn't pay his dock fees. I was glad to help out. And he paid me back. Every cent!"

"Why did Luke think George had lost money gambling?"

"This is where the story gets weird. Luke insisted he got it from a private detective."

"Huh?"

"That's what I said."

"Luke hired a PI?"

"He swore he didn't, that the PI approached him with the information."

"Why would the PI do that?"

"According to Luke, the PI had been tailing George for some time, observed a budding romance between us, and felt I needed to be warned about what kind of man he was."

"How noble of him. But PIs don't work for free. Someone had to be picking up the tab. If it wasn't Luke, then who?"

"Sheila's father."

"Sheila?"

"George's second wife."

"He was married more than once?" This was something she'd neglected to mention. I could understand why: in some people's books—Luke's, probably—two marriages meant two-time loser.

Erin looked slightly guilty. "I thought I told you. Anyway, the fact that he was married twice doesn't reflect badly on George.

His first wife was an alcoholic. She was in and out of treatment programs but couldn't keep off the bottle. He only stayed with her because he felt a divorce would be hard on their son. Then he met Sheila. She was young and beautiful and like George, an avid sailor. They fell madly in love. His wife took him to the cleaner's when he asked for a divorce. But he didn't care as long as he could be with the woman he loved."

"What happened to her?"

Erin sighed deeply. "That's the tragic part. On their honeymoon, they ran into a terrible storm off the coast of Australia. Sheila was washed overboard and drowned. George was devastated. He spent several years wandering around the world without any sense of purpose. Eventually, he wound up in Spouters Point and . . . well, you know the rest. George said he felt like he'd been given a second chance at happiness when he met me. I felt the same. But now he's dead, and I don't know what I'm going to do!" She began to sob so violently the packing boxes around her shook.

I put my arms around her again and held her close. While my body absorbed some of the fury of her grief, my mind ranged back over her words. If true, what she'd told me about Kavanagh's gambling, his two marriages, and the fact that his father-in-law had hired a private detective to tail him raised questions about Kavanagh's character. The answers to these questions might hold the key to his murder. But it was the police's job, not mine, to find those answers. My job was to comfort my friend, and that's what I did. I rode out the storm with her until the great, heaving sobs that wracked her frame and mine were replaced by occasional sniffles.

The ringing phone interrupted the momentary calm that had settled over us. Erin tensed. "You answer it. If it's Luke, I don't want to talk to him."

"Oh, hi, Miranda," Mark said. "I'm glad you're there. How is she?"

If Erin hadn't been nearby, I might have reported, "She just had a good cry, and that helped." Instead, I said, "Okay, I guess—under the circumstances."

"Can I speak with her?"

I passed the phone to Erin. "It's Mark."

Her side of the conversation consisted of a string of emphatic "no's," followed by a hesitant "I'll think about it."

"What was that all about?" I asked after Erin hung up.

"Mark doesn't think I should be alone. He tried to persuade me to move back to the family house. When I kept refusing, he invited me to stay with him and his family."

"And you said you'd think about it?"

"Yes, but I don't know . . . it's kind of crowded with Mark, Jane, the kids and all the stray animals he's taken in. I'd be in the way, feel like a stray myself."

"But Mark's right: it isn't good for you to be alone. If you're not ready to move in with family, I could stay here with you for a while."

"Thanks, Miranda, but what about Nate? And your work?"

"He'll understand. And my work can wait. Besides, I can always make a quick trip back to Cambridge to get what I need."

"I don't know," Erin repeated, her gaze taking in the jumble of boxes and tote bags. "This place is a mess. It's hardly comfortable for one person, let alone two."

"Not now, it isn't. But a little unpacking would do wonders."

We spent the next hour or so putting things away. As I was unloading Erin's books from a box, a brightly colored brochure sailed to the floor. I picked it up and studied it. Under the picture of a vessel that resembled the *Susan Kilrain* was the caption: "Experience the life of a 19th-century whale man with a voyage on board the *Achusnet.*"

"What's this?" I held out the brochure.

"Oh, just something I was thinking of doing at some point. Before I met George."

"Sounds like fun," I remarked, hoping to distract her temporarily from her grief.

"It would be—if you don't mind hard work with little sleep, bad food, and bouts of seasickness."

"Maybe it's not my kind of fun, but surely you'd enjoy sailing on a replica whaler."

"I guess," Erin said without enthusiasm.

It was lunchtime when we finished unpacking. I hadn't eaten anything since the muffin I'd grabbed at Luke and Maggie's, and I was hungry. Erin wasn't but agreed to keep me company at Spouters Point Pizza. Afterward, we went to a market where I persuaded Erin to stock up on groceries.

When we returned, I decided to call Nate and let him know my plans. He didn't answer the phone in our room at the inn. Perhaps he'd gone out for a bite, too. I left a message at the desk for him to call me. I also tried his cell phone without success. Either he'd forgotten to turn it on or the battery had run down.

Erin said she was tired and lay down on the futon in a corner of the room to take a nap. Looking for something to occupy me while she slept, I examined a pile of books we'd stacked on the floor. One title caught my eye: *Fastnet, Force 10, The Deadliest Storm in the History of Modern Sailing.* I flipped through black-and-white photos of mountainous seas, a de-masted sailboat floating adrift and, most chilling of all, a rescue worker from a helicopter recovering the body of a dead seaman.

Erin had taken me sailing a number of times, and even taught me the rudiments, but never under conditions like this. If I'd ever needed convincing it was a dangerous sport, this book more than made the case.

Kavanagh's second wife had perished in a storm at sea. I wondered if her body had been recovered. If not, this would've made her loss even more painful for her husband and her father, who were denied the closure that comes with burial.

I shut the book and picked up Erin's well-thumbed copy of *Moby-Dick*, which, thankfully, wasn't illustrated. Melville's dense prose had its usual soporific effect on me. I was beginning to nod off when the phone rang. Anxious not to wake Erin, and hoping it was Nate, I grabbed the handset.

"Me again," Mark said. "How is she?"

"Asleep," I whispered.

"Good." Mark lowered his voice also. "Listen, I know it's hard for you to talk right now, but think you could persuade her to come and stay with Jane, me and the kids?"

"We talked about it, but she wants to remain here for the time being. I've offered to keep her company."

"That's awfully kind of you, but it's just one room, and the last time I was there, it was filled with her stuff."

"We'll manage."

"Okay, but you'll need something to sleep on. How about I bring over an air mattress, sheets and a blanket or two?"

"That would be great."

"See you in a bit."

I tried the inn and Nate's cell again without reaching him. Maybe he'd gone over to Jimmy's. I got the number from information, but no one answered. Oh, well. Nate and I would connect eventually.

Mark's "in a bit" became an hour. Erin was still asleep when he arrived with the air mattress, so we kept our voices down. "Sorry I didn't get here sooner, but I figured I might as well feed some of my strays on the way." By strays, I knew he meant homeless people as well as cats and dogs.

Working quietly so as not to disturb Erin, Mark and I had begun to set up the air mattress when the phone rang. This time, it was Nate. "Where've you been?" I asked. "Didn't you get my—"

"I'm at the Spouters Point police station. Jimmy's been arrested."

"Why?" In my excitement, I forgot to keep my voice down. "Does it have to do with Russell and the dance contest?"

"No, Kavanagh's murder."

"*What!*" Out of the corner of my eye, I saw Mark and Erin, now awake and sitting up, staring at me.

CHAPTER 8

"Santander Jim is a mate from hell,
With fists o' iron an' feet as well."
—Sacramento, Sea Shanty

I was deliberately vague about what had happened to Jimmy. I told Erin and Mark only that he'd gotten into trouble due to a misunderstanding, and that I wanted to see what I could do to help. Mark said he'd stay with Erin. He'd brought his mandolin and as I left, he began to play and sing to her.

I took a cab to the police station. Nate and Reba were waiting outside. Their somber expressions said it all. "It's no use. They won't let us see him. Told us to come back tomorrow morning," Nate informed me. To Reba he said, "I might as well take you home."

"What exactly happened?" I asked Reba in the car.

"I was out doing errands when the police came. When I got home, Jimmy was gone, Kyle was shrieking and Patty was in tears. Patty said the police told Jimmy they wanted to ask him some questions about a man who was found murdered at the Spouters Point Museum this morning. Jimmy said he didn't know anything about it. They insisted he did. Said they had a witness who'd seen him arguing with the victim the night before. He kept denying it, and the cops got mad. 'You won't talk here, we're taking you down to the station,' they said. Jimmy tried to slam the door on them, but they pushed their way in and dragged him off. Now he's charged with assaulting a police officer."

"Unbelievable!" I could barely contain my indignation.

"Any other cop, and things might've been different." Reba shook her head.

"What do you mean?"

"The arresting officer was Mike Curtin. His family has a long-standing grudge against us. Curtin's from around here. He grew up hearing stories about the bad Indians on the 'rez.' We only had a little land left then. Later, after the feds recognized us as a tribe, we sued to recover our lost land. It included the Curtin family farm. They were furious when we bought it back with government money. They hated us when we had nothing. Now they hate us because of our success."

"Yeah, but the cops are way off base if they think Jimmy had anything to do with that guy's murder," Nate said. "Did he even know George Kavanagh?"

"If he did, he never mentioned him," Reba said. "And he certainly never brought him to the house."

"It must've been someone else who was seen with Kavanagh, someone this witness—whoever he is—mistook for Jimmy. Jimmy was home last night, wasn't he?" Nate asked Reba.

Frowning, she fiddled with the clasp of her seat belt. "He was in the living room watching TV when I went to bed. The TV was still on when I woke up around midnight. I assumed he was there, but it never occurred to me to check. I wish—"

"Don't worry," Nate interrupted. "This is all a huge mistake. We'll get it straightened out in the morning."

Back at the Swifts', Nate continued to reassure Reba and helped calm Kyle and Patty. But once we were in the car again, he turned grim. He brooded silently until we were almost to the inn. "What's up?" I asked finally.

"I don't like the looks of this. First, Jimmy's accused of winning the dance contest unfairly, then of having it out with a guy he doesn't even know, and the next day, the guy turns up—"

"Jimmy and Kavanagh could've known each other," I cut in.

"What d'you mean?" Nate asked with an edge in his voice.

"Luke told Erin that Kavanagh lost a lot of money at Clambanks. If it's true, that's where he and Jimmy could've met."

Nate looked thoughtful as he pulled into the parking lot. We continued talking while we walked toward the inn. "I doubt it," Nate said. "Jimmy works outside on the grounds, not inside at the tables, where it's more likely he would've run into Kavanagh."

"I know. I'm just suggesting it as a possibility."

Nate shook his head. "Seems like a long shot to me. What I think's going on is that they're trying to get Jimmy to take the rap for a murder someone else committed."

Oh, no, I thought, sensing that Nate was about to launch into one of his conspiracy theories. "Who's 'they'?" I asked, even though I knew and dreaded the answer.

"The cops, of course. You heard what Reba said about Curtin's having it in for Jimmy."

"Yes, but what about this eyewitness they claim to have?"

"I'll bet there is no witness. It's a ploy on the police's part to con Jimmy into confessing to something he didn't do."

"Well, if there *is* an eyewitness, I think I know who it is."

Nate stopped and faced me. "Who?"

"Higginbotham. I saw him go into a huddle with Curtin as we were leaving the museum this morning. And he was at the dance contest the other night, so he could've recognized Jimmy from there."

"What! Why didn't you tell me?"

"At the time, I didn't think it was important."

"Not important!" Nate roared. He spun around and hurried toward the car.

"Where are you going?"

"I need to talk to that guy."

"I'm coming with you." I ran to the car, and was just reaching for the door handle when Nate pulled out and sped away with a squeal of rubber. Dammit! In the mood he was in, he might beat the shit out of Higginbotham. My first impulse was to call a cab and go after him. But something held me back. Wounded pride? If he didn't want me, I wasn't chasing after him. Let him get into trouble. Serve him right for shutting me out. But if he really did beat the shit out of Higginbotham, he'd end up in jail. Was that what I wanted?

I spent the next several minutes in an agony of indecision. By the time I'd made up my mind to follow him, it was too late. I'd never catch up with him now. I'd have to wait this one out and hope for the best. But waiting wasn't easy. I went back to our room at the inn and paced, torn between anger at Nate for rushing off without me and fear of what might happen between Higginbotham and him. After a while, my bridge-burning instincts got the better of me. Despite his promises to curb his rage, Nate wasn't going to change. He would always fly off the handle at the slightest provocation. But I wouldn't be around to pick up the pieces. I'd go back to Erin's, where my presence was appreciated. Having a relationship with a man like Nate was just too difficult.

I started gathering my things. The sight of our two tooth-brushes leaning against one another in a plastic cup in the bathroom gave me an unexpected pang. We'd bought them when we'd come for the powwow because we'd both forgotten to bring ours. They were a pair . . . like us. But why let myself be swayed by two stupid toothbrushes? I yanked mine out with such force I knocked the cup over. Nate's toothbrush lay on the counter like a fallen figure. I left it there.

I finished packing and, duffel bag in hand, went to the door.

Nate walked in, ashen-faced. He looked at me and at my bag. "Jesus," he murmured. He put an arm around me and drew me close. I held myself stiff and resistant in his embrace. His fingers found their way under my blouse and he began stroking my back. I gave in to him. Reaching under his shirt, I touched the bare skin of his back also. But even as I reveled in the feel of him, a question nagged at me. "What happened with Higginbotham?"

Nate removed his hand and laced fingers with me. "Sit down and I'll tell you." We sat on the bed. Nate took a deep breath and let it out slowly. "I found him in the yard of that church at the museum." He must mean the First Congregational Church. I pictured the quintessentially New England church with its spire pointing sternly heavenward like a preacher's admonishing finger.

"His poodle was crapping on the grass in front. And Higginbotham was watching it with this smug expression. 'You gonna clean that up?' I said. 'No.' He sneered. 'Want to make something out of it?' I could tell he was spoiling for a fight, and I was tempted to let him have it."

"Did you?"

"I told him I wanted to talk about the guy he claimed to have seen arguing with Kavanagh the night he was killed. 'What about him?' Higginbotham said. 'How can you be so sure it was Jimmy Swift?' I asked. 'What's it to you?' he said. 'He a friend of yours?' 'Matter of fact, he is,' I said. 'If you're trying to get him off the hook, forget it. My story stands. End of conversation.' He turned his back on me and started walking toward his sailboat with his stupid little dog. I stared at the pile of crap his dog had left. I felt like rubbing the prick's nose in it."

As Nate spoke, I heard the anger build in his voice and could tell from his body language—eyes narrowed and chin and chest thrust forward, as if he were about to spring—that he was back in that moment of rage. "But . . . you didn't?"

"I came this close." He held his thumb next to his index finger so there was barely any space between them.

"What stopped you?"

"Getting into a fight with Higginbotham would only make things worse. I'd land in jail where I couldn't help Jimmy. And you'd be mad, maybe even dump me." His gaze settled on my duffel bag on the floor beside us. "Is that what you were going to do? Go back to Cambridge?"

"Actually, I was on my way to Erin's. It's not good for her to be alone right now, and she refuses to move back in with her family. I said I'd stay with her for a while."

"Why didn't you tell me?"

"You didn't give me a chance."

He gave me a searching look. "You want a ride there now?"

He obviously didn't want me to leave, and I didn't want to either. "Mark was with her when I left. Let me phone and see how things are." I made the call and was relieved when Mark offered to spend the night with Erin.

"I'm glad you're staying, Miranda," Nate said in a husky voice. "How about we hop into the Jacuzzi together, then—" He nodded at the bed.

"Great, I'll start the water." I went into the bathroom and turned on the faucet, then the jets. When the tub was almost full, I undressed and climbed in, thinking Nate would join me soon. When he didn't appear, I called to him. No answer. Perhaps he couldn't hear me over the roar of the jets. I shut them off and was about to call again when I heard his voice in the other room. He was talking to someone on the phone. "Terrific. Be good to see you again." He hung up.

Nate came into the bathroom and started to take off his clothes. "Who were you on the phone with?"

He unbuttoned his shirt with a guilty look. "Forgot to tell you, but after Higginbotham blew me off, I thought more about the best way to help Jimmy. Decided he needed a good lawyer. So I called Gloria."

"Gloria?"

"Gloria Ramos. She's agreed to take Jimmy's case."

"You're kidding!" Gloria Ramos was one of the hottest criminal lawyers in Boston, known for her advocacy of controversial cases. She was also young, hip and beautiful.

"She's driving down first thing tomorrow." Nate fanned his fingers over his pants zipper, shielding a telltale bulge.

Now, *who* was that for?

CHAPTER 9

"Glou'ster boys they have no sleds
They slide down hills on codfish heads."
—The Codfish Shanty

The next morning, Nate dropped me at Erin's apartment on his way to meet Gloria Ramos at the police station. Mark was cooking breakfast when I walked in. I'd had a bagel at the inn, but the smell of bacon was irresistible. I accepted Mark's offer of two crispy slices, along with my second cup of coffee for the day.

"What's going on with Nate's friend?" Mark asked after we'd sat down with our food.

I'd been hoping they wouldn't inquire—at least not right away. With a sigh, I put down the bacon I'd been about to bite into. "He was arrested last night."

Mark looked concerned. "What for?"

"This is where it gets strange. Apparently, Vernon Higginbotham overheard him arguing with George the night he was killed."

"What!" Erin looked up from her plate where she'd been crumbling bacon into ever smaller pieces.

"That was my reaction. I wasn't aware Jimmy and George even knew each other. Were you?"

Erin shook her head.

"Anyway, when the police went to question Jimmy, he

wouldn't talk to them, they got mad, there was a scuffle, and they arrested him for assaulting an officer."

"Pigs," Mark muttered.

"It does sound like they overreacted," I said. "But the upshot is Jimmy's in jail, and Nate and a lawyer friend are trying to get him out."

Mark chewed thoughtfully on his toast, as if digesting the information. "You said Higginbotham identified Jimmy. He knows him?"

"Higginbotham must've remembered Jimmy from the pow-wow. He was sitting behind us when Jimmy competed in the men's fancy dance. But it's odd Higginbotham was even there. He doesn't strike me as someone who'd go in for that sort of thing."

"Seguan's big around here," Mark said. "It draws all kinds of people. Maybe he heard about it and was curious."

"Maybe, but it still bothers me."

"Why don't you ask him about it?"

I rolled my eyes, remembering the brushoff Higginbotham had given Nate last night. "Getting information from him's about as easy as getting blood from a stone."

"The guy does have a bad case of lockjaw," Mark acknowledged. "But his wife sure likes to run off at the mouth. Maybe you should try her."

While Mark and I spoke, Erin mixed pieces of crumbled bacon into the runny yolk of her fried egg, making an unappetizing mess. Now, she put down her fork and said, "But how could Jimmy and George have known each other?"

"Jimmy works at Clambanks," I said. "So, if what Luke's PI said about George's gambling is true, that's where they could've met,"

Erin picked up her fork again and went back to mixing egg and bacon. "Okay, maybe George did go to Clambanks once or twice," she said finally. "So do a lot of people. That doesn't make him a compulsive gambler. What were he and Jimmy supposedly arguing about?"

"We don't know yet."

Erin broke off bits of toast and added them to the mix in her plate. Mark watched her with a pained expression. "Why don't I take that?" She handed him the plate without a word. Mark and I finished our breakfast, and he took our mugs and plates to the sink. "I should put in some time at the museum today. Will you guys be okay here?"

Erin shrugged. I nodded.

"See you later then."

"Wait, I'm coming with you," Erin called when he was almost to the door.

Mark turned back to her with surprise. "Sure?"

"It'll give me something to do, take my mind off . . . you know. I just won't go anywhere near George's boat."

"All right. How about you, Miranda?"

"I'll come, too."

Mark and I left Erin in the shipyard, which was located at the other end of the museum and well out of view of Kavanagh's boat. While she sanded the hull of a schooner as if her life depended on it, we headed toward the wharves on the other side of the village green. Mark went to take part in a demonstration on board the *Susan Kilrain*. I decided to look for Flo.

Police tape blocked access to Kavanagh's sailboat but not the one next to it. Higginbotham sat on deck with a newspaper, Happy lying beside him. Seeing no sign of Flo, I was about to walk away when Happy barked. Higginbotham looked up and frowned at me. "What do you want?"

"Just looking for Mark Meloy," I fibbed.

"As you can see, he's not here," Higginbotham snapped.

"Right." I'd have to find a way to approach Flo when her husband wasn't around. I started back toward the shipyard building, thinking I'd hang out with Erin for a while.

The path I followed skirted the village green, then took me past the dock, where a replica fishing schooner called the *Mason T.* was moored. I noticed Luke on board the *Mason T.*, surrounded by a small group of children and adults. I stopped to watch.

"Cod is why we're here," Luke said. "It's why this country was settled. Long before Columbus, fishermen came to these shores for cod. They dried and salted the fish before they went back to Europe." He lugged a large cod from a cooler at his feet and laid it on a table in front of him. "This is how they prepared it for salting. First, they cut off the head with a long, rectangular knife." He demonstrated this. "Then they split the fish down the middle and took out the guts. They tossed these overboard." He dumped the mess into a pail. "But they saved the cod liver." He held it up.

"They put the liver in a wooden cask, let it rot, and strained the liquid into cod liver oil. They had to open up the fish as much as possible for the salt to reach all parts of it. We squeamish Americans will only eat the flesh, but in Newfoundland they eat all parts of the cod, including the cheeks, gills, and tongues. The only part they won't eat are the eyeballs."

"Gross!" a boy in the audience exclaimed. I thought so, too. The mention of eyeballs reminded me how Luke had probed an imaginary whale's eyeball with a killing lance the day before Kavanagh's murder. Before I could follow this train of thought to its logical conclusion, I turned on my heel and walked away.

"Miranda!" Luke caught up with me. "I saw you watching the cod splitting demonstration. Is Erin here, too?"

"Over at the shipyard."

"Ah. Do you think I should . . . ?" He looked hopefully in

that direction.

"I'd leave her be for now. She's still pretty fragile."

Luke wiped the sweat from his forehead, leaving behind a small bit of fish gut. I tried not to stare, but my eyes kept coming back to it. "God, I wish I'd never told her that stuff about Kavanagh!" he burst out. "But I honestly thought she should know who she was mixed up with."

"That business about Kavanagh losing a small fortune at Clambanks," I began.

"She told you?"

"Yes. She said it came from a private investigator hired by Kavanagh's second wife's father."

Luke must have heard the skepticism in my voice. "Erin didn't believe me either. She thinks I made the whole thing up."

"Your being approached by a PI someone else hired does seem kind of unlikely."

"But that's what happened," Luke insisted. "Sunday afternoon, this guy came up to me out of the blue, identified himself as a PI, and—"

"You think he was legitimate?"

"He showed me a license. Then he said he'd been tailing Kavanagh, noticed my sister was involved with him, and felt she should be warned."

"Because of the gambling?"

"That and worse," Luke said grimly. "His client, the father, suspected Kavanagh was responsible for his daughter's death."

Despite the warmth, I felt a chill. "Erin told me Kavanagh's second wife was washed overboard during a storm."

"I'm only repeating what the PI told me. I had my concerns about Kavanagh from the start, but I never expected anything that bad."

"Your concerns were?"

"The difference in their ages, the fact that he'd been married

79

twice before, and that he might be after Erin's money."

"Erin has money?"

"She doesn't make a big deal out of it—lives modestly, dresses simply because that's her nature. But the truth is that Erin, Mark and I each have a trust fund that was set up by our grandfather. He was an inventor who patented a lifesaving device that made him a fortune."

"But if I, as a good friend, didn't know about the trust fund, what makes you think Kavanagh knew?"

Luke shrugged. "A guy like him has his ways of finding out."

"Anything else?"

"Erin's young and naive and easily taken in by a man like Kavanagh."

"She's thirty-five, for heaven's sake!" I suspected that in Luke's eyes Erin's age didn't make any difference; she would always be the baby sister he needed to look out for. My brother acted the same way toward me.

"When I found out he was a gambler and possible murderer, that really did it. No way was I going to let things go any further. And when Maggie came home and told me they were engaged . . ." Luke's fist clenched. The fish gut on his forehead throbbed like an exposed vein. I couldn't help wondering to what lengths he might have gone to prevent Erin from marrying Kavanagh.

As if he read my mind, Luke suddenly relaxed. "Now, of course, I wish I'd handled things differently. I should've broken the bad news about Kavanagh gradually instead of unloading it on Erin all at once. And I probably should've checked out the PI's story before I even went to her."

"Who was this detective, anyway? Do you remember his name?"

A fly buzzed in Luke's face. He shooed it away. "I didn't catch it."

"But you said he showed you his license."

"Flashed it at me is more like it."

"Too bad, because the police will want to talk to him."

"I'm sure he'll come forward once he finds out Kavanagh was murdered." Luke looked at his watch. "I've got another demo in a few minutes. See you." After a last, pensive glance toward the shipyard, he hurried off.

As I made my way there, I thought about what Luke had just told me. His not remembering the PI's name struck me as strange, unless it was a case of deliberate amnesia: he'd hired the PI himself and didn't want Erin to know. But if this were so, how had the PI found out Kavanagh's father-in-law suspected him of having a hand in his daughter's death? I had a hard time imagining that a detective hired by Luke would go to that much trouble.

Then again, maybe Luke had instructed him to dig up all the dirt he could. Or there was no PI, and Luke had played gumshoe himself. He could've followed Kavanagh to Clambanks, and he could've read about Kavanagh's second wife's death on the Internet and made up the story about her father's suspicions.

But this didn't square with the Luke I knew. Or thought I knew. I added the PI to my mental list of mysteries related to Kavanagh's murder.

"What's the matter?" The question jolted me from my thoughts. Erin had stopped sanding the ship's hull to look at me.

"Nothing. Why?"

"You were shaking your head and muttering."

I smiled. "Caught in the act—again."

A ghost of a smile appeared on Erin's face. "I could use some help. Here." She tossed me a piece of sandpaper.

We worked in silence. Sanding, I discovered, was a strenuous but essentially mindless activity, which left me free to think of other things—like what was happening at the police station.

I hoped Gloria Ramos would be able to spring Jimmy, but at the same time, I felt a prick of jealousy at the thought of Nate and her. She wouldn't have dropped everything and driven down here for just anyone.

A half hour later, I'd built up a sweat and my arm was starting to ache. I stood and stretched. "Think I'll mosey over to the pier and see if Flo's around."

I hadn't gone far when my cell phone rang. "Good news!" Nate exclaimed. "Gloria convinced the cops to drop the charges and let Jimmy go. In exchange for his cooperation, of course."

"That's great. Where are you now?"

"I'm driving Jimmy home. Then Gloria and I are going out for a little celebration."

Bad news. Aloud I said, "I'd like to join you. How about picking me up at the museum?"

"Well . . . all right."

The hesitation in his voice raised my hackles even more.

CHAPTER 10

"And the schooner is painted already,
She is painted in red and violet—"
—*Albertina,* Sea Shanty

"Mmmm . . . now this is lobster!" Gloria Ramos sucked a final morsel of butter-drenched meat from the tail. She licked her glistening lips, and with a shake of her mahogany mane, leaned back and smiled at Nate through half-closed hazel eyes.

You didn't have to be a rocket scientist to sense the chemistry between them. A chemistry that had been evident from the moment I'd gotten into the car. Gloria had sat in front, elegant in an aquamarine silk suit with a short skirt that showed off her long, shapely legs. Apparently, she'd recently given Nate a big kiss because a smudge of her bright red lipstick remained on his cheek.

The smudge moved as Nate returned her smile. "Figured you'd like it here."

"Here" was Clawz, a lobster in the rough place, where patrons sat outdoors on red picnic tables at the water's edge.

"And you deserve it after what you did today," Nate said.

"I was glad to help out—this time."

"What d'you mean?"

"Well . . ." Gloria broke off lobster legs from the carcass and lined them up on her plate.

As she spoke, she picked up the legs one by one, holding

83

them, cigarette-style, between long, crimson-tipped fingers, while she inhaled slivers of white flesh.

"This is only the beginning. You think it's bad now, it's probably gonna get worse. The cops don't like your friend, and they're not satisfied with his answers. They're gonna be watching him closely in the coming days. Watching him and putting pressure on him. 'Cuz right now he's all they've got."

"You mean—" Nate began.

Gloria waved him into silence with a lobster leg. "I'm not saying their investigation won't open up, and they'll start looking at other suspects. But your friend's in the hot seat now. The cops are gonna break him if they can. And he strikes me as easily broken."

"He's scared," Nate said. "He knows that cop Curtin is out to get him."

"You're sure that's all it is?" Gloria probed.

" 'Course, I'm sure. There's no way Jimmy could've even known Kavanagh."

"What about Clambanks?" I chimed in.

Nate scowled at me.

"What about it?" Ignoring me, Gloria directed the question to Nate.

"Miranda heard that Kavanagh may've been a regular at Clambanks. Jimmy works there, but outside on the grounds, so it's unlikely that—"

"Cops know about this?" Gloria interrupted.

"Luke might've told Curtin," I said.

"Who's Luke?" Gloria asked, again directing the question to Nate.

"The brother of a friend of Miranda's. She'd just gotten engaged to Kavanagh and Luke didn't approve."

Gloria sucked on a leg reflectively. "So the brother's a possible suspect. That should help—"

"Now wait a minute," I broke in hotly.

"Jimmy," Gloria finished, still ignoring me.

"Yeah," Nate said. "Except that Luke's buddies with Curtin. They went to high school together."

"Not good," Gloria muttered.

I stared at them, appalled. Nate acted as if Jimmy was the only one who mattered, as if my friendship with Erin and her family didn't count. If that's the way it was going to be . . . I pushed back my chair, ready to leave.

"What about the Clambanks angle?" Gloria asked abruptly. Her question kept me in my seat.

"What about it?" Nate replied.

"Cops know about it, they're gonna be all over the place, asking questions. And if they find someone who saw Jimmy and Kavanagh together—"

"They won't find anyone," Nate said.

"I hope not because if they do, your friend's credibility will be shot."

"You don't believe him?"

Gloria shrugged. "That's not the issue. The issue is that the cops don't. As I said before, they're gonna put pressure on him, and he has to keep his cool. I can't run down here every time he gets on the wrong side of the law."

"I thought you said—" Nate began testily.

"I have other clients. I'm due in court tomorrow for the bus terrorist case. You been following it?"

"Of course," Nate said. "Been in the papers almost every day for the past couple of weeks."

"You check out Thursday's *Globe*." Gloria reached across the table and tapped Nate's forearm with a crimson nail. "I think you'll find there will be some interesting new developments."

"I'm sure there will, knowing you. But getting back to Jimmy—"

"Relax," Gloria cooed, massaging Nate's arm with her finger. "Have I ever let you down?"

"I don't think you realize how important this is. Jimmy's like family. I'd hate to see him—"

"Trust me." She leaned forward seductively and locked eyes with him.

"Okay," Nate said after a long moment. "You want another lobster? Dessert?"

"What I'd really like is . . ." She batted heavily mascaraed lashes at him.

Dammit! Gloria was about as subtle as a ten-ton tank. And Nate seemed to be falling for her.

"Yes?" he asked softly.

"No!" I wanted to yell. Instead, I made a sound that was half choke, half gag.

"You all right?" Nate asked.

"A piece of shell stuck in my throat."

"Drink some water," Gloria ordered, the first words she'd spoken to me since we'd been introduced. She shoved a glass at me. Then she resumed her forward-leaning, siren pose. Chest thrust toward Nate, she reminded me of a figurehead on a ship. The bad ship, *Gloria*.

"Actually, I'd love dessert," she said to Nate. "But not here. There's gotta be some sweet, little café nearby."

She must have confused Spouters Point with Boston's North End, which is filled with "sweet" little cafés, I thought.

Nate stood. "I don't know of any, but I'll ask."

Gloria watched him disappear into the restaurant. What now? Would the notorious Gloria Ramos finally give me the time of day? Apparently not. As soon as Nate was gone, she whipped out a compact and began applying a fresh coat of crimson, no doubt in readiness for another assault on his cheeks. Ignoring her back, I stared out at the waterfront.

Gloria's shriek was loud enough to be heard by passing ships. She jumped up and raised a fist heavenward like the Statue of Liberty, except she held no torch, wore no crown, her expression enraged rather than solemn. White goo dripped from her mahogany hair onto her aquamarine suit. Gloria Ramos, Esq. had been targeted by a terrorist. A winged terrorist with a bad case of diarrhea.

CHAPTER 11

"An' if we drown while we are young,
It's better to drown, than wait to be hung."
—'Way, Me Susiana!, Sea Shanty

"It wasn't *that* funny," Nate insisted. Yet the smile tugging at the corners of his mouth told me otherwise. Gloria had left in a rage over her ruined clothing, and now Nate and I lingered over coffee at Clawz.

"It was. And when you doused her with water like she was a house on fire."

"Okay, okay." He held up a hand, forestalling another burst of laughter from me. Ordinarily, I don't take pleasure in another's misfortune, but Gloria's none-too-subtle come-on to Nate, combined with her refusal to acknowledge my presence, had exhausted any good will I'd felt toward her.

"I had to do something," Nate said. "You sure weren't any help."

"I was trying hard not to crack up."

"Thank God, you didn't. I can't afford to offend Gloria. You heard what she said. Jimmy's in the hot seat. He needs all the help he can get."

"But at Luke's expense? The two of you seemed awfully eager to seize on him as a suspect."

Nate glanced at the water, where a powerboat churned past. "You have to admit he's got motive and means. Opportunity, too, for all we know. And he's tight with Curtin, so the cops aren't gonna give him a hard time. Whereas Jimmy . . . you heard how they put the screws on him."

"I did and I'm sorry the deck seems to be stacked against him right now. But I know Luke. Much as he disapproved of Kavanagh, I don't think he's capable of murder."

Nate's eyes bore into me. "You think Jimmy is?"

"I didn't say that."

"You could've been thinking it."

"Will you stop putting words in my mouth and thoughts in my head? I'm on your side, remember?"

"Okay, I was outta line," Nate conceded. "But it makes me so mad when white people automatically blame an Indian based on who he is."

"It makes me angry, too. But even your friend Gloria wondered what was going on with Jimmy."

"She doesn't know him like I do."

"You and she seem to know each other pretty well," I couldn't resist adding.

Nate shrugged. "She defended me when I was arrested in a demonstration a while back."

"Ah . . . I didn't think she'd rush down here for just anyone."

Nate removed his sunglasses and looked at me. "If you're trying to find out whether we were involved, the answer is yes. But Gloria and I are history." He took my hand in his. "I'm with you now. Very much with you," he added with a seriousness that was both thrilling and unnerving because it ran counter to our usual banter. I was more comfortable with the banter because it let us avoid heavy-duty discussions about commitment and the future I wasn't ready for yet.

"I'm with you, too," I said quickly. "Now that's settled, what do you want to do next?"

Nate studied my palm as if it held the answer. "I don't know.

Wish I could anticipate the cops' next move. Because if they're gonna put more pressure on Jimmy, I want to be there. But I can't hang around indefinitely. Got a bank job back in town tomorrow and other things I need to take care of."

Nate freelanced as a security specialist, checking out systems for banks and other businesses and, if necessary, helping them upgrade, a skill he'd acquired during his years as an AIM activist when he'd done his share of breaking and entering.

"Suppose I could cancel," he mused aloud. "And I *would* if it weren't for Sam. His school's started making noises about us putting him on medication for ADHD again. I want to show them he can do fine without it. But that means I've got to be there, providing structure, seeing he does his homework, and gets to bed on time."

Under the custody arrangement Nate had with his ex-wife, Sam spent part of the school week with one parent, part with the other, and weekends with either his father or mother.

"When will you leave?" I asked.

"Tonight or early tomorrow morning. You want to ride back with me or stay here with Erin a while longer?"

"I told her I'd stay. Which reminds me. I should see how she's doing."

I called Erin at the museum on my cell. She told me Mark had persuaded her to have dinner with him and his family and spend the night. She said I was welcome, too. When I explained that Nate was leaving soon, Erin urged me to drive back with him. She said she'd be okay at Mark's. If she needed me, I could always return in my own car with my work materials. After some hesitation, I agreed.

"So," I asked Nate, "what do you want to do for the rest of the time we're here?"

He considered this a moment. "We're checked out of the inn, but it's a weeknight so we might be able to get a room there. Or go somewhere else."

I grinned. "Sounds good to me."

The inn was full, but we found a room at another B & B nearby. Anticipating a leisurely afternoon of lovemaking, I went into the bathroom to shower and change. When I came out, Nate was sitting on the bed, fully clothed, with a gloomy expression on his face.

"What is it?" I sat down beside him.

"I can't stop worrying about Jimmy being in the hot seat."

"Then let's do something about it."

"What?"

I was silent, thinking. "Clambanks," I said finally.

"Huh?"

"Let's go there and—"

"What good will that do?"

"You said you wished you could anticipate the cops' next move. They need to establish a connection between Jimmy and Kavanagh, and that's the place to look for it, assuming what Luke said about Kavanagh's gambling is true."

"There is no connection," Nate insisted. "The whole thing's a conspiracy on the part of the cops, Higginbotham and God only knows who else to nail Jimmy for a crime he didn't commit."

"Maybe so, but don't you think we should at least rule out the possibility of a connection?"

Nate seized a tuft of bedspread and pressed it tightly between his thumb and index finger. "All right, we'll go."

CHAPTER 12

"Next mornin' when I woke, I found that I was
  broke,
I hadn't got a penny to me nyme;
So I had to pop me suit, me John L's an' me boots
Down in the Park Lane pawn shop Number Nine."
  —*Maggie May,* Sea Shanty

We exited the elevator onto the main concourse of the Grand Dottaguck Tower. I started walking toward the casinos. Nate stopped me. "Where're you going?"

"To the casinos to see if we can find someone who remembers Kavanagh."

"Uh-uh. The guys who work the tables aren't allowed to talk about customers to just anyone. But I happen to know somebody."

While Nate went to speak with his friend, I sat down facing a plate-glass window, which offered a dramatic view of the surrounding woods. I watched a hawk soar over the treetops. The bird looked as if it were suspended in the air by invisible strings. That was how I felt: suspended, in limbo. The other seats were empty. There was no one to study in secret and speculate about, no conversations to eavesdrop on. I looked at my watch. Ten minutes had passed. I wished I'd brought something to read.

Finally, feeling restless, I got up to explore. I strolled past a series of shops and restaurants, which gave the concourse a mall-like appearance. Before long, I felt myself succumbing to the malaise that comes over me in malls, making me want to run to the nearest exit before my brain turns to mush. I had to force myself into a casino. Almost immediately, the noise and bright lights overwhelmed me. I didn't understand how anyone could remain for any length of time in such a stultifying place. The people feeding the slots reminded me of workers on an assembly line, each repetitive movement robbing them of a little more of their humanity until they were transformed into automatons. Those at the gaming tables showed more life, but they stared at their cards or at spinning roulette wheels with an intensity that was frightening. Even the snippets of conversation and occasional bursts of laughter sounded more nervous than not. Much was at stake. The very air was heavy with hope, disappointment, and despair.

As a child, I'd resisted the urge to play the slots on family trips through Nevada. But carnival games were another matter. I still remembered trying to toss Ping-Pong balls into a fish bowl in a vain effort to win a goldfish my parents could just as easily have bought me. I also remembered the sense of letdown I felt when I finally gave up and walked away, empty-handed. I left the casino in a hurry.

"Decide to gamble after all?" Nate caught up with me.

"I was just checking out the scene. Did you find out anything?"

"Let's sit down and I'll tell you."

We returned to the seats by the windows. "My friend found a blackjack dealer who remembered Kavanagh," Nate said. "Guy works in the only smoke-free casino here."

At least Kavanagh had chosen a healthy environment for his gambling.

"Apparently Kavanagh was a regular. Played the slots, some table games like blackjack and Caribbean stud, but mostly he was a back-better."

"What's that?'

"When you were in the casino, did you happen to notice tables where people were standing behind the players?"

"I think so."

"Those people aren't just friends or fans. The guys in the rear bet on the guys who are seated. Kavanagh liked to do that. Usually he picked winners. But according to this dealer, he lost big one time when a pick of his was having a bad night."

"So Luke's PI was right about Kavanagh's gambling losses," I said.

"Yeah. Luke probably went ballistic when he found out," Nate said.

Sensing where this was going, I said, "Now that we know Kavanagh was here, the next step is to see if there's anyone who might've seen him with Jimmy."

Nate rolled his eyes. "How're we gonna do that? We can't establish a connection where none exists."

"The cops aren't going to give up so easily."

"Okay, okay," Nate grumbled. "We'll go outside and I'll talk to some of the guys on the grounds crew."

"Good." I rose and headed for the elevator.

"Hey, not so fast!" Nate called. "Don't you want to bet on a horse?"

"There's no track."

"They've got a state-of-the-art Ultimate Race Book, where you can place a bet."

"Let's get out of here." Laughing, I took him by the arm.

Outside, Nate went off to speak with men on the grounds crew, while I waited in the parking lot. A little boy wearing shorts, a t-shirt, and a dime-store Indian headdress tumbled out of a nearby car and began whirling around in an empty space. He reminded me of the kids I'd seen competing in the Junior category at Seguan. I'd watched them on Saturday—only four days ago. It seemed a lot longer because of all that had happened in the meantime.

The boy's mother emerged from the car, and taking him firmly by the hand, dragged him off toward the casinos. Fifteen minutes later, Nate returned. He'd talked to two men. One knew Jimmy but had never seen Kavanagh; the other had just started working at Clambanks and didn't even know Jimmy. I wanted him to try more people, but he refused. "This is a waste of time. Besides, I'm not comfortable asking questions behind Jimmy's back. We can stop by his house and I'll ask him again if he knew Kavanagh. I want to see how he's holding up, anyway, before I head home."

As we approached the Swifts', we heard banging, Kyle's barking noise, then a loud cawing, as if a flock of crows were inside. Nate and I exchanged glances. Something was up. Patty answered the door. "Everything all right?" Nate asked.

"Yeah. Mom and Kyle were just playing a game of hubbub."

"Uh-uh," Nate said with mock alarm. "Better get them to quit. Miranda doesn't approve of games of chance."

"Oh, c'mon." I punched his arm playfully.

Inside, Kyle and Reba sat opposite each other at the dinette table. Reba started to get up when we entered, but Nate motioned her to sit. "Don't let us interrupt you. I just wanted to say good-bye to Jimmy before I go home."

Reba frowned slightly. "He went out a little while ago. But if you don't mind waiting, he should be back soon."

"Fine." Nate sat on the couch. I walked over to the table. "So what's this game you're playing?" Reba showed me a wooden bowl that contained five pieces of shell, each of which was white on one side and purple on the other. "Players take turns banging the bowl on the table three times, while calling out 'hubbub,' " she said. "A player scores when four or five pieces of the same color show up in the bowl. He gets a twig or chip from a pile on the table. He also gets another turn. The game goes on until one player's gotten all the twigs. Want to try?"

While I hesitated, Kyle barked and pointed at Nate. "Okay, buddy, you're on," Nate said. "When Miranda sees how much fun it is, maybe we can persuade her to join us."

Nate was right. Hubbub was noisy, fast, and fun—a big departure from the games I'd observed at Clambanks. When Nate was on the verge of winning, I even joined in the cawing, which is done to distract the player who is ahead. After Nate and Kyle finished their game, I played with Nate and was surprised at the rush of adrenalin I felt when I was close to winning. I became even more excited when I actually won.

By then, it was nine o'clock and Kyle's bedtime. He'd gotten very wound up from the game, so Nate offered to go to Kyle's room with him and help calm him down, filling in for the boy's father who still hadn't returned. While Nate was with Kyle, Patty disappeared into her room, and Reba and I made small talk. Having just spent the last couple of hours trying to establish a connection between her husband and the murder victim, I felt awkward. I was relieved when Nate came back into the room. "We better head out," he said. "Tell Jimmy I'm sorry I missed him, but he knows where to reach me in case—" He broke off.

"What?" Reba asked anxiously.

Nate shifted his weight. "In case the cops give him a hard time again."

"Do you think they will?" Reba sounded even more worried. "Jimmy said the lawyer got them to drop the charges."

"Of assault yes, but that may not be the end of it."

Reba groaned.

"It'll be okay," Nate assured her. "If the cops come around again, Jimmy just needs to keep his head. And call me."

"What about the lawyer?"

"She'll stay involved."

"Good, but with a reputation like hers, she must be very expensive."

"Didn't Jimmy tell you? Gloria's agreed to represent him on a pro bono basis."

"Really? That's wonderful. Otherwise, we couldn't afford her. There's Kyle's dolphin money, of course, but . . ." Her voice trailed off.

"Dolphin money?" Nate looked puzzled.

Reba ran a finger around the rim of the wooden bowl on the table. "We've been saving to send Kyle to a dolphin therapy program in Florida. Kyle's pediatrician told us about it. He said it's great for disabled kids. They swim with the dolphins and—"

"That makes them better?" Nate appeared skeptical.

"Not exactly. The dolphins are used to motivate the kids to work on specific tasks. For each task the kids accomplish, they get to pet, stroke, or swim with a dolphin and a therapist in a special enclosed lagoon."

"Sounds fun, but does it really work?" Nate asked.

"I spoke on the phone with a woman whose child has cerebral palsy. He's been attending the program since he was four, and she said he's made amazing progress. That's what we want for Kyle."

"You'll get it."

Reba placed a hand on Nate's arm and gave him a long look. "Thank you for everything you've done."

In the car, Nate was silent and seemed abstracted. "Still worried about Jimmy?" I asked.

He nodded. "Wish he'd been there so we could've talked more. But I'm not sorry we stopped by on account of you and hubbub."

"What d'you mean?"

He turned to me with a smile. "I love it when you let yourself go like that. Think you can hold the feeling until we get to the B & B?"

I smiled back. "I'll try."

Our lovemaking was some of the best ever, pleasure breaking over me like an enormous wave. Afterward, I drifted into a peaceful sleep, unbroken by dreams until it was almost morning.

Nate and I played hubbub against a blackjack dealer at Clambanks. The prize was a trip to Florida for Kyle and enrollment in the dolphin program. We won and took Kyle to Florida, where we joined him in the water. His mouth opened in an "O" of delight as he held onto the fin of a partially submerged dolphin. A crow cawed loudly overhead. Kyle screamed and let go. The dolphin had morphed into Kavanagh's dead body.

CHAPTER 13

"Oh, we had aboard o'us a little cabin-boy,
Who said, 'What will you give me if the galley I
*   destroy?'*
'Oh, ye can wed my daughter, she is my pride and
*   joy,*
If ye sink her in the Lowlands Low.' "
                    —Lowlands Low, Sea Shanty

I woke to the sound of running water. Water and singing. Indian singing that to me just then sounded wonderful. Moments later, Nate emerged from the bathroom with a towel wrapped around his waist. Drops of water beaded his broad chest. Beautiful. He sat on the bed and touched my hair lightly. "You awake?"

"Mmmm."

He bent and kissed me. "I feel great. Slept like a baby thanks to . . ." Grinning, he reached under the covers and stroked me. My body arched with pleasure. I decided not to tell him about my nightmare. He deserved a break from worries about Jimmy.

Nate dropped me off at my apartment in Cambridge before heading to his place in Plymouth. As usual, my cat, Love, conveyed his displeasure at my absence by running away and hiding. I fed him, went through the mail, and checked phone and e-mail messages. There was one from my editor on *America: The Republic's Glory and Greatness,* reminding me that the next chapter, "An Industrial Nation," was due on Friday, two days from now. I went to work, and before long Rockefeller, railroads, and the Wizard of Menlo Park replaced Kavanagh's murder and the suspicion surrounding Jimmy at the forefront of my consciousness. By early evening, I was ready for a break and a check-in call with Erin.

"How's it going?" I asked.

"Okay. I guess." She sounded doubtful.

"What's up?"

Erin sighed heavily. "I've spoken with George's first wife."

His alcoholic first wife, if I remembered correctly. "That must've been difficult."

"Actually, she was surprisingly nice. Not at all what I expected. We talked about having some sort of service. It won't be at a church because George wasn't religious. We decided to take his boat out and scatter his ashes at sea. Pam thinks that's what he would've wanted. His father-in-law, too."

"Pam's father?"

"Sheila's. Pam's father passed away a while ago."

"Ah. What about George's parents?"

"They're no longer living."

"So, it will be just you and—"

"Pam, George Junior, and Anson Graf-Jones, Sheila's father. They all live in Greenwich, so they won't have to travel far for the service."

What an awkward and ill-assorted group. I didn't envy Erin being thrown together with three people she might never have met but for George's death. It seemed a sad commentary on the state of contemporary marriage. I had a further thought: If I died tomorrow, who would show up for my funeral? A hodge-podge from the past and present like the group that was coming to Kavanagh's service? Dead, at least I'd be spared the embarrassment of watching Nate and my ex-husband, Simon, struggle to find a patch of commonality.

"We're having a gathering afterward at the Spouters Point Inne," Erin said. "I hope you can make it."

"Of course. When is it?"

"This Friday."

So much for my deadline. "I'll be there."

"Thanks, Miranda. There's something else I wanted to tell you. Remember Winston Woo?"

"Who?"

"The Korean student I rescued from the rigging Sunday afternoon. He went out that night and never came back."

"Really? Did he get discouraged and return to his college?"

"We contacted Gellis College and he's not there. They've promised to let us know if he shows up. We also telephoned his family in Cambridge. They own a restaurant called the Korean Hotpot. Do you know it?"

"I've never eaten there, but I've heard of it."

"Anyway, his parents don't understand English very well, so it was hard communicating. But they said he wasn't at home."

"Maybe he's visiting friends or other relatives."

"Maybe, although . . ."

"What?"

"He left most of his gear behind, including a journal he'd been keeping. We took a look at it in the hopes it might give us a clue about where he'd gone. There was all this stuff about me."

"What sort of stuff?"

"Sexual fantasies. It was really pretty embarrassing. I guess he has kind of a crush on me."

It didn't take me long to connect the dots: If Winston was obsessed with Erin, perhaps his disappearance the night of the murder wasn't just a coincidence. "Do the police know about this?"

"Yes. They want to talk to him. But first they have to find him."

As soon as I got off the phone with Erin, I called Nate to report this latest development.

"That's good news," he said. "Takes the pressure off Jimmy. He can relax and so can I. Sam's with me now, and he'll be staying through the weekend. Maybe the three of us can do something fun."

"I'd like to, but I promised Erin I'd go to a gathering in George's memory on Friday."

"When you get back, then. I miss you already," he added in a voice that made my toes curl.

After we said good night, I tried to refocus on my work, but thoughts of Nate, Jimmy, Erin, and now, Winston kept intruding. I hoped the police found him soon—if indeed he was the murderer. I had a hard time imagining the skinny kid who'd dangled, terrified, from the rigging thrusting a killing lance through Kavanagh. Still . . .

Under a cloudy sky, I walked the several blocks to Inman Square, where the Korean Hotpot was located. A few people carried umbrellas tucked under their arms, a reminder that heavy rain was forecast for later in the day, the tail end of an August hurricane that had already wreaked havoc along the Carolina coast. When I arrived at the restaurant around two, the lunch crowd had dispersed, leaving only a few college students hunkered over bowls of noodles. A small, gray-haired Korean woman in a plain black dress approached me with a menu.

"Mrs. Woo?" She looked too old to be Winston's mother, but with so many older parents nowadays, it was always a good idea to ask.

"Daughter," the woman said.

"Is she here? Can I speak with her?"

"I get. No eat?"

"Just tea, thanks."

I sat down at a table. The old woman disappeared behind a beaded curtain at the rear of the restaurant. A few minutes later, another woman with short, dark hair and a worried expression emerged from the back. She carried a tray with a pot of tea and two cups, which she put on the table. I stood and held out my hand. "Mrs. Woo, I'm Miranda Lewis. I'd like to talk to you about your son."

"You teacher?" She regarded me warily.

"No, I—"

"Look like teacher."

"I'm not, but my friend is a teacher."

Mrs. Woo appeared puzzled. "Friend of Wendell's teacher? Wendell good boy, no trouble at school."

"I'm sure he is. It's your other son Winston I wanted to talk to you about."

"Winston good boy, too. Very smart. Go to college." Mrs. Woo's face lit up with pride.

"I know."

"You from college?"

"No, the museum."

"Museum?"

"The Spouters Point Maritime Museum, where Winston's doing an internship." I understood why Erin had found it so difficult to communicate over the phone. Face to face, I wasn't faring much better.

"Very smart. Choose pencil," Mrs. Woo said.

"I'm sorry?"

"No sorry. Choose pencil is good." Mrs. Woo sounded as frustrated as I felt with my inability to make myself understood. "You talk Wendell. Learn English in school. You wait." She disappeared into the back of the restaurant. I drank tea and waited.

Outside, the rain had begun. Giant drops lashed the window, making me wish I'd thought to bring an umbrella.

Minutes later, the grandmother left the restaurant with an umbrella, returning with a boy who looked several years younger than Winston. She brought him to my table and said something in Korean. I stood and introduced myself. The grandmother left and Wendell and I sat.

I was in the midst of explaining my Spouters Point Museum connection when Mrs. Woo arrived with two steaming bowls filled with noodles, beef, and vegetables. "Thank you, but I'm really not—"

"You eat," Mrs. Woo said. Wendell needed no persuading. He picked up his bowl, skewered a bundle of noodles with his chopsticks, and popped them into his mouth. My appetite whetted by the rich, tangy odor, I tried to secure a noodle. It promptly slid back into the bowl. Mrs. Woo brought me a knife, fork, and spoon. She hovered nearby while I took several bites of the delicious soup. Picking up where I'd left off, I said, "My friend is worried about your brother because—"

"You don't have to speak so loudly," Wendell interrupted. "I understand you fine."

"Sorry." I lowered my voice. "Anyway, my friend is worried because your brother left the museum on Sunday night without telling anyone where he was going. We thought you might've heard from him, or have an idea where he's gone."

Wendell spoke to his mother in rapid-fire Korean. Her eyes widened with alarm. "Winston good boy. Very smart. Never trouble. Choose pencil."

"Why does she keep saying that?" I asked Wendell.

He rolled his eyes. "Korean families make a big deal out of their child's first birthday. They have a party, dress the kid in traditional clothes and sit him on a table with various objects. They believe the object the child chooses will influence his future. Winston's choice of a pencil meant he'd do well in school. He has. My parents are real proud of him."

I detected a note of bitterness in his voice. "I'm sure they're proud of you, too."

Wendell shrugged. "I didn't choose a pencil. Back to your question, we haven't heard from Winston in over a week."

"Any friends or relatives in the area he might be visiting?"

"His only family is right here. As for friends . . ." He shook his head, then his eyes narrowed. "What's this really about? The cops were here asking about Winston, now you. Are you a cop, too?"

"No, I'm just . . . a concerned party. If you hear from him, or if he does come home, please get in touch." I wrote my number and Erin's at the museum on a piece of paper and gave it to Wendell. He stuffed it into a pocket and vanished behind the beaded curtain without another word.

I turned to Mrs. Woo, who was still standing nearby, regarding me anxiously. "The soup was delicious. What do I owe you?" I took out my wallet.

"No pay." Mrs. Woo pushed the wallet away. "Take home."

Before I could argue, she picked up my bowl and disappeared into the kitchen, returning with a cardboard container.

"Thank you very much."

"Thank you very much," Mrs. Woo echoed. She didn't sound happy. I felt bad because my visit had stirred up more worries about Winston.

At the door I hesitated. The rain was still coming down in torrents. I started to put my jacket over my head when I felt a tap at my elbow. The grandmother stood beside me, umbrella in hand. She walked with me to the bus stop and waited until it came. "Thank you." I got in, taking care not to step in the stream of brown, rushing water that had formed in the gutter.

"You welcome."

As the bus pulled away, I glanced back. The grandmother was still standing on the curb at the edge of the brown stream, solemn as a mourner at a grave site in her black dress with her dripping black umbrella.

CHAPTER 14

"We lowered him down with a golden chain,
Our eyes all dim with more than rain."

—**Mister Stormalong, Sea Shanty**

By the time I'd put the finishing touches on the "Industrial Nation" chapter and e-mailed it to my editor, I-95 South had begun to clog with Friday afternoon traffic. I was going to be late for the reception in Kavanagh's memory and that was that.

Three hours later, I arrived at the Spouters Point Inne, tired and frazzled. The hostess steered me toward a function room beyond the main dining room. Before going in, I decided to freshen up in the downstairs restroom. A heavily made-up woman in a low-cut dress stood in front of the mirror, slathering on a new coat of lipstick. She looked vaguely familiar. I went into a stall. The toilet flushed before I could sit down. Damn. Automatic flushing toilets always unnerved me. It flushed twice more before I finished. The faucet was automatic, too, yet when I held my hands under it, nothing happened.

"Hold your hands like this." The lipstick woman stuck her hands under another faucet, bringing forth a flow of water.

I followed her example, but again nothing happened. "Guess I don't have the right touch."

"Must be busted. Try this one."

I did and it worked. "Thanks. You obviously have a way with these things."

Lipstick shrugged. "Win a few, lose a few. And right now, I'm one helluva loser." Her face drooped and I could smell the alcohol on her breath.

"What's the matter?" I asked more out of politeness than genuine interest.

"Oh nothing, 'cept my boyfriend left me high and dry."

"I'm sorry."

"Yeah, just when I thought everything was hunky dory, he goes and dumps me."

I took another look at her and realized where I'd seen her before. She was the woman Nate and I had observed arguing with her boyfriend the night Kavanagh was murdered. I told her I was sorry again and went upstairs.

The reception took place in a large, low-ceilinged room with a view of the water, now gray under an overcast early evening sky. Tables and chairs filled some of the cavernous space. One table contained food, another floral arrangements and photographs of the deceased. A music stand with various instruments lined up beside it occupied one corner. Evidently, Mark and the other museum musicians had been playing earlier.

The room was sparsely populated. Either most of the guests had already come and gone, or not that many had showed up in the first place. Those who remained were clustered in small groups. I glimpsed Erin in a grouping of museum staffers that included Mark and his wife and kids, as well as Luke's wife and kids. Luke himself stood apart, still the pariah apparently. Sergeant Curtin strolled over and spoke with him. Nate believed Curtin wouldn't give Luke a hard time on account of their being high school buddies. I wondered how true this was. They certainly looked relaxed and at ease with each other now.

My gaze shifted to another group of somewhat older, more well-heeled men and women. They must be the Greenwich contingent of Kavanagh's first wife and friends from that time in his life. A distinguished man in his late sixties or early seventies who looked like he belonged with the Greenwich crowd stood by himself, gazing pensively at the photographs displayed on the table. Vernon and Flo Higginbotham, with Happy in her arms, hovered near the food table. To my disgust, I noticed she was surreptitiously feeding the poodle canapés.

Erin spotted me and hurried over. "Miranda! I was afraid you weren't going to make it."

"Sorry. I got started later than I'd planned, and hit rush-hour traffic."

"Well, I'm glad you're here." She gave me a big hug.

I was tempted to ask how the scattering of Kavanagh's ashes had gone, but decided not to. Erin looked as if she was barely holding it together. The wrong words, or even too sympathetic a look, and she might lose it completely. She bit her lip and glanced away. "I think you already know most of the museum people," she said after a pause, "but why don't I introduce you to George's first wife?" She guided me over to the Greenwich group. "Pam, I'd like you to meet my friend, Miranda Lewis."

An attractive woman with gray-streaked brown hair, who looked to be in her mid-fifties, Pam Kavanagh had a wholesome, clean-scrubbed air that reminded me of Erin. The resemblance between them was so strong that Pam could have been Erin's mother or older sister. Based on appearance alone, Kavanagh seemed to have chosen similar women for his first and third wives.

Pam Kavanagh introduced me to her son, George Junior, a nice-looking young man in his twenties with his father's startlingly blue eyes, and several friends and neighbors from Greenwich. I exchanged a few polite remarks with them, then Erin and I started back toward the museum crowd.

"Doggie's eating all the food!" Mark and Jane's youngest son pointed an accusing finger at Happy.

"He's just having a little snack," Flo Higginbotham countered. "There's more than enough for everyone."

Her husband scowled at the boy, enough to send him running back to his mother. The distinguished man by the photographs remained impervious to the commotion. I asked Erin who he was.

"Anson Graf-Jones, Sheila's father. Would you like me to introduce you?"

I nodded, curious to meet him.

"Lewis, did you say?" Graf-Jones asked after Erin had introduced us. With tanned, chiseled features, small, pale, almost colorless eyes, and a shock of gray-blond hair, he struck me as the epitome of the Connecticut Yankee. "I used to know a family by that name. They wintered in Manhattan and spent the summers at Point O' Woods."

Point O' Woods, I knew from my sole visit to Fire Island, was an exclusive, old-moneyed enclave of charming, shingled houses at the eastern tip of the island. "I'm from California originally."

"Ah . . . the West Coast." His tone held just enough disdain to show he considered it the *wrong* coast.

"Erin, can I speak with you for a moment?" Maggie appeared at Erin's side. Erin excused herself. Graf-Jones turned back to the photographs. I moved in to get a look myself. They showed Kavanagh at various stages of life: as a boy, college student, young husband and father, and finally as a middle-aged man. Several of the latter photos had obviously been taken by Erin, because I saw the Spouters Point Museum in the background. There was one I couldn't see very well because Graf-Jones blocked my view.

"Excuse me." I craned my neck around him. Three smiling figures posed in front of a sailboat I recognized as Kavanagh's. On one side stood Kavanagh himself, on the other a handsome younger man. In the middle was a stunningly beautiful young woman with long, blond hair and perfect teeth. Sheila probably. I thrust my head closer for a better look. Both men had their arms around her. Kavanagh's hand cupped her shoulder, the younger man's dangled downward. His tanned forearm and the blue face of his wristwatch stood out against her white polo shirt.

"Your daughter?" Graf-Jones nodded imperceptibly. "She's lovely." Another imperceptible nod. Behind us, Mark and the other musicians began to play a song about coming home to old New England:

> *"And the waves we leave behind us*
> *Seem to murmur as they flow,*
> *'There's a hearty welcome waiting*
> *In the land to which you go!*
> *And the girl you love so dearly . . .'"*

Beside me, I heard a muffled sob. Graf-Jones's shoulders heaved. He seized the photograph of his daughter and left the room abruptly. I stared, open-mouthed, after him. Pam Kavanagh caught my eye and came over. "What happened with Anson?"

"Something in the song set him off. Maybe the line about 'the girl you love so dearly'?"

Pam Kavanagh sighed. "You're probably right. Anson and I have only a nodding acquaintance because we belong to the same country club. But others who know him better say he hasn't been able to accept the loss of his daughter."

I remembered something Luke had told me. "I heard he thinks George might have been responsible for his daughter's death, and that he even hired a private investigator to look into it."

"A detective? My goodness!" Pam Kavanagh appeared surprised. "I don't know anything about that, but I wouldn't put it past Anson. He's a very determined man."

"Do you—I mean, do you think he's right to blame George?"

Pam Kavanagh smiled wryly, as if aware of another question I might've asked: if she blamed her former husband. "For Sheila's death, no. It was a tragic accident, one of those things that can happen in a bad storm at sea. As for the rest of it, who's to say where the blame lies?" She paused and stared thoughtfully out the window at the overcast sky, the gray, churning water. "There was a time when I blamed them both—Sheila for stealing him away, George for turning our lives into a cliché. You know: middle-aged man dumps wife of twenty-seven years for beautiful younger woman. I was very angry and bitter. Especially when George made me out to be something I wasn't to justify leaving."

She must be referring to her husband's portrayal of her as an alcoholic. Now that I'd met Pam Kavanagh, I didn't think she had the unhealthy look of an alcoholic or even a recovering one.

"But I'm past that now, thanks to Andy."

"Andy?"

"*My* younger man," Pam Kavanagh said with proprietary pride. She gestured toward the Greenwich contingent. A man with round, ruddy cheeks and a thick head of curly black hair smiled and waved. Pam Kavanagh waved back. "Now, if you'll excuse me." She moved away.

"One more thing."

"Yes?" She turned back to me with a slight frown.

"Who's the other man in the photograph with George and Sheila?"

A shadow crossed her face. "Alex Broussard. He was the shipbuilder in Maine who built the *Sheila Anne*."

"You used the past tense."

"Alex was swept overboard with Sheila."

"What!" I couldn't contain my surprise. "Why was he even

on the voyage? I thought it was George and Sheila's honey-moon."

Pam Kavanagh gave me another wry look, this time without a smile. "Remember that song from *Damn Yankees*? 'Whatever Lola Wants, Lola Gets'? That was the way it was with Sheila."

CHAPTER 15

*"Then the cabin-boy did swim all to the larboard
side,
Sayin' 'Capen, take me up, I am drifting with the
tide.'
'I will sink ye, I will kill ye, if ye claim my child as
bride,
I will sink ye in the Lowlands, Low.' "*
—Lowlands Low, Sea Shanty

The reception over, Erin and I went back to Mark's for dinner, a meal frequently interrupted by his many adopted cats. They tossed toys into the air—one landed in my plate—chased each other around the room, leaped onto laps and even the tabletop and generally made a nuisance of themselves. I could understand why Erin had been reluctant to stay here, and also why she was ready to leave when dinner was finished.

Back at her apartment, we opened a bottle of wine left over from the reception and settled down for a heart-to-heart. Erin stared into her wineglass. "Well, it wasn't as bad as I thought it was going to be."

"The reception or the scattering of ashes beforehand?"

"Both, though I was really dreading the ashes part. But Pam Kavanagh was so sympathetic and supportive, it made the whole thing much easier."

"I hope you don't mind my saying this, but she doesn't strike me as the alcoholic George portrayed her."

Erin ran a finger around the rim of her glass. "I know what you mean. I don't understand why he felt he had to make her out to be such a monster."

"Unless it was to justify his leaving her for Sheila."

"Still . . ." Erin lapsed into a pensive silence. I suspected she was beginning to realize George wasn't the paragon she'd thought him. "What happened with Graf-Jones, by the way?" she asked finally. "One minute he was talking with you, and the next, he disappeared without saying good-bye."

"Pam Kavanagh told me he's never come to terms with losing his daughter. So perhaps the occasion brought back painful memories that became too much for him."

"I hadn't thought of that, but you may be right," Erin said.

"Someone else was swept overboard with Sheila. Did you know about that?"

Erin stared at me with surprise. "No. Who?"

"Alex Broussard, the shipbuilder who built the *Sheila Anne* and who accompanied George and Sheila on its maiden voyage."

"Really? George never mentioned there was anyone else on board. How did you find this out?"

"Pam Kavanagh. I noticed a young, good-looking man in a photo of George and Sheila. When I asked Pam who he was, she told me the story."

"This is certainly news to me." Erin put her glass down and chewed a nail.

I gave her a few minutes to let the information sink in, then, as gently as I could, I asked, "Did George ever talk about what happened during the storm?"

"A little. He said he was resting in the cabin below, and Sheila was keeping watch in the cockpit when a rogue wave capsized the boat. Flying objects knocked him unconscious. When he came to, the boat had righted itself, but Sheila was gone."

Sheila and Alex Broussard, I corrected mentally.

"She probably would have been wearing a safety harness," Erin continued, "so it either broke or—"

"Those things can break?" I asked, horrified.

Erin pointed to a book I'd noticed earlier: *Fastnet, Force 10, The Deadliest Storm in the History of Modern Sailing.* "In that race six men were swept overboard when their safety harnesses broke."

I shuddered inwardly. "You said 'or.' What's the other possibility?"

"It was cut."

"Why would someone cut a safety harness?"

"When the boat capsized, Sheila may have been trapped under the cockpit. She could've cut the harness to save herself."

I flashed back to a high school outing to a beach in Southern California. We'd been having a great time riding the swells on a rubber raft when a huge wave slammed into the boat and flipped it over. I'd been trapped underneath. I considered myself a strong swimmer, and had spent a lot of time in the ocean in my younger days. Yet I'd come away with a healthy respect for monster waves. "I wonder what happened to Alex Broussard."

"Probably the same thing that happened to Sheila: his safety harness broke, or he was trapped and cut it. Or he was lost trying to rescue her."

"What did George do when he regained consciousness?"

"He found himself alone in a damaged boat with a broken radio and no life raft. So he did the only thing he could—tried to keep the boat afloat until help arrived."

"You said there was no life raft. What happened to it?"

"Most likely washed overboard. That's what happened to nearly a dozen life rafts in the Fastnet race."

"Sheila and Alex Broussard could've used the life raft,

couldn't they?"

"If they did, it was never found. But I can't believe they'd abandon ship without George." She shook her head slowly.

She doesn't have a suspicious bone in her body, I thought. I, on the other hand, had no trouble imagining the latter scenario, especially if Sheila and Alex had been lovers and had felt crowded by her husband. "Don't you think it's odd Alex Broussard went along in the first place?"

"He was the shipbuilder. He may've wanted to go on the maiden voyage to test the boat's seaworthiness. Or George and Sheila felt they needed an extra hand."

Or Sheila wanted him there. The song title came back to me: "Whatever Lola Wants, Lola Gets."

"How were things back in Cambridge?" Erin changed the subject.

"Okay. I finished another chapter of *ARGG,* and paid a visit to Winston's family."

Erin sat up straighter. "You did?"

"I figured I might as well since the family restaurant isn't far from my apartment."

"Did they have any idea where he might have gone?"

I shook my head. "Like you, I had a hard time communicating because his mother doesn't understand English very well. But I spoke with his younger brother. He didn't have a clue about Winston's whereabouts either."

"I hope to God he's all right," Erin said.

Another silence settled over us, this time broken by the ringing of my cell phone. It was Nate. "What's up?"

"I'm at Jimmy's."

"Why? What's happened?"

"Reba called late this afternoon. The cops have been giving Jimmy a hard time again. They say they have new evidence linking him to Kavanagh. Reba's afraid Jimmy's starting to lose it."

"What's the new evidence?"

"They found a waitress at Clambanks who remembers serving Jimmy and Kavanagh coffee."

"And?"

"That's it. They haven't got zip."

"They caught him in a lie, though."

"Big deal. Besides, the waitress could be mistaken. Or the cops could be bluffing. I don't want to talk about it anymore."

"Okay, but what about Sam?"

"I brought him with me. We're spending the night. You with Erin?"

"At her apartment."

"I'd come by to see you, but I'm beat. I'll be in touch tomorrow. Maybe we can make some plans."

We said good night and I turned back to Erin. "That was Nate," I began. She didn't reply but continued to stare into space, eyes narrowed, as if she were straining to catch a last glimpse of a receding object before it vanished altogether.

CHAPTER 16

"How he wasted and wasted away in those few long-lingering days, till there seemed but little left of him but his frame and tattooing."

—Moby-Dick

The next morning, Nate called and invited me to join Jimmy and his family on a hike to the top of Stargaze Hill, one of the highest points in Rhode Island. The outing was Reba's idea. She hoped it would do Jimmy good to get outdoors and visit a place that was important to their people.

I met Nate and company at the trailhead. Right away, I was struck by how much Jimmy had changed in less than a week. Dark circles rimmed his eyes, and his chin and shaved head bristled with stubble. He seemed more jittery than ever. "You drive down this morning?" He rocked on the balls of his feet.

"No, I arrived late yesterday for—" I broke off at a warning signal from Nate. "A get-together some friends were having."

"Let's get started," Reba said.

Jimmy and Nate led the way, Jimmy wearing a backpack, Nate bearing Kyle on his shoulders. Sam followed, one hand holding a cooler, the other a media player. Reba and I brought up the rear, Patty having opted to stay at home.

"This land belongs to your people?" I asked Reba.

"Yes. Long ago, our ancestors hunted caribou here."

"They hunted snakes, too," Jimmy called back.

"That was over in Big Otter Swamp, hundreds of years later," Reba said. "Times were hard then. There were no jobs on the reservation, so one man went into the swamp looking for snakes. He tied towels around his legs for protection. The snakes wrapped themselves around his legs, and he took them and put them in a bag. He sold them to an old man who came to the reservation to buy them."

I shuddered inwardly at the thought of snakes coiling themselves around the man's legs.

"Are there snakes around here now?"

"Sure," Jimmy said. "Copperheads and—"

"Only a few and just in the swamp," Reba corrected him. "Most of the snakes are harmless garter snakes. Getting back to the caribou . . ."

She launched into a description of the natural history of the area—how it had been covered by a glacier that left behind a depression, which became Big Otter Swamp. While interesting, her account was probably a way to avoid talking about what must be uppermost in her mind: the fact that her husband was not only a murder suspect, but acted guilty as well.

Eventually we came to a place where the trail ascended steeply over a jumble of rocks. At the summit, the woods gave way to an open area of rocky ledges that offered a sweeping panorama of the surrounding countryside. Reba pointed with pride to the Dottaguck Museum of History and Culture, a long, low-rise structure. Beyond, the gold turrets of the Clambanks casino complex glistened in the sun. Immediately below, a lovely pond, partly covered with green-and-red lily pads, mirrored the blue sky, powder-puff clouds, and the beginnings of fall foliage.

"Great views," I enthused.

"Two hundred years ago, our sachem, Ottommaocke, came to this spot to look for enemy campfires when we were at war with the Assawogs," Reba said.

Jimmy stood at the edge of a ledge, frowning down into the woods. He looked as if he, too, were searching for an unseen enemy. His feet shifted, sending a rain of pebbles down the mountainside. Nate steered him away. "C'mon, bro, let's eat."

Our picnic consisted of fried chicken, green salad and potato salad, and brownies for dessert, with beer for the adults and soda for Sam and Kyle. Jimmy drank more than he ate, his Adam's apple bobbing with each swig of beer. Scrunched into a crevice like a stunted plant, Kyle put down his chicken leg and barked excitedly, gesturing toward a spot where sunlight made the quartz veins in the rock sparkle like diamonds.

"Like that, huh?" Nate broke off a piece of shiny rock and gave it to Kyle. The boy's pinched face opened into a smile, as he turned the rock around and around in the sun.

"I'll get more for you." Jimmy gathered a bunch of quartz rocks and thrust them at Kyle. "Here, take 'em." The rock Kyle was holding slipped through his fingers, as he tried to grasp the others. He wailed with distress.

"Stop it!" Jimmy raised a hand. Kyle shrieked louder.

"Leave him be," Reba said firmly.

Jimmy turned away. His flare-up with Kyle reminded me of the one I'd witnessed at the powwow. He'd been under a lot of pressure then, and was even more stressed now. Still . . . I glanced around. Reba's head was lowered, her face in shadow. I couldn't see Nate's eyes behind his reflector sunglasses, but a deep furrow was etched in his broad forehead. Even Sam seemed affected by the outburst. He removed his earphones and stared quizzically at Jimmy.

"I need another beer." Jimmy grabbed a can from the cooler, finished it, and reached for another.

"Have some brownies," Reba said. "Patty made them this morning." We all took one except for Jimmy, who went on drinking. After a while, he mumbled something about catching rays, and stretched out on the rock. Moments later, he was snoring. The sun, food, and beer made me sleepy, too. Nate put his arm around me and I snuggled close, resting my head on his chest. I dozed.

Someone tapped my arm. Opening my eyes, I saw Sam. He pointed at a large bird of prey, hovering in the air above Jimmy, its outstretched wings mimicking his splayed arms and legs. "Is that a hawk?" I whispered.

"No way," Sam whispered back. "It's an eagle."

"Really? I didn't know there were eagles around here."

"Must've flown over from somewhere else," Sam said.

Beside me, Nate stirred. I nudged him awake and pointed. The eagle remained suspended over Jimmy, its image superimposed on his. Jimmy woke with a start, saw the bird, and cried, "Get away from me!" The bird shifted slightly. Jimmy grabbed a rock. Nate knocked it out of his hand. "Have you gone crazy? That's an eagle!"

"It's evil," Jimmy muttered. Nate drew him aside and they spoke in low voices. I helped Reba pack up the remains of the picnic. Sam lent Kyle his earphones so he could listen to music on Sam's media player. The eagle continued to hover over the place where Jimmy had lain. Nate and Jimmy rejoined us. "We should head back now. Ready for another ride, buddy?" Nate hoisted Kyle onto his shoulders.

No one said much on the downward hike. Jimmy's outburst with Kyle and the eagle's strange appearance had cast a pall over us. The bird's image stayed with me, a Rorschach blot on the brain.

In the parking area, I thanked Reba and Jimmy for including me on the hike. "Why not come back to the house?" Reba asked.

I glanced at Nate, who responded with an imperceptible shake of the head. "Thanks, but I've got work to do at home." Better this white lie than admit I'd be spending the rest of the weekend with the fiancée of the man Jimmy was suspected of murdering.

"Miranda takes her deadlines very seriously," Nate said when Reba started to protest. He walked me to my car, hugged me and promised to call when he could.

The opportunity came when I was back at Erin's apartment, waiting for her to return from the maritime museum. "How are things?" I asked.

"Not good. The cops stopped by and hassled Patty while we were at Stargaze Hill."

"Ouch. They haven't found any more evidence linking Jimmy to Kavanagh, have they?"

"No, and the waitress thing is probably one big bluff."

"Then why does Jimmy act so guilty?" The words were no sooner out of my mouth than I regretted them.

"You really don't get it, do you?" Nate's voice was laced with scorn.

His words stung. My first impulse was to strike back, tell him my question was valid, and he was wrong to use that tone with me. I counted slowly to ten. Then I said, "I'm trying."

"Then try harder. Put yourself in his shoes. Imagine what it's like to be an Indian accused of a crime you didn't commit by a bunch of prejudiced white cops."

"But the way he lashed out at Kyle, and that business with the eagle," I persisted.

Nate's tone softened. "I know. He shouldn't have turned on Kyle or tried to harm that eagle. They're special birds. They fly high in the sky, where the air is pure, and carry messages to the Great Spirit. When you pray with an eagle feather, the bird's spirit in the feather takes your prayer all the way to God's ear."

"Why did Jimmy say the eagle was evil, then?"

"Told me he'd been having a nightmare about an evil bird, and when he woke up, he mistook the eagle for the dream bird.

I'd like to believe him but . . ."

"What?"

"Years ago, after Jimmy got clean, I gave him an eagle feather. I wanted him to feel good about himself. Today when I asked him if he still had it, he got all nervous and defensive. I think something's happened to that feather. If it has, he's in trouble."

"Just because he may've lost or damaged a feather?"

"To hold an eagle feather in your hand is to be like an eagle: kind, strong, and free. You take care of it, it takes care of you. But if you don't . . ." Nate let the sentence hang.

"What're you going to do?"

"Talk with him more. Let him know again I'm here for him. Wish I could stay until this blows over, but I gotta get Sam back for a big piano recital tomorrow afternoon. When are you going back?"

"Tomorrow probably."

"Maybe we can get together after Sam's recital. Sooner, if things calm down here."

Although the conversation ended on a positive note, I didn't feel good. I wished Nate and I could've spoken in person, maybe even had make-up sex. Instead, I felt the distance between us, emotionally as well as physically. He said I didn't get it. Would I ever, in his view? And would he ever understand my need to point out things he was too stubborn to see?

CHAPTER 17

"Then she robbed them of silver,
She robbed them of gold;
She robbed them of costly wear-o
She took his broad sword
instead of an oar,
And she paddled her way
Back to the shore."
—The Maid on the Shore, Sea Shanty

Nate called the next morning while Erin and I were having breakfast. He wasted no time getting to the point: "Jimmy's disappeared."

"What?!" I put down my coffee mug with a clatter.

"His side of the bed was empty when Reba woke up this morning. At first, she thought he'd gone out for a walk or an errand. Then she noticed some of his clothes were missing, and that his car was gone. That's when she woke me."

"Any idea where he is?"

"Reba called everybody she could think of, and nobody's seen him. We've also driven around looking for him with no luck. I'm guessing he might've headed to Providence."

"Why?"

"He's got friends there from his druggie days. I'm going to check out some of his old haunts."

"God, I hope you find him."

"Me, too. But it may take a while. I don't know if I'll be back in time to get Sam to his recital."

"You want me to drive him there?"

"Only if I can't. It's a pretty big deal. He's been practicing for months. He'll be really disappointed if he doesn't take part, and so will his teacher, his mom and me."

"Okay, I'll be waiting to hear from you."

"Thanks, Miranda."

"I don't see why Dad has to go chasing after Jimmy today of all days," Sam fumed two hours later when I picked him up at the Swifts'. "He said he'd take me fishing, but he dragged me down here. Now, when I need to get back for my recital, he bails and—"

"He wouldn't have done it if finding Jimmy weren't important," I defended Nate.

Sam scowled, clamped on his earphones and withdrew into his music. We were almost to the entrance to the highway when he announced he was hungry.

"We'll pick something up on the way," I said.

"No, here. I'm starving."

"There must be a McDonald's somewhere around."

"Are you kidding? I don't eat that fast food."

"Where do you want to go?" I was tempted to add, "your royal highness," but restrained myself.

"The Sea Shanty."

"Where's that?"

"I'll get us there."

The Sea Shanty was a shack on a back road in the vicinity of the maritime museum. Despite its out-of-the-way location, the place was crowded. Sam managed to snag one of the few tables, while I stood in a long line to place our order. The line moved with glacial slowness. Glancing over at Sam, I saw him fiddling with his cell phone. Finally, I reached the counter, ordered, waited, got our food and paid. I started toward the table only to discover Sam gone. I was annoyed. I'd gone out of my way to bring him here, and now he'd wandered off without telling me.

I went to the men's room, knocked and called his name.

"Frank here," an older man's voice yelled back.

Annoyance gave way to concern. Where could he be if not the men's room? He couldn't have just vanished into thin air. Or could he? What if someone had lured him outside? Heart pounding, I ran out into the parking area. A car was just pulling away. I hurried over. "Have you seen a teenage boy with long dark hair?" I asked the woman behind the wheel. She shook her head, but a little girl sitting in the back and drinking through a plastic straw pointed toward a dumpster in the rear of the building. Sam stood on one side of it, peering into a tangle of brush beyond.

"What're you doing here?" I demanded. "You should've told me you were going out."

"Sorry. It was too noisy inside to talk on my cell phone, so I came out and—"

"Come in and eat your lunch," I interrupted impatiently. "We need to get back on the road."

Sam's mother, Kathy, was already waiting in the recital hall at the music school with two saved seats when we arrived. She was a short woman with straight dark hair parted in the middle, an olive complexion, and almond eyes that gave her an exotic look. She also possessed a dazzling smile. But she wasn't smiling now. She was biting her nails. "I thought you'd never get here," she said to Sam. "Where's your dad?"

"Off on a wild-goose chase."

"What?"

"We'll explain later." I sat down next to Sam. Fortunately, he wasn't on until nearly the end of the program. The performers ahead of him included small children who struggled through simple pieces like "Old MacDonald," and slouching teenagers who somehow managed to play Bach and Beethoven with finesse. When Sam's turn came, he handed me his cell phone and asked me to take a few pictures of him. I thought this was unnecessary, as his mother was already going to film him with her camcorder, but I did so anyway.

Sam's rendition of a piece by the jazz musician Herbie Hancock drew a huge round of applause that made me glad I'd taken the trouble to get him here. When the recital was over, Sam wanted to see the pictures his mother and I had taken. I gave him the cell phone, and watched as one image after another appeared on the screen. After four pictures of Sam in various stages of performance, the image of a woman crouching by a dumpster came into view.

"Who's that?" I asked.

"A homeless woman I saw outside the Sea Shanty," Sam said.

"Can I have a closer look?" Sam gave me the cell phone.

"Now, will you please explain why your dad isn't here?" Kathy demanded.

"Jimmy was acting pretty weird, then he like disappeared, and dad . . ."

My gaze riveted on the woman on the screen, I stopped listening.

A few hours later, I studied the image of the crouching woman on my computer. At my request, Sam had e-mailed me the picture. Seeing her on a bigger screen convinced me she was the homeless woman Nate and I had met at the dumpster behind the Spouters Point Inne the night of Kavanagh's murder. She had the same dirty, matted blond hair, same wrinkled, brown skin, same wide, staring eyes with a feral gleam. But what really caught my attention was the expensive-looking watch she wore. A watch with a blue face. I'd noticed a similar watch on someone else recently. Who?

Then I remembered.

CHAPTER 18

"Oh my men must be crazy,
my men must be mad,
My men must be in deep despair-o,
For to let you away
from my cabin so gay
And to paddle you back to the shore."
—The Maid on the Shore, Sea Shanty

I lost track of how many times I shut down my computer only to restart it and open the file with the homeless woman's picture. Her face held a strange fascination for me. Like the illustration of the Wicked Witch in *Snow White and the Seven Dwarfs* when I was a child, I was alternately repelled and drawn to her.

Every time I stared at her ravaged features, another image rose up in my mind. It was the image of a very different woman. She was beautiful with long blond hair and perfect teeth. The only link—tenuous at best—between the images was that there was a watch with a blue face in each. In the picture on my screen, the homeless woman wore the watch, but in the image stored in my memory, the watch circled the wrist of a handsome young man whose arm was casually draped around the beautiful woman's shoulder. Alex Broussard and Sheila, the probable lovers who'd been swept overboard.

I knew it was crazy to connect the homeless woman with

Sheila based on a watch. Yet the more I studied the former's picture, the more I thought I saw a faint resemblance between them. They were like faces in a makeover gone awry: one was the stunning "before," the other, the hideous "after." Or a female version of Dr. Jekyll and Mr. Hyde.

I squinted at the screen until my eyes watered and the image blurred. I blinked, refocused and stared again. Finally, tearing my gaze away from the computer, I yawned and stretched. I was punch-drunk with exhaustion, and when I got this way, it affected my judgment, causing me to imagine all sorts of ridiculous things. I'd go to bed and everything would be fine in the morning.

But daylight brought no return to my senses. The notion that these two disparate faces belonged to the same person haunted me. I felt I couldn't rest until I'd settled the matter. I picked up the phone and dialed information for Greenwich. Graf-Jones's number was unlisted, but I was able to get it from Pam Kavanagh. A man who identified himself as John Lent, Graf-Jones's secretary, answered. It hadn't occurred to me he'd have a gatekeeper, and a surly one at that. I'd just begun to explain who I was when he cut in, "What do you want?"

"I have a photo I'd like to talk to Mr. Graf-Jones about."

"A photo of what?"

"I think it might be his daughter."

"A recent photo?"

"Uh-huh."

"You and a million others," Lent muttered. "I'll see if he wants to speak to you." His tone conveyed that he thought this highly unlikely.

I waited and waited. I was about to hang up when Graf-Jones came on the line. "Who did you say you are? My secretary wasn't clear."

"Miranda Lewis. We met Sunday evening at—"

"One of the New York Lewises?"

"Yes." Let him believe that if it got me what I wanted.

"You say you have a recent photo of someone resembling my daughter?"

"Correct. Only I can't be sure until I've compared it with other photos of her."

There was a long silence. Finally, he said, "Why don't you mail me the photo, then I can see if it's Sheila or not?"

"I'd rather bring it to you. That way, we don't have to worry about it getting lost in the mail. Besides, I live close by," I lied.

Another silence. Then: "I suppose that would be all right. I'm lunching at the club at noon, so it will have to be before then."

A quick phone call, and the guard at the gate buzzed me through. I drove past stately brick colonials, Tudor mansions and Italian villas, some clearly visible, others half-hidden by trees or tall fences, until I came to Graf-Jones's residence. The Gothic revival house, with its buttresses, pointed-arch windows and steeply pitched roof, reminded me of a castle perched on a knoll overlooking the Long Island Sound.

A youngish man with the buzz cut and muscular build of an ex-Marine answered the door. The secretary or, rather, bodyguard, John Lent. Despite my best efforts to dress for the part in Connecticut country club casual, he eyed me suspiciously as he showed me to Graf-Jones's study.

Graf-Jones sat behind a large desk with a ship model and several framed photographs of his daughter. More photographs of Sheila, along with paintings and photographs of sailboats, covered the walls, which were paneled in gleaming wood like the interior of a yacht. Glass cabinets held trophies, along with scrimshaw and boat models. The room seemed part mini maritime museum, part shrine to his dead daughter.

He rose when I entered. Although I'd only seen him a few

days ago, I'd forgotten how imposing he was. Graf-Jones was well over six feet tall with a long, lean body, a large head and the small, pale eyes of a lizard. He extended a hand. His grip was firm, yet his expression conveyed a certain wariness. "So you're a Lewis." He studied my face, as if searching for a trace of family resemblance.

"Yes. By marriage."

"Ah. Which one of Edward's sons did you marry?"

"Philip." Thank heaven I'd done my homework and looked up the family on the Internet before leaving.

"I thought his wife's name was Elizabeth."

"They divorced. I'm his second wife."

"I didn't know there was a divorce. But then it's been some time since I've been in touch with them."

"Would you like to see the photo now?" I asked to forestall further questions about my background.

"All right." Graf-Jones's hand trembled as he took the photo of the homeless woman. He turned away so I couldn't see his face while he examined it. His shoulders rose and lowered in a sigh. But when he turned back to me, his features were set in hard lines of denial. "There is absolutely no resemblance between my daughter and this woman. Sheila was beautiful. This woman is a hag." He put the photo face down on his desk. "I don't know how you could have imagined she was my daughter. Did you ever meet Sheila?"

"I only saw a photograph of her."

"Where was that?"

"At the reception Sunday night."

"For George Kavanagh?"

"Yes."

Graf-Jones studied me more closely. "I thought you looked familiar. You're a friend of that young woman who was having a . . ." He paused, as if seeking the right word. "A relationship with George."

"They were engaged."

"I don't care what they were," Graf-Jones snapped. "Why did you tell me you were a Lewis when you're actually a friend of that young . . . ?" He left the sentence unfinished, but I suspected he intended a derogatory name.

"Because I'm both a Lewis and a friend of Erin Meloy's. The two aren't mutually exclusive."

"Don't be impertinent." He glared at me.

"I'm sorry."

Graf-Jones turned away again, gripping the edge of his desk. When he turned back, his features were composed, and his voice calm, if a bit stiff. "I accept your apology. Now, if you don't mind, I have a few questions for you."

I nodded for him to proceed.

"Who took the photo you brought?"

"I did. I'm an amateur photographer, always snapping pictures of people and things that interest me."

"I see. Why did you think this woman might be Sheila?"

"I noticed a faint resemblance between her and a picture of Sheila at the reception. Then, too, there's the watch."

"Watch?"

"The woman in my picture is wearing a watch similar to one the builder of the *Sheila Anne* wore in the other photo. A watch with a blue face." I turned the photo over and pointed to it.

Graf-Jones removed a pair of reading glasses from his pocket and bent over the picture, squinting at it like a jeweler examining a gem. "An Omega Seamaster®, if I'm not mistaken. Sheila did give Alex Broussard a Seamaster® as a gift. It was her way of thanking him for his superb craftsmanship. But the fact that this woman is wearing such a watch means nothing. From the looks of her, she probably stole it."

"You don't think there's any chance your daughter is still alive?"

Graf-Jones shook his head. "If she were, I would have heard from her."

"Or the private detective you hired would have found her?"

Graf-Jones's eyes narrowed to slits. "Who said I hired a private detective?"

"It's just something I heard." He didn't need to know the information had come to me from Erin via Luke.

"You should learn not to believe every rumor you hear," Graf-Jones said icily. I did my best to look chastened. Whether it was my repentant look or the fact that Graf-Jones thought me a New York Lewis, he relented somewhat. "If I sound harsh, it's because I was besieged by people claiming to have seen Sheila in the beginning. Some were well meaning, but most, I suspect, were simply after the reward I offered."

"I didn't know there was a reward. I came because I honestly thought this woman could be Sheila."

"That may be . . . but do you have any idea what it's like to have one's fondest hopes raised one moment and dashed the next?" As he said this, his hand floated briefly in the air before slamming into the desktop. The ship model and the framed photographs of his daughter rattled. The photo of the homeless woman fluttered to the floor.

"I'm sorry," I said again.

"It's all right. I don't doubt your good intentions, but now it's time you left. My secretary will see you out." Graf-Jones tapped a bell on his desk.

The door opened so quickly, I suspected Lent had been listening on the other side. I retrieved the photo and turned to go. "Thanks for agreeing to see me."

"You're welcome. Give my regards to your husband and father-in-law."

"I will."

Graf-Jones followed me to the door. "By the way, where did you say that photograph was taken?"

"I didn't."

"It doesn't look like anywhere in Greenwich."

"It's not." He'd made things difficult for me, and now it was payback time.

"Where then?"

"What does it matter? The woman in the picture isn't your daughter."

"I'm merely curious. There can't be many places in this area where people are reduced to scrounging for food in dumpsters."

He was seriously out of touch if he believed that. "More than you think."

Graf-Jones moved closer, towering over me. "Where did you take the picture?" I glanced behind me. John Lent stood in the doorway, arms folded across his chest. I was hemmed in between a giant lizard and a pit bull.

"I thought your secretary was going to show me out."

"Answer the question."

"I take so many pictures, it's often hard to remember. But this one . . ." I made a show of studying it. "This one was taken at a roadside restaurant in New London."

Graf-Jones signaled Lent to let me pass. The secretary guided me to the main entrance. "Or maybe it was Bridgeport?" I said as I stepped out the door.

CHAPTER 19

"Oh, your men was not crazy,
your men was not mad,
Your men was not in deep despair-o.
I deceived all your sailors
as well as yourself,
And I'm still the maid on the shore."
—The Maid on the Shore, Sea Shanty

My satisfaction at having the last word was short lived. By the time I left Greenwich and headed north on I-95, I was beginning to doubt the trip had been worth it. All I'd gotten from Graf-Jones was a string of denials. He'd denied hiring a private detective, and he'd denied that the homeless woman was his daughter. Still, his obvious interest in where the photograph had been taken suggested uncertainty.

I wondered if Nate was having any better luck in his search for Jimmy. I hadn't heard from him since yesterday afternoon. And in this case, I didn't think no news meant good news. I pulled off the highway to telephone. His answering machine picked up when I called his home, so I tried his cell.

"Glad you called," he said. "Would've called myself but I've been driving flat out and—"

"Driving where?"

"Minnesota."

"You're kidding! Whatever for?"

"After I struck out finding Jimmy in Providence, I went back and talked to Reba to see if she had any other ideas where he might've gone. She told me she overheard him talking on the phone with a friend in Minnesota from his days on the powwow circuit. She didn't think anything of it at the time, but now that Jimmy's disappeared, she thinks that's where he could be headed."

"Really?" I found this hard to believe.

"Makes sense to me. He's got friends in the West who'd let him hide out with them without asking any questions."

"Okay, but do you have to be the one to go all that way to get him?"

"Better me than some trigger-happy cop."

"Nate—" I started to protest.

"How are things in Cambridge?" he asked, forestalling further argument.

"I'm not there." I told him about my visit to Graf-Jones.

"That's the craziest thing I've ever heard," Nate said when I finished.

His words hit me like a slap across the face. "It's not any crazier than what you're doing."

"No? I have good reason to believe Jimmy's headed west, while you're basing everything on a watch. Besides, her own father denied the woman's his daughter."

"But he was awfully interested in where the picture was taken."

"Big deal. You're barking up the wrong tree. You want to do something useful, why don't you find out if Luke's got an alibi for the night of the murder?"

So he was still on that track. "You're the one who's barking up the wrong tree if you think Luke killed Kavanagh," I yelled, my voice rising with my irritation. "Hasn't it ever occurred to you that Jimmy's on the lam because—"

"He's guilty?" Nate exploded. "You've thought that all along, haven't you? You and the cops. You white people are all the same. Something bad happens, you blame the non-white guy."

"I'm on your side, dammit! I love you, Nate." There, I'd said it, a confession made in anger and frustration rather than fondness.

Nate was silent a long moment. Finally, he said, "I love you, too, Miranda. I'm sorry for what I said. It's just that this thing with Jimmy is tearing me apart."

And tearing us apart, I thought. Aloud I said in what I hoped was a calmer voice, "I hope you find him."

"Me, too. We'll talk soon."

I buried my head in my arms, leaned against the steering wheel and had a good cry. When I was finished, I felt empty, purged. I'd go to the maritime museum, find Erin and spend the night with her rather than driving back to Cambridge.

On the way there, I passed the turn for the back road leading to the Sea Shanty. Passed it, turned around and went back. Maybe Nate was right in thinking me crazy to connect the homeless woman with Sheila, but a combination of curiosity and a desire to prove him wrong made me return to the place where she'd last been sighted.

I went inside, ordered a large coffee and sat down at a table with a view of the parking lot and the dumpster. I drank my coffee and waited.

After a while, an employee carried two large bags of trash to the dumpster and flung them in. I hoped this would be the cue for the homeless woman to appear. She'd been here yesterday, and the homeless people I'd observed in Cambridge tended to frequent the same spots. Fifteen minutes passed with no sign of her. I decided to check the tangle of brush behind the dumpster. As I passed it, I caught a whiff of its contents. The odor of rotting food hung in the air like a miasmatic cloud. Ugh!

I scanned the brush, searching for a break in the seemingly impenetrable mass. Stray pieces of trash—used napkins and tissues, plastic straws, and several cardboard food containers—were either snared in the branches or littered the ground at the base of the bushes. Near the spot where a French fry container lay, I discovered an opening that would enable me to get through without scratching myself bloody.

I emerged from the brush into an empty landscape. Tall grass interspersed with weeds sloped down to a swampy area, filled with cattails. More garbage was strewn on the ground by the cattails. The wind could have blown it there, or someone could have brought it to this place.

I scurried down the slope toward the cattails. A duck flew honking into the air. A plastic bag hung like a shroud over a cattail. A gust of wind carried it aloft. Aside from the duck and a lot of garbage, there didn't seem to be anything here. Before heading back up the slope, I gave the cattail grove a final onceover. Another, stronger gust raked the grove. The cattails swayed wildly, parting to reveal a mound of earth and what looked like a reed hut.

I pushed my way into the cattails. Tawny fluff from the spikes blew into my face and clung to my clothes and hair. The tails themselves proved surprisingly sharp to the touch. The ground underfoot felt spongy, but at least I didn't sink into total muck. I passed through the front line of cattails and came to the mound with the hut. It looked like something a muskrat might have built, only bigger. At the opening to the hut, I spotted a patch of blue. I knelt to get a better look. It was the fluffed end of a sleeping bag.

Behind me, cattails clattered an alarm. A whoosh of air ruffled the hairs on my neck. I felt a searing pain at the back of my skull. Stars like Fourth of July sparklers danced before my eyes, dissolving into blackness.

CHAPTER 20

"Oh, they whacked me up, an' they whacked me
*   down,*
The Mate he cracked me on the crown,
They whacked me round an' round."
—*The Shaver,* Sea Shanty

Pain throbbed in the back of my head, as if someone were pummeling me with padded gloves. I felt something wet and slimy under my cheek. My blood and gore? I didn't have the strength to find out. Finally, I eased myself up. A wave of nausea overcame me. I lowered my head, sucking in air, until it subsided. Then I looked around.

I was alone in the cattail grove. The wetness and slime I'd felt came from a puddle with small, pale green algae plants floating in it. At least my injury wasn't as serious as I'd thought. But where was the hut with the sleeping bag? I noticed an area of flattened reeds. Otherwise, the cattails stood upright, swaying gently in the breeze like dancers in grass skirts.

I crawled out of the grove into tall grass and weeds. Ahead, on a low rise, I could see the barrier of brush. I groped my way forward, feeling like Sisyphus pushing the boulder that was my aching head up the hill.

At the edge of the brush, I paused before thrusting myself through. Branches clawed at me, temporarily distracting me from the pain in my head. I came out into the parking lot, and used a corner of the dumpster to haul myself up.

A woman about to get into her car with a bag of food noticed me and came over. "Are you all right?"

"My head's killing me. Somebody knocked me out back there." I motioned toward the brush.

"Oh, my goodness! We better call 911."

An ambulance and a police car arrived almost simultaneously. The responding officer was Sergeant Curtin. He waited while the EMTs, an older man and a younger one who looked like they could be father and son, dealt with me. After examining the bruise on the back of my head, the older EMT held up fingers for me to count and asked me a few simple questions. "You don't seem disoriented," he said, "but it would be a good idea to go to the hospital and have them take an X-ray."

I told him I didn't think this was necessary. They had me sign a waiver, gave me a cold pack and pain medication and drove off. Then it was Curtin's turn. "So, Ms. . . . ?" he began.

"Lewis," I filled in, holding the cold pack against my head.

He pushed a shock of hair the color of moldy hay away from his forehead and squinted at me behind his glasses. "Erin Meloy's friend?"

"Yes, I was at the museum when her fiancé's body was found."

"I remember. You and your Indian boyfriend."

He seemed to stress the word *Indian,* but maybe I only imagined it.

"You said someone hit you on the head?"

"Back there." I gestured toward the brush.

Curtin frowned. "What were you doing there in the first place?"

"Looking for a homeless woman I saw here the other day."

Curtin's frown deepened. "How come?"

"I think she might be Sheila Kavanagh, the second wife of the man who was killed."

Curtin's eyebrows lifted above the frames of his glasses. "I thought Erin and he were engaged. Are you telling me the guy was a bigamist?"

"He may not have known his second wife is still alive. She was supposed to have been lost at sea."

"She's the one who hit you on the head?"

"I think so. Come, I'll show you where it happened."

Reluctantly, Curtin followed me through the brush and down the hill to the cattail grove. Together, we examined the trampled mass of reeds where the hut with the sleeping bag had been.

Curtin stated the obvious: "Whoever was here has cleared out."

"That doesn't mean she can't be found."

"Okay, but I'm gonna need a description."

"I have a photo."

Back at my car, I showed him the homeless woman's picture. "Have you seen her around?"

"I might've, but I can't be absolutely certain. Since the Indians started their casino, we've been getting a lot more folks either on the dole or homeless. It's hard to keep track of 'em all. Sure as hell hasn't made my job any easier."

The resentment in his voice reminded me of Curtin's long-standing grudge against Jimmy and his family.

"You'll keep an eye out for her?"

"See what I can do, but I'm not making any promises. We've got a murder investigation on our hands."

"This woman could be connected to it. She was at the Spouters Point Inne that night."

"Really now?"

His patronizing tone infuriated me. He was as dismissive as Nate, though probably for different reasons. Beneath the cold pack, my head began to throb. "Yes, really," I snapped. "I'd think you'd want to talk to everyone who might have information, instead of just focusing on—" I stopped short of saying "one person of interest."

The eyes behind the glasses narrowed. "Not trying to tell me how to do my job, are you? We're doing the best we can. Doesn't help when people go missing. First that Korean kid—"

"Winston Woo?"

"That's him."

Focused on Jimmy's disappearance, then the mystery surrounding the homeless woman, I'd pushed Winston to the back of my mind. Now I remembered that he, too, was considered a "person of interest."

"Any leads on his whereabouts?"

Curtin shook his head. "What about you?"

"Me? How would I—"

"I meant about the other guy who's missing. The Indian guy. You got any idea where we might find *him?*"

My head was throbbing in earnest now, and I felt dizzy. I put my free hand on the side of my car to steady myself. "Why would I?"

"Your boyfriend's a friend of his."

"Sorry, but you're barking up the wrong tree." Unconsciously, I echoed Nate's words.

"Too bad." Curtin started toward his patrol car. As an afterthought, he turned and stabbed a finger at the cracked taillight on my rattletrap Peugeot. "I could cite you for that. Get it fixed."

CHAPTER 21

*"By the merest chance the ship itself at last rescued him; but
from that hour the little negro went about the deck an idiot;
such, at least, they said he was. The sea had jeeringly kept his
finite body up, but drowned the infinite of his soul."*

—Moby-Dick

"What on earth happened to you?" Erin asked when she walked
into her apartment and saw me.

"If I tell you, promise you won't say I'm crazy like Nate did.
And that was before I was injured." I patted the cold pack
pressed against my head.

Erin sat down beside me. "I promise."

I told her about my hunch about the homeless woman, my
visit with Graf-Jones, then my getting knocked out in the cattail
grove.

Erin looked at me with amazement. "I don't know what to
say. My mind's spinning. Maybe it would help if you showed
me this woman's picture."

I gave it to her; she studied it and shook her head. "I've seen
pictures of Sheila, and it's hard to imagine this woman is her."

"Even after undergoing a terrible ordeal?"

Erin studied the picture again. "Maybe . . . I just don't know."

"I might not have made the connection myself if it hadn't
been for the watch she's wearing."

"What about it?"

"It's a Seamaster. Alex Broussard, the guy who was washed overboard with Sheila, is wearing the same kind of watch in another photo."

"So? It could just be a coincidence."

"What if they were in the life raft together and she managed to survive, but he didn't? Could something like that happen?"

Erin stared abstractedly into space. "It's a big stretch," she said finally. "But people have been known to survive being lost at sea. There was one guy who was stranded for more than seventy days in a life raft. I even have his book."

She rummaged in a stack and handed me a paperback titled *Adrift*. The cover showed an emaciated young man in an inflatable raft holding three sticks tied together to form a triangle. I assumed the triangle was some kind of makeshift navigational device. I flipped through the pages. They were illustrated with photos and line drawings of the author spearing fish, catching birds, and struggling to stay afloat in the midst of towering waves. I closed the book. "So it is possible?"

"Yes, but if Sheila were still alive, wouldn't she have gotten in touch with George, or her father?"

"You'd think so, unless . . ." I paused. *Unless George had tried to kill her by deliberately setting her adrift with her lover, and she was still afraid of him.* But even if that were true, it didn't explain her not contacting her father.

"What?" Erin prompted.

I shook my head. "I really don't know."

Erin lapsed into a moody silence, broken when she said, "You should show her picture to Mark. He knows many of the homeless people in the area, so he might recognize her."

"Good idea."

"I'm hungry and you probably are, too. I actually have food in the house, thanks to you and Mark."

She made us a cheese omelet and a salad. I felt somewhat

better after eating, but in a while, the pain medication began to wear off, and my head started throbbing again. I took another pill, and at Erin's urging, lay down on the air bed.

The bed smelled fresh and clean and felt comfortable—not at all like lying on the hard ground with only a reed roof separating me from the elements. Compared to the owner of the blue sleeping bag, I had it easy. Again I wondered who she was and where she'd gone. But not for long. Snuggling deeper under the covers, I was soon asleep.

Toward morning, a tuneful sea shanty roused us. Erin scrabbled for her cell and flipped it open. She listened intently, her face ashen in the gray light. "I'll be right there." With her free hand she reached for her clothes.

"What happened?"

"It's Winston. His body washed up at the museum."

CHAPTER 22

"Then the cabin-boy did swim all to the larboard side,
Sayin' 'Shipmates take me up for I'm drownin' with the tide.'
They hauled him up so quickly, but when on deck he died,
And they buried him in the Lowlands Low."
—Lowlands Low, Sea Shanty

The scene was eerily familiar: a body on shore in the gray, early morning light. This one had already been covered, and it lay in a different place, on a strip of sandy beach by the museum boathouse where one could rent small sailboats or row boats. Wavelets rocked the boats gently and lapped against the shore like beckoning fingers. But the body remained motionless, immune to the wavelets' appeal.

"Are you sure it's him?" Erin demanded in an agitated voice.

"Yes, but . . ." Mark looked at Curtin, who nodded at a medic. The medic uncovered the upper part of the body, and we caught a glimpse of Winston's pale, bloated face.

"Omigod!" Erin gasped. Mark folded her into his chest with one arm, and slipped the other around my shoulders. I pressed close, aware of a faint throbbing at the back of my skull. I hoped to forestall a full-fledged headache by drawing comfort from

Mark's warmth and sheer aliveness in the face of a second chilly death.

"It's horrible, all right," Flo Higginbotham babbled. "First George, now this. Poor Hap can't do his business with Daddy without—"

"Be quiet," Vernon ordered.

From this, I inferred that Higginbotham and his dog had been the ones to make the discovery. Flo, her husband, and the small crowd of museum staffers and student interns who had gathered were silent as the medics lifted the body onto a gurney and bore it away. Then one of the students, a young woman in a red parka, asked of no one in particular, "Do you suppose he took his own life?"

Curtin responded with a question of his own: "What makes *you* think that?"

"Well, he . . ." The girl hesitated, flustered at being put on the spot.

"He had mental problems," a male student in a Gellis College sweatshirt finished for her.

Curtin scribbled something in his notebook, then, turning back to the young woman, he said, "In answer to your question, we won't know until the medical examiner does an autopsy. Until then, we'll be considering all possibilities, including foul play."

At the mention of foul play, the students huddled more closely together. "Pretty creepy, if you ask me. Two drownings here in a little over a week," the sweatshirted student voiced what the others were undoubtedly thinking.

"Winston didn't drown at the museum." Standing alone at the edge of the crowd, Luke spoke for the first time.

"How do you know?" Curtin asked sharply.

"If he had, his body would've been discovered a lot sooner. He probably went into the water somewhere in the vicinity of

149

the bridge."

"The drawbridge?" another male student asked. We all stared in that direction. The clunky, greenish metal drawbridge that spanned the Spouter River was just lifting to let a couple of sailboats glide under.

"No, the highway bridge," Luke said. "A deer was hit by a car on that bridge and washed up on shore here about a week later."

"That far away?" Curtin asked.

"Yup, the tides carried it."

Curtin made a note of this. "If anyone thinks of anything else, please get in touch." He handed out his card to the students and museum staff. He was about to give one to Vernon Higginbotham, but Higginbotham waved him away. "I've already told you everything I know."

Curtin turned to go. Disengaging myself from Mark, I went after him. "When you notify Winston's family, be sure to ask to speak to his brother, Wendell."

"Why?"

"He's the only one in the family who speaks English well."

"You friends of theirs, too?" Curtin asked with a trace of sarcasm.

"We've met."

Curtin removed his fogged-over glasses, wiped them with a pocket-handkerchief, and put them on again. "You seem to have your finger in a lot of pies, Ms. Lewis. Careful you don't get burned."

I was tempted to retort, but the pain was building in my head. I let him walk away. Then, rummaging in my bag for the pain medication the EMTs had given me, I popped a pill in my mouth before I rejoined Erin and the others. Mark still had his arm around Erin. "We're going back to my house," he said. "Want to come with us?"

I hesitated. I'd feel better if I went with them, but part of me wanted some time alone to process what had happened. "I'll follow in a bit." I massaged Erin's outer arm and she managed a wan half-smile. "Don't be too long."

They left, and Luke and the other museum staffers scattered. The Higginbothams headed back to their boat. A small group of students remained, speaking in hushed voices.

"Think he jumped?" I overheard a girl say.

"No way. He was terrified of heights. Got so freaked out climbing the rigging, he would've fallen if Miss Meloy hadn't rescued him."

"That's what could've happened on the bridge," someone else said. "He freaked and fell."

"Yeah, but if he was so scared of heights, why'd he even go there in the first place?"

"Someone could've lured him to the bridge, then given him a shove. You heard what that cop said. They're not ruling out foul play."

"I still think . . ."

The students drifted away, disappearing into the fog. A clear soprano voice pierced the silence: "Winston, we hardly knew ye." Other voices picked up the words of the ballad.

Winston, we hardly knew ye. A fitting epitaph for a boy, who, either from shyness or a sense of not belonging, had held himself aloof. A lump formed in my throat at the thought of those who did know and love him—his brother, his parents, and his grandmother. On rainy days, she would wait in vain for him at the bus stop with an umbrella. The boy who had demonstrated he was destined for great things by choosing a pencil was never coming home.

I walked back to my car and drove to the highway bridge, where Luke thought Winston had gone in. Pulling over, I stared at the gray-green water below. But not for long. Looking down made my headache worse. I leaned against the headrest of my seat and closed my eyes, while I tried to make sense of things.

Nate said I should be checking out Luke. Was he right? Was it just a coincidence Luke knew the exact place where Winston had landed in the water? But why kill that poor troubled kid? Unless Winston had seen something he shouldn't have.

Whoa! I was making a big leap here. I needed to pull back and wait until the cops determined whether foul play was involved. I turned the key in the ignition, but the next minute shut off the engine. I hadn't spoken to Nate since yesterday afternoon. He'd want to know about this latest development. Before making the call, I pressed my palm against my still throbbing head. The pain medication hadn't kicked in yet, but I might as well get this over with.

My cautious hello evoked an even more guarded response from Nate. Perhaps he realized how he'd wounded me during our last exchange, and wanted to avoid a repeat performance. Or something else was going on. "What's the matter?"

"Nothing."

"You don't sound like everything's fine."

"Helluva of way to begin a conversation, asking what's wrong."

"Okay, give me an honest answer and we can move on."

"Who says I'm not being honest?"

"I *know* you."

Silence, then in a resigned voice, he said, "All right. I had a little accident."

My heart rate accelerated and so did the throbbing in my head. "What happened?"

"Must've dozed off 'cuz the next thing I knew I was off the road, heading across someone's field."

"Jesus, Nate!"

"Look at it this way: at least I didn't drive off a mountain."

"You were damned lucky. What about the Jeep?"

"Hit a boulder that tore out part of the insides. I'm holed up at this farm waiting to see if I can get it fixed. Guys at the garage in town aren't sure they've got the right parts. Might have to order them, and God only knows how long that'll take. In the meantime, Jimmy—"

"Can wait. This never would've happened if you hadn't pushed yourself too hard. You've got to—"

"Don't tell me what to do!"

I fought back a rising tide of anger by counting slowly to ten.

"You still there, Miranda?" Nate asked.

"I'm here. Here and worried about you."

"Here is Cambridge?"

"Rhode Island."

"How come?"

"I decided to spend the night with Erin rather than doing a round-trip on the same day. And it's a good thing I did because—"

"Sure that's the only reason?"

"Yes. Why?" I asked warily.

"Oh, I don't know, just thought you might still be on the trail of that homeless woman."

Damn the man! He knew *me* too well.

"While I was here, I figured I might as well check out the spot where she was last seen."

"And?"

I sighed. He was as relentless as I was about getting the truth. "All right, if you must know, I got whacked on the head after I found a sleeping bag in a cattail grove."

"You're worried about me!" Nate exclaimed. "I've got a few bruises from my accident, but you've probably got a bump the size of a baseball."

Instinctively, my fingers traced the lump. "It's not that big."

"Sure?"

"Yes, now will you—"

"Okay, we'll stop comparing war wounds and get back to business. You think the homeless woman knocked you out?"

"Most likely."

"She was only defending her territory. You better leave that poor woman alone."

"Are you telling me what to do?" I asked half-jokingly.

"It's good advice."

"Mine wasn't?"

"Seriously, Miranda, promise me you'll stop harassing that woman. She's already the victim of an unjust society, and you're making her life worse."

I wasn't convinced the homeless woman was the innocent victim Nate thought her. Not with that feral gleam in her eyes. The very memory of it sent chills down my spine. But in the interest of harmony, I said I'd stop.

"Good. Now, was there something else you wanted to tell me before we got going on this?"

"Remember the Korean kid at the museum who went missing?"

"Yeah. They find him?"

"His body washed up at the museum this morning."

Nate whistled softly. "Poor kid! What's the cops' take on it?"

"They don't know yet. His death could've been an accident, a suicide or foul play was involved."

"At least they can't blame Jimmy for this one."

"I'm not so sure about that. The body had been in the water a while."

"Christ! I've got to find Jimmy before—"

"You need to slow down and take better care of yourself."

"Don't start again."

"I mean it, Nate. You don't even know for sure Jimmy's in

Minnesota."

"Reba said—"

"That he might've gone there. But what if he didn't? You could be risking your life for nothing."

"Stop right there," Nate said in a voice that brooked no further discussion.

"At least think about what I said."

"We'll talk more later."

Sure we will, I thought after we hung up. *If you don't get yourself killed in the meantime.*

And for what? A wild-goose chase? I felt an urgent need to find out if Nate really was embarked on a fool's errand.

CHAPTER 23

"There is a young captain
who sails the salt sea;
Let the wind blow high, blow low-o
'I will die, I will die,' the young captain did cry,
'If I can't have the maid on the shore!' "
—The Maid on the Shore, Sea Shanty

I got the number of the Dottaguck Museum of History and Culture and called Reba from my car. She sounded surprised and a bit wary when I asked if we could meet.

"I'd like to see you, Miranda, but today isn't good. I've got one meeting after another."

"After work then?"

"Maybe. I'll see what I can do and get back to you."

When I arrived at Mark's, Erin was sitting on the ragged, fur-covered living-room couch, surrounded by kittens. One was curled up purring in her lap, another was using her trousered leg as a scratching post, and a third perched on the back of the couch, batting at her hair. The kittens provided a distraction from the morning's sad discovery, but my mind kept returning to that scene. Although we didn't speak of it, I knew Erin and Mark were thinking about it also. We drank coffee and talked in a desultory fashion. The caffeine and quiet conversation did wonders for my headache. I was almost completely pain free by the time Mark rose and said he needed to do some errands.

"I know what that means," his wife Jane said. "You're off to feed your ferals." To me, she explained, "He's got two colonies of feral cats he feeds every day." As Mark started for the door, she called after him. "Pick up another quart of milk while you're out. We're running low."

The mention of feral cats reminded me of the homeless woman. I followed Mark outside.

"You want to come with me?"

"No, thanks. I have something I'd like you to look at." I retrieved the picture of the homeless woman from my car and showed it to him. "Have you seen this woman around?"

Mark stared at the picture, and his expression became guarded. "Why do you want to know?"

"I'm trying to find her. I think she might be Sheila Kavanagh."

"Who?"

"George's second wife."

Mark looked astonished. "The one who was lost at sea?"

"Yes. Have you seen her?"

"No," he said without meeting my eyes.

"Are you sure? Take another look." I held out the picture, but he waved it away.

"Why is this important?"

"Nate and I saw her going through the garbage behind the Spouters Point Inne the night George was killed."

Mark tugged hard on his albatross earring—so hard I was afraid he'd pull it out. "I haven't seen her," he repeated. "But I'll let you know if I do."

I was almost certain he was lying. He knew this woman and was protecting her by not revealing her whereabouts. Like Nate, he undoubtedly viewed her as a poor unfortunate who'd already had enough trouble in her life. I hoped he'd have a change of heart.

I rejoined Jane and Erin in the living room, where we pretended to be amused by the kittens, drank more coffee, and made more desultory conversation. I hated being idle. I wished Reba would call and tell me she'd found a break in her schedule.

Maggie's arrival with a basket of freshly baked scones provided another temporary distraction. She'd no sooner placed the basket on the coffee table than a kitten leaped in, upsetting it. Scones tumbled onto the floor. We picked them up, dusted them off, and we each had one. Luke had apparently called Maggie with the news about Winston. She'd come to commiserate with Erin and find out more about what had happened. While Erin retreated to the bathroom, I went over the story for Maggie's benefit. When she got up to leave about a half hour later, I offered to accompany her on the short walk back to the farmhouse.

"Will you be staying a while?" she asked as we cut across the lawn.

"As long as Erin needs me. I don't think it's good for her to be alone, especially after this new shock."

"God, I wish she'd move back in with us!" Maggie blurted.

"Maybe she will once things calm down between her and Luke."

"If they ever do," Maggie said glumly. "He sure blew it. He should've broken the bad news about Kavanagh more gently. And he didn't have to boycott the party. He could've gone and put up a good front like the rest of us. And afterward, he should've—" She broke off, frowning.

"What?"

She kicked at a stone. "I don't know. It might not have done any good anyway."

"What?"

Maggie sighed. "I wanted him to go and apologize to her that night."

"But he didn't?"

Maggie kicked another stone, sending up a cloud of dust. "I don't think," she began, then almost immediately corrected herself. "No," she declared. "Luke never left the house that night."

Maggie's shift from doubt to categorical denial made me suspect Luke didn't have an ironclad alibi but that, if pressed, Maggie would stand behind him.

I tried another tack. "I agree Luke could've handled things better. But he was caught in the middle between Erin and that PI . . . if there was a PI."

"There was. Or rather is," Maggie said. "I know because I found his card when I was checking Luke's pants pockets before putting them in the wash."

If she'd dropped a bomb at my feet, I couldn't have been more surprised. Luke had said he didn't remember the PI's name, that the man had only flashed his license at him. Now it turned out he had the man's card. What was going on here? "Do you still have it?"

"Yup." We went inside, and after rummaging in a kitchen drawer filled with odds and ends, Maggie produced a business card with "Anthony Venezia Investigations," a phone number and a New London address.

"Mind if I keep this?"

"Go ahead."

I left with my prize. At least that's what I hoped it was.

CHAPTER 24

"We'll hoist him up to the main yard-arm,
We'll hoist him up to the main yard-arm.
An' drop him down to the depths o' the sea,
An' drop him down to the bottom of the sea.
We'll sink him down with a long, long roll,
Where the sharks'll have his body, an' the devil have
his soul."
*— **The Dead Horse**, Sea Shanty*

Reba finally called to say she could see me late in the day. She met me at the entrance to the Dottaguck Museum of History and Culture. The modern building in the middle of the forest was as incongruous as Clambanks. Reba greeted me warmly, but beneath her friendly manner, I sensed the same wariness that had been in her voice earlier.

"How about a quick tour of the museum while we talk?" Reba asked as she ushered me inside.

"Fine."

I followed her into a large exhibit hall showing various aspects of early Dottaguck life. Beside a display of a Dottaguck woman carrying a basket of lobsters on her back, I stopped and got to the point. "I'm worried about Nate. He fell asleep at the wheel and his car went off the road."

Reba looked alarmed. "That's terrible! Is he all right?"

"He was lucky—this time. But I'm afraid once the Jeep is

160

fixed, he'll have another, worse accident. He's pushing himself so hard, and we don't even know if Jimmy's really in Minnesota."

Reba stiffened and took a step away from me. "Jimmy's not anywhere around here. And Nate searched all his old haunts in Providence. So there's a good chance he's with his Minnesota friend." She glanced at her watch. "We'd better move on if we're going to finish the tour before closing time." She walked quickly from the exhibit hall into the next one, which she passed through without stopping. I finally caught up with her at the doorway leading to a third exhibit hall. "Please slow down. I'd like to finish our conversation."

"I don't want you to miss the Dottaguck village. It's our most popular exhibit."

"Okay, but—"

She left before I could complete the sentence. Once again, I hurried after her, even though all the rushing around was bringing back the headache I'd been fighting all day. I caught up with her at the entrance to the Dottaguck village. A guard stood beside shelves containing audio-guides. Reba took one, and tried to give it to me.

I shook my head, determined to question her further about Jimmy's whereabouts. "You think there's a good chance Jimmy's in Minnesota, but you're not entirely sure?"

"That's right."

"What if he's not there? What if Nate's off on a wild-goose chase?"

Reba continued to hold out the audio-guide with an almost pleading look in her eyes. When I still refused to take it, she pressed it against her chest, as if to erect a barrier between us. "I know you're concerned about Nate, Miranda. Let's hope his accident will serve as a wake-up call and make him slow down."

"Maybe, though—"

"We'll do a quick walk-through of the village, then there are some other exhibits I'd like to show you." Reba led me into the village. We'd barely stepped inside when her beeper went off. Frown lines sprouted under the fringe of her bangs. She listened a long minute, then strode toward the exit at the other end, talking as she went. "Something's come up. Meet you back here in ten, maybe fifteen."

"Wait!" I started after her, nearly colliding with a visitor coming out of an exhibit. "Sorry," I said, as the rank odor of tobacco and whiskey engulfed me. I peered into a face whose most prominent feature was a bulbous nose crisscrossed with purple veins. Black-rimmed glasses framed the man's eyes. His shock of dark brown hair looked like a toupee. He was dressed in slacks and a garish sports shirt covered with butterflies. Judging from his dissipated appearance and loud shirt, I pegged him for a casino patron.

"What's the big hurry?" he asked. "Interesting stuff here."

"I don't have time now." I turned to go, he turned in the same direction and we almost collided a second time. The same thing happened again. And again. Finally, I made it past him and continued toward the exit.

The open village gave way to an area that was enclosed by a palisade. Behind me, I saw the casino patron also heading for the exit. Hoping to avoid a further encounter, I ducked behind the palisade. Inside were several wigwams. In one I noticed the figure of a medicine man shaking a rattle over a sick man. The medicine man's face was painted a lurid red and black. He reminded me of someone, but I couldn't think who. Then I remembered. Russell Long Knife had looked that way at Jimmy's house and later at the powwow: alien and filled with menace. My spine tingled.

"Wouldn't wanna wind up like that—half-dead with nothing but a witch doctor's voodoo to cure me." The casino patron leered at me. I was about to point out his remark was offensive when I realized I'd been having similar thoughts. I'd identified the medicine man as a savage and therefore terrifying. I hated to think that underneath my politically correct facade, I harbored the same prejudices as Curtin and this yahoo from Clambanks. I fled the palisade.

I came out of semi-darkness into light, then back into semi-darkness again, as I passed from one exhibit hall to another, barely seeing what was there, in my determination to escape the casino man's leering face and Nate's damning words: *You white people are all the same; something bad happens, you blame the non-white person.*

I noticed a theater and peeked in. It was empty and quiet. I took a seat in the front, hoping to collect myself before Reba returned. A few minutes later, the movie began, and I was thrown back into the very world I'd been trying to escape, a world where whites and Indians viewed each other with fear and hatred.

The movie told the story of the Dottaguck War. In this war, one death led to hundreds more in a vicious cycle of violence. At one point, a group of English soldiers delivered the severed head of a Dottaguck Indian to their leader. I gasped at the gruesome sight. Laughter sounded behind me. The casino man had taken a seat in the last row. He waved. I turned back to the screen. His presence made me uneasy, but surely he was harmless.

I refocused on the movie, where the tension was building as the camera cut back and forth between scenes of the English army's advance and the unsuspecting Dottagucks carrying on their daily lives at their stronghold, Mawnaucoi. I heard movement from behind. The casino man had left his seat and was scuttling forward. The hairs on the back of my neck stood on end. Maybe he wasn't so harmless after all. My muscles tensed in readiness for flight.

All of a sudden, there was a ripping noise, and sound and picture were sucked into the void. The lights came on. The casino man slid into a seat just behind me. My blood went cold. Who was he and what did he want?

"Hey, we've lost the picture!" I called up to the projection booth. A staff person appeared at a side door. "Sorry, but we're experiencing difficulties. We should have the problem fixed shortly."

I headed for the aisle. The casino man rose. As he leaned toward me, the butterflies on his shirt seemed to fly at me. He opened his mouth, releasing a cloud of whisky and nicotine. "Can't take the heat, better stay away from the fire."

I stared at the black-framed glasses bridging his vein-riddled nose. If I pulled off the glasses, would the nose come, too? "Are you threatening me?" I demanded in a voice loud enough to be heard by the staff person in the doorway.

The casino man smiled and shook his head. He turned and sauntered toward the exit. I waited until he was gone before leaving myself. Outside the theater, I glanced at my watch. Fifteen minutes had passed. Reba was probably waiting for me back at the Dottaguck village. I'd begun to retrace my steps when she burst through a glass door leading to the outside. She looked as hot and bothered as I felt. "Miranda! What're you do-ing here?"

"When you didn't come back, I thought I'd check out some of the other exhibits. What kept you?"

"I had to deal with a problem." She glanced nervously over her shoulder.

"Outside?"

"Uh . . . yes."

Beyond the door lay an open, grassy area, flanked by a hillock planted with corn. The scene looked perfectly peaceful.

"What happened?"

Reba smoothed the bangs breaking like a wave over her forehead. A stray leaf fluttered to the ground.

"Looks like you've been in the woods."

She fiddled with her badge. "I have. The site of an old Dottaguck fort's in there. We've been excavating it, and the students who were digging today thought they'd made a major discovery. Our resident archaeologist is out of town, so I went to see what they found. What they thought was an ancient bone belonged to a deer that died recently."

"The fort sounds interesting."

"There's not much to it," Reba said quickly. "Just a clearing in the woods with part of a modern palisade. You'll get a better idea of what it was like from that." She pointed at a miniature replica. "Sorry I don't have time to give you more of a tour, but I've got to run if I'm going to get Kyle to a doctor's appointment." She started to leave, then as an afterthought, turned back. "Don't worry about Nate, Miranda. He's a big boy. He can take care of himself."

Yeah, sure, I thought. A big, stubborn boy with an anger problem. Far from reassuring me, Reba had stoked my suspicions that Jimmy wasn't in Minnesota. Why else would she have given me the brushoff? I stared at the door to the outside. She'd discouraged me from visiting the fort site. That's where I'd go.

Exiting the building, I headed across the open grassy area. At the beginning of a pine needle trail into the woods, I stopped. The last time I'd plunged into unfamiliar territory, I'd gotten whacked on the head and I was still hurting from the blow. But this was a museum; there were no bad guys lurking here. Or were there? I wondered, thinking of the casino man. He was a weirdo all right, but I saw no sign of him now. Perhaps he'd tired of his game with me and returned to the casino.

I started down the trail. After a while it brought me to a clearing with part of a recently constructed palisade. Inside the palisade, white markers had been placed at various points to indicate the sites of past digs. I saw no signs of recent activity, however. I walked to the far edge of the clearing and peered over the remains of a stone wall into a tangle of trees and bushes. Again I saw no evidence of digging.

Reba had lied to me. In the pressure of the moment, she'd concocted a story to explain her presence in the woods. Like many lies, it contained an element of truth. There had been digging at the site, just not now. What *had* she been doing here?

Approaching footsteps cut off my speculations. It was probably just a staff person, but I wasn't taking any chances. One end of the palisade looped back on itself to form a bastion. I crouched inside. My heart thudded and my head throbbed as the footsteps came nearer. From a slit in the stakes, I caught a glimpse of butterflied shirt.

Casino man! He could've wandered here on his own, but I suspected he'd deliberately followed me. I held my breath as he walked past the bastion into the middle of the clearing. He stood there a long moment, looking around. Then he turned and left, passing within a few feet of my hiding place. I waited until his footsteps died away, then I waited a bit longer. At last I made my way cautiously back to the museum building. I reached the glass door only to find it locked. The museum was closed for the day.

I glanced around. A stone wall skirted the open, grassy area. It was too high for me to scale at the point where I stood, but it became progressively lower the farther away it extended. I followed the wall until I came to a paved road that brought me into a service area with truck bays. I continued walking, hoping to reach the parking lot.

"What'd think you're doing?" a voice from behind demanded.

I froze. When I got up the nerve to turn around, I fully expected to find myself face to face with the ubiquitous casino man. Instead, a security guard confronted me. "Don't you know the museum's closed?"

"I went to look at the site of the old fort, lost track of time, and when I came back the door to the inside was locked."

The guard shook his head. "You didn't go any farther than the fort, I hope?"

"No. Why?"

"The area beyond it is part of Big Otter Swamp. It's so nasty even the archaeologists don't like to go in there."

If what he said was true, the swamp would make a good hiding place. I gazed in that direction, lured by the possibility of discovery. But no, even I wasn't foolish enough to venture there a second time today.

CHAPTER 25

"My trim little frigate is a very smart craft,
My trim little frigate is a very smart craft.
She's armed to the teeth both fore 'n' aft,
Sharp at the bows with a fine view abaft."
                    —The Gals O'Chile, Sea Shanty

I sat in my car in the museum parking lot, discouraged about how little I'd accomplished. First Mark, then Maggie, and finally Reba had sidestepped my questions, leaving me with doubts about their truthfulness, but no concrete evidence. And without proof Jimmy wasn't in Minnesota, Nate would continue to pursue what I was more and more convinced was a wild goose chase. Now what?

I remembered the PI's card Maggie had given me. He might be a useful source of information, if he were willing to talk to me. I dialed his number, got an answering machine and left a message.

Who else was there? My thoughts drifted to Higginbotham. He seemed to have a knack for being on the scene at just the right moment. This morning, he'd discovered Winston's body, and before that, he claimed to have overheard Jimmy arguing with Kavanagh. He could've recognized Jimmy from the pow-wow. His presence there still bothered me. Maybe now was the time to approach his waterspout wife, Flo. I popped my last pain pill, got the number and dialed. Luckily, she answered the phone.

"I was wondering if we could get together for a little poodle talk," I said.

"What?"

"You know, talk about our poodles. I can't remember if I told you, but I have a toy poodle that looks very much like your Happy. Or rather, I used to. Poor Pepe died a month ago. I miss him terribly." This was stretching the truth quite a bit. While I liked dogs, I'd never cared for toy poodles and couldn't imagine owning a spoiled pooch like Happy. But I figured it was a surefire way to connect with Flo.

She took the bait. "Why, you poor thing! I had no idea you'd lost your baby."

"I try to put on a brave front, but I'm hurting inside. It would help so much if I could talk with a fellow poodle lover who knows what I'm going through. Could we possibly have lunch tomorrow?"

"Why wait until tomorrow? You come right over here, and have yourself a good cry."

My opinion of Flo went up a fraction of a notch. She might be a foolish woman, but she wasn't unsympathetic.

"Oh no, I wouldn't want to intrude. Your husband—"

"Don't worry about him. He's off on an errand and won't be back till later."

Perfect. I stopped on the way to buy a bottle of wine and a bag of doggie treats. The museum was closed when I arrived, but Flo had told me I could get in through the gate behind the Spouters Point Inne. She sat on the deck of the *Happy 111* with a glass of wine and the poodle curled in her lap. As I came on board, Happy leaped off Flo and ran barking at me. I set the treats bag on the ground, leaving the poodle to tear it open with his teeth.

"That's so sweet of you to bring my little cutie pie a snack," Flo said. "He gets positively ravenous this time of day."

"So did my Pepe, and these treats were his favorite."

"You sit down, have a drink and tell me all about it."

For several minutes, Flo and I sipped wine and shared memories—manufactured on my part—of our dear poodles. I didn't have to tax my imagination too much because Flo did most of the talking.

"I knew you'd understand!" I gushed when Flo stopped motor-mouthing long enough to help herself to some potato chips coated with her famous "homemade" onion dip. "Some people don't understand how I can grieve for my dog when two people have just died. I wouldn't dream of bringing up Pepe in front of Erin now that she's lost her fiancé. I feel so bad for her. It must be hard for you and your husband, too. You were such good friends of his."

"We miss him, all right," Flo said. "Would you like to look at a few pictures of the first two Happys?"

"I'd love to."

"I'll get an album."

She returned with four bulging albums. My heart sank. After I'd oohed and aahed over dozens of snapshots, I brought the subject back to what I really wanted to talk about. "It's fortunate your husband was on deck the night George was killed."

"Why?" Flo asked absently, her gaze fixed on a photo of one of the Happys wearing a party hat and seated at a table in front of a birthday cake.

"Because he was able to steer the police to a possible suspect. Did you happen to see or hear anything that night?"

"What?"

I repeated the question.

Flo put down the album and looked at me. "I took a sleeping pill. Put me out like a light."

Too bad. I tried another tack. "Your husband must've recognized that Indian from the powwow the night before."

Flo frowned. "What powwow?"

"The one the Dottagucks hold every year near Clambanks. Your husband was sitting behind us during the fancy dance contest Saturday night."

"He was?" Flo's frown became more pronounced.

Her ignorance of her husband's presence at the powwow made me wonder. I knew that couples, especially long marrieds, sometimes needed a break from each other. But why would Higginbotham have kept his attendance at the powwow a secret?

"Are you sure it was Vernon?" Flo asked.

"Positive. He was wearing these pants with little white poodles embroidered on them."

"I gave him those," Flo said proudly. "I saw pants with black labs in a catalog, and that gave me the idea. Then I found a seamstress to make a pair with—"

Barking interrupted her. Happy leaped off the sailboat and ran down the dock. Speak of the devil. I rose quickly. "Thanks for the wine and sympathy."

Flo stared at me with surprise. "Don't you want to look at more pictures?"

"Another time."

I beat a hasty retreat, narrowly missing Higginbotham as he approached the sailboat with Happy at his heels. I could easily imagine the conversation between his wife and him that would follow.

"What the hell was she doing here?"

"Her poor little poodle died, and she needed a shoulder to cry on."

"Bullshit!"

In my car, I got out a small notebook I keep for jotting down ideas. I decided to see if I could make some connections based on what I knew so far. I wrote down three men's names, and after each, I scribbled a few phrases:

"Higginbotham—K's friend, saw J at powwow, heard K & J arguing.
Jimmy—employee at Clambanks, met K there? Fancy dancer, contest winner, H saw at powwow.
Kavanagh—H's friend, gambler at Clambanks, met J there? Back-better, heavy losses."

I drew lines showing the links between the three, and studied my drawing. Higginbotham and Jimmy had the powwow in common, while Jimmy and Kavanagh had Clambanks in common. Clambanks and the powwow. What was the connection there, aside from the obvious one that Clambanks was owned by the Dottagucks, the powwow sponsored by them? Clambanks involved gambling, the powwow dance contests. They were as different as apples and oranges. And yet . . . an idea began to take shape at the back of my mind, but it was too indistinct to put into words. *Think, Miranda, think.*

As I struggled to bring the idea into sharper focus, my cell phone rang. "Ms. Lewis," an unfamiliar male voice said, "it's Tony Venezia. You wanted to speak with me?"

CHAPTER 26

"So early in the mornin',
Sailors love the bottle-O!
Bottle-O! Bottle-O!
Bottle of very good whiskey-O!"
—So Early in the Morning, Sea Shanty

The man who met me at the bar in the Ambergris Inne looked vaguely familiar. Maybe because he reminded me of statues of Roman emperors with his long, straight nose and lidded gray eyes. But, instead of lying flat in sculpted curls, his hair stood up in a salt and pepper brush. And instead of a toga, he wore tight-fitting jeans and a gray t-shirt that seemed designed to show off his well-muscled torso.

"So," he said, sitting opposite me at a wooden table, "what's this about?"

"George Kavanagh. You were tailing him, right?"

Tony Venezia motioned to a waitress, who came and took our orders, mine for a glass of Chardonnay, his for a single-malt Scotch. "What makes you think that?"

"Luke Meloy said so."

Venezia glanced toward the bar. "Wish they'd hurry up with the drinks. I'm thirsty."

He signaled to the waitress, who spoke with the bartender. The bartender poured our drinks, and the waitress brought them over. Venezia tapped his glass. "I'll have another one, and bring it now." He took a swig of Scotch. "What were we talking about?"

I sighed inwardly. He was about as forthcoming as a clam. "Kavanagh. Did Luke hire you to dig up dirt on him?"

Venezia gazed at me through lowered eyes. "He tell you that?"

"No, he said Kavanagh's second wife's father hired you."

"Correct."

"But if the father was paying you, why did you approach Luke?"

Venezia nodded approvingly as the waitress placed his second drink on the table. "I had my reasons."

"Because your employer wanted to sour the romance between Kavanagh and Erin Meloy?"

"Why would he want to do that?"

"You told Luke Graf-Jones suspected Kavanagh of having a hand in his daughter's death."

Venezia polished off his first Scotch and started in on the second. "The old man had a hard time accepting she was gone. He wanted me to either find her, or find out what really happened at sea."

"Did you? Find out what happened, I mean?"

He shook his head. "Came up with zip."

"You don't think Sheila could've survived?"

He stared meaningfully at his nearly empty glass. "You good for another round? All these questions are making me even thirstier."

I hadn't realized I was paying for the first two rounds, but apparently that was the deal. Before Venezia drank himself under the table, I showed him the picture of the homeless woman. "Could she be Sheila?"

He snorted. "Are you kidding? Sheila was knock-down gorgeous; this woman's a dog." He looked at me intently. "Where'd you take this?"

"Bridgeport, New London. I don't remember."

"Doesn't matter. If she's Sheila, I'm the Queen of England."

"Sure?"

He planted his elbows on the table and thrust his face in mine. "I'm good at what I do, Ms. Lewis. Very good. If Sheila were alive, I would've found her."

"Maybe so, but you don't always act like a professional."

Like a dog's raised hackles, his brush of hair stood up even straighter. "Whaddya mean?"

"You blew your cover with Luke."

"I'm a softie at heart. Couldn't just stand by while that loser led that poor, unsuspecting girl to the altar."

"Why didn't you go to Erin directly?"

"Wouldn't of believed me. She was crazy about him. Her brother, on the other hand—"

"Didn't approve of the relationship from the start?"

"You got it. No guy in his right mind would want his sister to hook up with a creep like that. He was a gambler for Chrissake. And not even a good one."

"What do you mean?"

"He was lousy at cards. Most he could do was stand back an' try an' pick winning players."

"A back-better?"

"Yeah."

"What's so bad about that?"

Venezia shrugged. "Not much skill involved there."

"But isn't gambling more about luck than skill? You bet on something and hope you're lucky?"

"And if you're not, you lose!" Venezia cried. His third glass of Scotch was almost empty, and he was starting to slur his words. "Then you take a chance on something else. Win a few, lose a few. Lose big-time, and you start getting desperate. You're ready to put money on anything. Like Kavanagh with—" He broke off so abruptly, it was as if someone had clapped a hand over his mouth.

"What?" But even as I asked, the idea that had begun to take shape in my mind snapped into focus. Clambanks and the pow-wow. Suddenly I saw a possible connection between them, and between Jimmy, Kavanagh and Higginbotham. I felt giddy with excitement.

Venezia stabbed a finger at me, as if to pierce my thought bubble. "Nuh-uh. This kind of information doesn't come cheap. There's a terrific restaurant nearby. Bit pricey, but nothing like a first-rate meal to loosen my tongue." He flashed me his best cat-who's-just-swallowed-a-canary smile.

I rose and smiled back. "Why should I spring for dinner when you've already told me everything I need to know?"

"But . . ." His smirk gave way to a look of astonishment. I dropped the cash for my wine on the table and walked out.

CHAPTER 27

"In a bloodboat Yank bound round Cape Horn
Me boots an' clothes wuz all in pawn."
—A-Rovin', Sea Shanty

At last I'd come up with something. I couldn't wait to share my
new theory with Nate. I drove to the Spouters Point Museum
parking lot, now practically empty, and called him.

"I think I finally figured out why Higginbotham was at the
powwow that night."

"Why?" He sounded tired and not particularly interested.

"Gambling!" I exclaimed.

"Huh?"

I told him about my conversation with Flo, and how she
hadn't known about her husband's presence at the powwow.
"Why wouldn't he have told her unless he was doing something
he wasn't supposed to?" I asked rhetorically.

"Yeah, but what makes you think he was gambling?"

"Kavanagh got him into it. He was a back-better, remember?
And he lost heavily at one point. So he needed a way to recoup
his losses. The PI said—"

"What PI?"

"The one who was tailing Kavanagh. After I saw Flo, I had a
drink with him."

"How'd you get a hold of him in the first place?"

"Maggie. She found his card in Luke's pants pocket, I called him, and we met."

"You've been busy, all right." I heard a note of grudging admiration in Nate's voice.

"Anyway, the PI said that when a gambler like Kavanagh loses big-time, he gets so desperate he's willing to put money on anything. In Kavanagh's case, this could've been the dance contests at Seguan."

"The PI told you Kavanagh bet on the dance contests?"

"He didn't have to. I figured it out myself. I think Kavanagh organized a betting pool that included Higginbotham and some of his Clambanks buddies. That's why Higginbotham was at the powwow. It also explains why he left in a rage when Russell Long Knife dropped his dance stick. Higginbotham must've had a lot of money riding on Russell. After all, Russell was the favorite to win."

"But Russell lost and Jimmy won," Nate said slowly. "So maybe the contest really was rigged."

"How so?"

"Kavanagh could've cut a deal with Russell to throw the contest."

"Why would he do that?"

"If Kavanagh convinced his buddies to bet on Russell, while he secretly bet on Jimmy, he'd make out like a bandit, and they'd lose a bundle."

"I don't know. What about Russell's claim that his dance stick was tampered with?"

"That was just a ploy to cover his tracks and make Jimmy look bad. Russell arranged to have the dance stick conveniently disappear, so his story couldn't be checked. Good work, Miranda. You just might've come up with the reason Kavanagh was killed."

"You've lost me."

"You know what they say about thieves."

"There's no honor among them, but—"

"Don't you see? Kavanagh must've promised Russell a share of his winnings in exchange for throwing the contest. Then, when Russell came to collect, Kavanagh tried to short-change him, they argued and Russell killed Kavanagh."

"But Higginbotham claims it was Jimmy he saw arguing with Kavanagh."

"In the dark he could've mistaken Russell for Jimmy. As far as most white people are concerned, all Indians look alike, anyway."

I winced at the jab, but let it pass. "What about the waitress who saw Jimmy and Kavanagh together at Clambanks?"

"Jimmy, Jimmy, Jimmy! Why do you always come back to him? What did he ever do to you?"

"Nothing, though—"

"Then cut it out! We need to be focusing on Russell and Higginbotham, because if the one didn't kill Kavanagh, the other did."

"Higginbotham because he realized he'd been tricked when he heard Russell and Kavanagh arguing?"

"Right. I'll use my connections to scope out Russell. I want you to see what you can dig up on Higginbotham. You get anything more from that PI?"

"No. He was such a sleaze. Wanted me to buy him an expensive dinner for additional information."

"That's the way those guys operate, at least some of them. Nothing's for free, Miranda. You should know that by now."

"So I messed up."

"I didn't mean to criticize you. I think you're doing great. This stuff about the betting pool and the rigged contest is the best news I've had in a long time."

I wasn't so sure about that, but again I kept my mouth shut. Why mention that the same scenario pointing to either Russell or Higginbotham as the killer could just as easily apply to Jimmy? Perhaps even more so. Nate believed what he wanted to believe, and despite my doubts, I hoped he was right.

CHAPTER 28

"He's moored at last an' furled his sail,
No danger now from wreck or gale."
—Mister Stormalong, Sea Shanty

I drove back to the bar in the hopes Venezia was still there. He wasn't. I called his number and left a message. Damn! Why hadn't I bought him dinner when I had the chance? Instead, put off by his presumption and eager to one-up him, I'd missed an opportunity to get more information.

At Mark's I learned Erin had gone back to her apartment. She looked about as glum as she had earlier in the day. I put a hand on her shoulder. "You okay?" I asked, though it was obvious she wasn't.

She shook her head and tears welled in her eyes. "I keep thinking about Winston, and the awful way he died. Thinking and wondering if . . ."

"What?"

"If he could've killed George, then killed himself."

"Because he was jealous of you two?"

Erin nodded miserably. "That stuff he wrote about me in his journal. If only I'd known."

"What could you have done? It wasn't your fault he developed a crush on you. Besides, I found out something today that suggests two other people had a stronger motive for killing George."

Erin stared at me, wide-eyed. "Really? Who?"

I sat down facing her, took a deep breath, and exhaled slowly. "Remember the private investigator who spoke to Luke? I met with him today. He repeated what he told Luke about George's gambling, but with some additions." I paused. Seeing Erin's stricken look, I said, "Sure you want to hear this?"

She sighed heavily. "No, but you might as well tell me."

I told her the gist of what I'd told Nate: how, desperate to recoup his losses, Kavanagh had probably organized a pool to bet on the dance contests at Seguan and how Higginbotham might have been involved in it. This would explain his presence at the powwow, where he'd seen both Jimmy and Russell Long Knife. He identified Jimmy as the person arguing with Kavanagh, but Nate believed it was really Russell Long Knife.

"Why?"

"Nate thinks George arranged with Russell, who was the favorite to win, to throw the contest. Then, while the others in the pool bet on Russell, George secretly put his money on Jimmy and came out the big winner. Nate believes Russell and George argued over dividing the loot, and Russell ended up killing George."

Erin's face twisted with anguish. She was silent a long time as she let this damning portrait of her beloved sink in. Finally, in a voice so subdued as to be barely audible, she said, "You mentioned two people with strong motives for killing George. Who's the other one?"

"Higginbotham. When he overheard Russell and George arguing, he realized he'd been had. He could've confronted George after Russell left and killed him. Only trouble is we don't have evidence to prove any of this."

Erin rose and began to pace around the small room, moving with the grace of a born athlete. Eventually, she stopped in front of me, feet spread apart, as if balancing on the deck of a rocking boat. "If what you say is true, then—" She broke off and her legs wobbled.

I reached out a hand to steady her. "I'm really sorry, Erin."

"Yeah, I know." Her legs folded and she sat. "I just wish George had come to me when he needed money. Then I could've repaid his debts, and he'd still be alive."

"He was probably afraid he'd lose you if you knew about his gambling."

"It would've been hard, but I could've handled it. It's not like I expected him to be perfect."

"No, but maybe he felt he had to appear that way. After all, most people try to put their best foot forward in the beginning. It's only later the warts start showing."

This hadn't been the case with Nate, however. He'd revealed his dark side at our first meeting in the parking lot at Plimoth Plantation. When we nearly collided, he chewed me out in a burst of road rage. Since then, I'd seen the ugly face of his anger enough times to make me wonder whether we could last as a couple. He was like a pressure-cooker, ready to explode at any moment, especially now that his good friend was a murder suspect.

"I guess." Erin frowned at her sneakers. The laces of one were starting to come untied. She undid and retied them with a double knot. "You said you needed evidence. How will you get it?"

I held out my hands, palms up. "I have no idea, but hopefully I'll think of something."

While Erin struggled with the notion of her fiancé as a deeply flawed person, I thought and thought and came up with nothing. No wonder. If the police hadn't found anything at the crime scene, how could I expect to? I tried to imagine the sequence of events leading up to the murder. Where had Higginbotham been when he'd overheard Russell—if it had been Russell instead of Jimmy—arguing with Kavanagh? Sitting in the shadows on the deck of his boat? Or returning from a walk with Happy?

Happy. Maybe I was on to something here. Higginbotham might've brought the poodle with him later when he squared off with Kavanagh. If I could just figure out how that nasty little barking, biting poodle could've been involved in murder.

CHAPTER 29

"Nantucket gals are very fine,
They know how to bait a codfish line."
—South Australia, or The Codfish Shanty

I felt like a fisherman, casting my line into the early morning fog. I used real fishing line Erin and I had purchased at a twenty-four-hour market the night before. We'd bought a bag of frozen bagels for bait, too.

The creature we hoped to lure was no fish, but a dog. Happy was obscured by the mist, but, as usual, we could hear him. I cast the line in the direction of his barks and waited tensely. Would he take the bait? Was this a crazy thing to be doing? Could the red marks I'd observed on Kavanagh's neck when his body was brought out of the water really be Happy's bite marks? Erin was a dim shape beside me. I wondered if she were having similar doubts.

The line jerked. "He's gone for it!" I whispered excitedly, tightening my grip on the pole.

Erin crept down the length of the line. The poodle was pulling hard. I was afraid the line would break and he'd make off with the bagel before Erin reached him. The line slackened. I heard angry barking. Erin must've taken the bagel away from Happy. I hoped her leather gloves protected her. I'd offered to do this part myself, but she'd insisted. Speed was essential. She had to toss a second bagel before Happy's jaws closed on her shins.

The barking continued, though not quite as loudly as before. Then it was quiet. Erin emerged from the fog, holding the bagel aloft like a trophy. Done! We high-fived quickly before we turned and ran. In the distance, we heard Higginbotham calling, his voice plaintive as a foghorn: "Happ-ee, Happ-ee, where are you?" If he'd been anyone else I would have felt sorry for him.

The officer behind the desk told us Sergeant Curtin hadn't come in yet, but was expected shortly. Erin and I sat on a bench beneath a wanted poster for Jimmy. I noticed that no picture of the homeless woman had been put up. Obviously finding her wasn't high on Curtin's list of priorities.

Ten minutes later, Curtin sauntered through the door, carrying a takeout coffee and a bag from Dunkin' Donuts. He exchanged pleasantries with the officer behind the desk, then turned to us. "Ms. Meloy, what can I do for you?" he asked, ignoring me.

"Can we speak privately?" I said.

"Of course. Come into my office," he replied, keeping his eyes on Erin.

Curtin's office was the size of a small closet. He settled behind a postage stamp–size desk and motioned for Erin to sit in the only other chair. She remained standing. "Miranda needs a chair, too," she said.

"Oh, right." Curtin went out and got another chair. When we were all seated, he said, "So what did you want to see me about?" Again he directed the question to Erin.

"We have some evidence related to George Kavanagh's murder." I removed a baggie from my tote and gave it to him.

He peered at the contents. "This is . . . a bagel?"

"Yes. The bite marks on it are from Vernon Higginbotham's

dog, Happy. We think that if you compare these marks with those on Kavanagh's neck, you'll find they match."

"Oh, really? You're telling me that little poodle bit Kavanagh, stuck him through with a killing lance, and tossed his body overboard?"

"Of course not!" I flared. "We believe Happy bit Kavanagh and his owner did the rest."

Curtin took a donut from his own bag and bit into it. "Why would Higginbotham kill Kavanagh?" he asked with his mouth full. "Weren't they friends, Ms. Meloy?"

"Yes, but as Miranda will tell you, George did something that really pissed off Higginbotham."

I told him about the possible betting scheme, how Kavanagh could've arranged with Russell to throw the contest and how Higginbotham could have been tricked out of a lot of money.

Curtin took another bite of his donut. "What makes you think there was a betting pool?"

"A combination of things I observed and stuff a private investigator who'd been tailing Kavanagh told me."

"I'd be interested in hearing what this investigator has to say. Why hasn't he come forward?"

"I'm sure he will," I said quickly. "Or you can contact him." I pulled out Venezia's card. Curtin made a note of the name and number.

"Maybe I will. In the meantime, let me explain a few things to you." He leaned forward and scowled at me. "First of all, this bagel you brought is worthless as evidence. We had a forensic odontologist examine the bites on Kavanagh's neck. He's ninety-nine percent certain they were made by a human. Human bites, Ms. Lewis. Like these!" He chomped down on his donut and held it out to me.

I recoiled instinctively. So much for that theory. I wasn't done yet, though. "Okay, but you've got to admit Higginbotham had a reason to kill Kavanagh."

"If what you say about the betting scheme is true, he did." Curtin waved the remaining piece of donut at me. "But by the same token, Jimmy Swift also had a motive for murder. He could've been the one who Kavanagh cut a deal with to rig the contest. Then Swift killed Kavanagh when they couldn't agree about dividing the dough."

"But Higginbotham—"

"There's another thing," Curtin interrupted. "Do you know how Kavanagh died?"

"He drowned?"

"Wrong. According to the medical examiner's report, drowning wasn't the cause of death because Kavanagh's lungs hadn't filled with water. Guess again, Ms. Lewis."

"Why don't you just tell us?" I shot back, refusing to play his game.

"It wasn't because of the killing lance either. He was already dead when it was thrust into him."

"How do you know?" Erin asked.

"Post-mortem wounds don't bleed," Curtin said. "When the heart stops, the blood clots. No, Ms. Lewis," he went on, directing his reply at me, "George Kavanagh died of cardiac arrest. And know what I think made him have a heart attack?"

No, I thought, but I have a feeling you're going to tell us.

"Fright," Curtin said. "He was so terrified, his heart jumped into overdrive, then shut down completely."

Erin blanched. A tremor went through me. In my mind's eye, I saw the medicine man's lurid face, as he leaned over another Indian's prone figure, heard the casino man's chilling words: "Wouldn't want to wind up like that, half-dead with nothing but a witch doctor's voodoo to cure me."

"This murder was the work of a savage," Curtin continued. "A savage who sank his teeth into the poor man's throat."

"No!" Erin moaned.

Curtin got up from behind his desk and went over to her. "I'm sorry, Ms. Meloy, I didn't mean to upset you."

The hell you didn't, I thought.

"You go home now," Curtin said gently as he helped Erin to her feet. "And don't worry. We'll find the savage who did this to your fiancé."

He guided her to the door. I followed. No point staying and arguing with the man; he was convinced Jimmy had killed Kavanagh, and that was that.

As we were leaving the station, Curtin came after us. "You forgot this." He handed me the baggie with the bagel. "By the way, you ever get that busted taillight fixed?"

CHAPTER 30

"Sing goodbye to Sally an' goodbye to Sue,
For we are the boy-os who can kick her through."
—Randy Dandy O, Sea Shanty

"I feel like such a fool," I vented outside the station.

"It seemed like a good idea at the time," Erin said generously. "How were you to know some forensic dentist decided those were human bite marks? They could've been the work of an animal. Happy certainly bites people."

"Yes, but by telling Curtin about the betting pool I've done the opposite of what I intended. Instead of casting suspicion away from Jimmy and onto someone else, I've convinced him even more that Jimmy's the killer. I wish . . ."

"What?"

"I don't know. I should probably go back to Cambridge before I cause more trouble."

"Please don't. It's been good having you here. Can't you stay a day or two longer?"

"Okay, but—"

Erin patted my arm. "Thanks, Miranda." She glanced at her watch. "I need to go. I promised Mark I'd put in time at the museum today. Want to come?"

"I'll catch you later. I'm going to try and finally make some progress on the chapter I'm supposed to be writing."

Back at Erin's apartment, I tried to focus on "Closing the

Frontier," but I just couldn't wrap my mind around it. Not with Jimmy on the lam, Nate and the police trying to find him, and me feeling like a jerk for making matters worse. Was there any way I could do damage control? Curtin had said he'd be interested in speaking with the private investigator. I wanted to talk to him more myself. I called his number, got his machine and left another message.

Now what? Once again, I tried to focus on "Closing the Frontier," but it was no go. On a whim, I looked up "A. Venezia Investigations" on the Internet. The one entry gave me the agency's New London address and phone number, which I already had. On the off chance I might be able to reach him at home, I got the New London directory online. It showed only the agency listing, but I noticed a listing for a Mrs. Rose Venezia. His mother or his wife? I had nothing to lose. I dialed the number.

"Hello, my name is Miranda—"

"I don't care who you are, take me off your phone list." Rose Venezia sounded tired and cross, like me when I get this kind of call, only with an Italian accent.

"I'm not a telemarketer. I'm trying to reach your . . . son?"

"My ex-husband. Call his office."

"I've already left several messages there. I thought you might know another number I could try. Please. It's really important I get in touch with him."

"He'll get back to you."

"But I need to speak to him. Now!" I did my best to sound frantic.

"You and a lot of others," Rose Venezia snapped. "You'll have to wait your turn. And don't call here again because I'm sick and tired of hearing from Tony's jilted girlfriends." She hung up.

Hmmm. So the man was a lady-killer. A lady-killer who drank

expensive Scotch and expected me to pick up the tab. I felt sorry for his ex-wife, but at the same time I was curious to learn more. And not just about the possible betting pool. I didn't quite buy his reason for approaching Luke about Kavanagh. Also, despite his insistence that if Sheila were alive, he would've found her, he'd been awfully interested in where I'd taken the photo of the homeless woman. Again, feeling I had nothing to lose, I got directions to Rose Venezia's from the Internet.

She lived in a residential neighborhood with modest but well-kept houses on the outskirts of New London. I rang the bell. "Who is it?" a woman's voice yelled.

I hesitated. If I gave my real name, she might not open the door for me. "Delivery," I called back, then ducked behind some bushes conveniently located beside the house. The door opened and a striking woman with large, dark eyes and a thick mane of hair gone completely white peered out.

I popped from the bushes and rushed the door, managing to get a foot inside. "Oh, Mrs. Venezia, please, I really need to talk to you!"

"Who the hell are you?"

"Miranda. I called earlier and—"

"Get out of here." She tried to shut the door, but I held my ground.

"Please. Just for a few minutes. I'm desperate. I don't know what I'll do if I can't talk to you." I looked at her beseechingly.

Rose Venezia glanced at a neighboring house. Following her gaze, I saw a woman's face in the window. "All right," she grumbled, "but only for a few minutes."

She steered me into a small living room crowded with furniture that was a mishmash of old-fashioned and modern. "Sit down and pull yourself together. Tony's not worth the fuss." She motioned me to the couch.

"But he seemed like such a nice guy," I sniveled. "A real

gentleman. When he stood me up the other night and wouldn't answer my phone calls, I got pretty upset."

Rose Venezia perched on the edge of a love seat. With her piercing dark eyes and white hair, she reminded me of a snowy owl. "Lemme give you some advice. Forget Tony. His motto is 'love 'em an' leave 'em.' "

"Is that why you got divorced? Because he was unfaithful?"

"Not exactly."

"What happened?"

"Look, I don't know you and—"

"Please talk to me. If I'm going to follow your advice and forget Tony, I need to know the worst."

Rose Venezia sighed. "Oh, all right. It's not easy being married to a PI. Tony'd get calls for jobs at all hours. Half the time, it'd mess up plans he'd made with me and the kids. But it was the year he spent in Australia that really did us in."

"Australia?"

"Yeah. Tony'd done a job for this rich guy before. Then when the guy's daughter was lost at sea off the coast of Australia, he hired Tony to find her. So Tony went to Australia and that's when the trouble started."

"How?"

"Well, as you may've noticed, Tony likes the good life. Always has. But until that rich guy started bankrolling him, he couldn't afford it. Tony was living high on the hog while he was in Australia, spending that guy's money. No wonder he stayed nearly a year."

"But wasn't he also trying to find his client's daughter?"

"In the beginning, yes. But I think he realized pretty quick it was a lost cause. And rather than give up his cash cow, he kept stringing the old man along."

This could be sour grapes talking. But a year did seem an awfully long time to spend on a search where there was little chance of success. "This rich man must've had a lot of faith in Tony, though, because he hired him for another job here in the States," I said.

"That's news to me. But if it's true, Tony's still pulling the wool over the old man's eyes. Bastard's raking in the dough, all the while telling me he doesn't have enough to meet his child support payments."

"How many children do you have?"

"Three boys." Rose Venezia pointed proudly toward a grouping of family photos on the mantel. "How about yourself?"

"None," I replied, truthful for the first time since my arrival.

"There's still time."

I stood. "Thanks for speaking with me, Mrs. Venezia. I feel better now."

"Good. I wouldn't want you collapsing on my doorstep. Not with the neighborhood busybody watching." She saw me to the door.

My visit with Venezia's ex made me all the more eager to speak to him again. But unless he replied to my messages, I didn't see how that was going to happen. I was back where I'd started from.

Midway through the return trip to Spouters Point, I realized things weren't as hopeless as they seemed. Rose Venezia had mistaken me for a jilted girlfriend. I wasn't the genuine item, but I knew someone who was.

CHAPTER 31

"The old man wuz a drunken geezer
He could not sail the Ebenezer
Learnt his trade on a Chinese junk
Spent mos' time, sir, in his bunk."
                    —Ebenezer, Sea Shanty

At two P.M. the bar at the Spouters Point Inne was practically deserted. A few men hunched over drinks, but I didn't see Lipstick. When I described her to the bartender, he told me she was a regular who usually showed up around five to catch the after-work crowd. I thanked him and was about to leave when one of the men at the shadowy far end turned in my direction. Luke. With a guilty look, he bolted.

"Does he come here often?" I asked the bartender.

"Lately, he does."

I returned to Erin's apartment and tried to settle down to work. But other thoughts intruded. What to make of Luke's drinking in the middle of the afternoon? No doubt, he felt bad about his estrangement from Erin, but was there more to it? He certainly had motive, means and opportunity, since his wife couldn't vouch for his whereabouts the night of the murder. And, as a museum staffer, he could easily gain entry to the grounds, get the killing lance and skewer Kavanagh. But Kavanagh hadn't died that way, I reminded myself. He'd had a heart attack after being bitten on the neck. I couldn't imagine

Luke attacking him so viciously. Or anyone else, for that matter. That's why I'd wanted to believe Happy had bitten him.

Too restless to concentrate, I kept looking at my watch, waiting for it to be time to return to the Spouters Point Inne. Finally, I gave up and drove there. I parked in the museum lot across the street from the inn and waited.

A car door slammed. Lipstick teetered across the pavement in a short skirt and high heels. I went after her. "Hi. Remember me? We met in the ladies' room at the inn a while ago. I couldn't get the faucet to work and you helped me."

She shrugged. "I guess."

"You were upset because your boyfriend ditched you. Did he ever turn up?"

"No."

"You didn't try to get in touch with him?"

"How could I? I only know his first name, and I'm not even sure that's his real name. Told me he was on some top secret job. CIA, I'm thinking."

"Too bad."

"Yeah, well, win a few, lose a few. He either hooked up with someone else, or his top secret mission ended and he split. You headed for the bar?" She inspected me more closely, as if sizing up the competition.

"I'm meeting a friend at the museum."

"Have fun."

"You, too."

So much for my hopes of locating Venezia via his last girlfriend. I glanced at my watch. The museum would be closing soon, but maybe I could still catch Erin. As I walked across the village green, I spotted Mark and another staff musician in the bandstand, putting away their instruments. "Any idea where Erin is?"

"Try the *Susan Kilrain*," Mark said. "She likes putting the old lady to bed."

The ship was quiet and appeared deserted. As I made my way below, taking care not to bump my head on the low ceilings, I could understand why some believed the whaler was haunted. It was easy to imagine the ghostly shapes of seamen lurking in its dim recesses. For a moment, I even thought the figure crouched in the cavernous hold was a phantom. But as I got closer, I realized that my "ghost" wore the clothing of a museum staffer. "Erin?"

The person turned. Luke had a silver flask in hand, and didn't look glad to see me.

"Sorry." I started to leave.

Luke strode quickly over, and grabbed me by the arm. "I've always liked you, Miranda," he said without a trace of friendliness in his blue eyes. "But lately, you've developed a bad habit of showing up in the wrong place at the wrong time."

"I said I was sorry. I didn't expect to find you here any more than—"

"At the bar at the Spouters Point Inne?"

"Right." I decided to confront the issue head-on. "What's with the drinking, Luke?"

He stared into the dark, empty space of the hold. "Helps take the edge off things. This hasn't been an easy time. Erin won't speak to me, and Maggie blames me for the way I broke the bad news about Kavanagh."

"But you apologized to Erin, didn't you? That night and afterward."

"That night . . . what do you mean?" Luke's eyes bore into me.

"The night of the party. Maggie said—"

"You've been talking to Maggie? What did she tell you?"

Luke loomed over me, a tall, strong man who'd played sports in high school and college, and had remained in shape as a museum staff person. I felt a tremor of fear. Why couldn't I learn to keep my mouth shut?

"Nothing."

"You're lying!" His grip tightened on my arm.

"What's going on?" Erin looked down on us from the ladder leading into the hold.

Luke released my arm and hid the flask behind his back. "Miranda and I were just chatting while I put the *Kilrain* to bed. But she's your baby, so I'll let you finish." Squeezing past Erin, he was up the ladder and out of the hold before either of us could say anything.

"What was that all about?" Erin asked.

"I came here searching for you, and found Luke drinking— for the second time today."

"When was the first?"

"I ran into him in the bar at the Spouters Point Inne this afternoon. He didn't like it that I caught him hitting the bottle twice. Or that I'd spoken to Maggie about him."

"When did you speak to Maggie?"

"The other day when I walked back to the house with her."

"What did she say?"

I hesitated, reluctant to reveal that Luke lacked a solid alibi for the night of the murder, when Erin was already so set against him. "She feels bad about how he broke the news about Kavanagh to you."

Erin's expression hardened. "He's the one who should feel bad."

"He does, or he wouldn't be drinking. If you two could only bury the hatchet."

"No! I may never forgive him."

"But—"

"I don't want to talk about it anymore. Let's finish up here and go home."

At Erin's apartment, we decided that after a day that had begun with an attempt to entrap Happy and ended for me with a tense confrontation with Luke, we were ready for some mindless entertainment. We got pizza and rented a couple of old James Bond movies. With their fast-paced action, exotic locales, and ingenious gadgets—not to mention their uncomplicated, black-and-white view of the world—I found these movies an excellent form of escapism.

Goldfinger served this purpose so well that we started watching a second movie. But in *The Spy Who Loved Me,* a monstrous character named Jaws, with huge steel teeth and a nasty habit of sinking them into his victims' necks, jolted us back to the present. "I've seen enough." Erin switched off the DVD player. "I'm going to bed."

I could've kicked myself for not remembering the Jaws character. But later, as I lay on the air bed, trying to sleep, I wished that such a cartoon-like figure of evil existed in real life, and was responsible for Kavanagh's murder. Then, I wouldn't have to suspect people I knew and liked.

CHAPTER 32

"The first mate's name wuz Dickie Green, sir
The dirtiest beggar ye've ever seen, sir
Walkin' his poop wid a bucko roll
May the sharks have his body an' the devil have his
soul!"

—*Ebenezer,* Sea Shanty

When the phone rang the next morning, I thought it was Nate, or maybe the PI. Instead, an unfamiliar male voice said, "Miss Lewis, it's Vernon Higginbotham."

"Who?" I couldn't possibly have heard him right.

"Vernon Higginbotham. I'm calling for my wife. Something terrible has happened. She wants to speak to you."

"Okay, put her on." I wondered what it was, and why she wanted to talk to me, of all people.

In the background, I heard muffled sobs, then Flo's distraught voice came onto the line. "Oh, Miranda, I can't believe that just the other evening you told me about losing your poor little baby. And now—now I've lost Hap!"

This time, I thought I hadn't heard *her* right. "What?"

"I've lost Hap."

"He ran away?"

"No. He was attacked and killed. Oh, I can't, it's too awful!" She began sobbing in earnest.

Surprise gave way to horror and genuine sympathy. "Flo, I'm

so sorry! Is there anything I can—"

I heard a crash, as Flo dropped the handset, then Higginbotham came back on. "She can't talk anymore. Good-bye."

Erin sat up in bed. "What's going on?"

"Happy's been killed."

"You're kidding! How?"

"That's what I'm going to find out."

Seated on the couch in the cabin, he with his arm around her, and she crying softly into his shoulder, they might have been any grieving couple. Higginbotham rose when I climbed down the ladder. "Thank you for coming." He spoke with a simple dignity I hadn't thought him capable of. He even shook my hand. Flo threw herself into my arms. "Oh, Miranda, I didn't know who else to turn to!"

Only then did I understand why she'd had her husband call me. I'd reached out to Flo for sympathy, and now she was reaching out to me—with the difference that my appeal had been fake, while hers was the real thing. Pushing aside my dislike of the Higginbothams and their dog, I responded to Flo as one human to another. I held her and murmured words of comfort until she calmed down a bit. "Why don't you lie down and try to rest?" I suggested.

"Yes, why don't you?" Higginbotham said.

"I don't know if I can," Flo said in a childlike voice.

"Of course, you can. Here, take this. It will help." He handed her a glass of water and a pill. Flo looked at me, as if seeking permission. I nodded and she took the pill. I went on holding her until her body went slack in my arms. Then I gently extricated myself and eased her down onto the couch. Higginbotham motioned me to follow him out on deck.

"What happened to your dog?" I asked.

Higginbotham's eyes narrowed. "What's it to you? You didn't

lose *your* poodle. Bet you never even had one. You were on a fishing expedition when you came to see my wife the other day, weren't you?"

Rather than answer his question, I repeated mine. Higginbotham glared at me a moment longer. Apparently deciding he might as well tell me, he said, "I woke up in the middle of the night. Happy was restless, so I took him for a walk. Must've smelled something, because all of a sudden he took off, just like he did yesterday morning."

"Yesterday morning? What happened then?" I was curious to hear his version of the day's escapade.

"He was attracted by something and ran away. I heard him barking. When I finally found him, he was chewing on a bagel. I didn't think any more about it until last night when . . ." His voice quavered and he broke off. Recovering, he said, "when the same person returned to . . ."

My heart beat faster. "How do you know it was a person?"

"Because I saw someone scurrying away after he'd killed our poor little darling." The anguish in Higginbotham's voice was as real as his wife's. I felt sorry for him, but only for an instant. "You're sure it was a person, not an animal?"

"Yes. The monster came back to finish the job he started yesterday morning. He lured Happy into his clutches and murdered him."

My blood went cold. "Why would anyone want to kill Happy?"

"Revenge. He wanted to get back at me for telling the police about George and him."

I felt dizzy. "You think Jimmy Swift . . . ?"

"Who else? In case I didn't get the message, he left his signature behind."

"What signature?"

Higginbotham clamped his teeth together. "He bit poor Hap

in the neck just like he—" Higginbotham covered his face with his hands and made hoarse noises that sounded like his version of crying.

I was too stunned to speak. Finally, I said, "Have you talked to the police about this?"

His fingers parted to reveal one malevolent eye. " 'Course I have."

CHAPTER 33

"Oh, this is the tale of John Cherokee,
The Injun man from Miramagadea,
With a hauley high, an' a hauley low!

They made him a slave down in Alabam,
He run away every time he can,
With a hauley high an' a hauley low!

They shipped him aboard of a whaling ship,
Agen an' agen he gave 'em the slip,
With a hauley high an' a hauley low!"
—Alabama, or John Cherokee, Sea Shanty

As I was leaving the museum, I spotted Mark walking toward me, head bent, frowning at the ground. He must have been deep in thought because when I called his name, he looked up, startled and even a little guilty, as if he'd been caught doing something he wasn't supposed to.

"Oh, hi, Miranda," he said absently, continuing on his way.

"Have you heard the news about Happy?" I followed him.

"Yes, it's horrible." Mark kept his eyes on the ground.

"Vernon Higginbotham's convinced a human killed Happy. But don't you think it's got to be the work of another animal?"

Mark said nothing.

"Know of any strays that might've gotten into a fight with Happy?"

"I'm late for a demo on board the *Kilrain*." Mark quickened his pace. "Catch you later."

I stared after his retreating figure. Why was Mark, who was usually so friendly and forthcoming, now giving me the cold shoulder?

Walking toward my car, I considered the possible repercussions of Happy's death and Higginbotham's belief that Jimmy was responsible. Higginbotham had gone to the police, which meant Curtin. Curtin knew Erin and I had been involved in the morning attempt to entrap Happy. But given his strong prejudice against Jimmy, he might be willing to believe Jimmy had attacked and killed Happy that night. However, before Jimmy was declared the culprit, a forensic odontologist needed to determine that the bites were made by a human. Then the DNA found in the bites had to be shown to match Jimmy's. I hoped the evidence would point to another animal as the killer, or if a human, someone other than Jimmy.

I got in my car and started to drive back to Erin's. I hadn't gone far when my cell phone rang. Keeping one hand on the wheel, I flipped it open.

"Miranda, what's going on there?" Nate's angry voice bounced off my eardrums.

"What do you mean?"

"Reba called. Curtin came to the house this morning, looking for Jimmy."

Uh-oh. The proverbial shit was hitting the fan even sooner than I'd anticipated. I pulled over rather than risk an accident.

"Claimed he had a search warrant, tore the place apart, scared the kids and gave Reba a hard time. Curtin's convinced Jimmy's hiding out nearby, all because of some nonsense about Jimmy killing the Higginbothams' dog. You know anything about this?"

"I just talked with Higginbotham, and he does think Jimmy

killed Happy. He saw someone fleeing the scene, and figured it was Jimmy getting revenge because Higginbotham fingered him for Kavanagh's murder."

"Christ! Of course, Curtin's ready to believe Higginbotham about Jimmy. In his book, Indians kill dogs."

"Do they?" I was taken aback.

"Sometimes. But that's another story. I'm coming back. I don't know if Jimmy's there or not, but I'm not going to stand by and let those bastards harass Reba and her family."

"Anything I can do?"

"See what you can find out on your end."

"My end?"

"What the white guys are up to."

The call over, I thought about my new assignment. Curtin was probably the most important white guy I needed to keep tabs on. But how? He already distrusted me because of my connection with Nate, and through him, Jimmy. When Erin and I had gone to the police station with the bagel, he'd ignored me. He had, however, turned on the charm with Erin. Maybe there was an opening there.

Erin was up, dressed and drinking a cup of coffee when I returned. I poured one for myself and sat down to fill her in on what had happened. When I was finished, she gave me a strange look. "I hate to ask this, but I have to. Do you think Jimmy killed George, then Happy?"

I swallowed hard. Nate and I had already had several run-ins over the same question, but this was the first time it had come up with Erin. It was a relief to speak honestly with her.

"I don't know if Jimmy is innocent or guilty, but I do know he won't get justice from Curtin. If the police find him and he tries to escape, they'll kill him. Then, we'll never find out for sure if he killed George. And Nate will be devastated. I love Nate the way you loved George. If there's any chance Jimmy's innocent, I'm going to help Nate prove it. Will you help me?"

Erin didn't miss a beat. "Yes, but what can I possibly do?"

"Call Curtin and tell him how upset you are by this new killing, and ask him to keep you informed about the progress of his search for the murderer."

"Why do you think he'll talk to me?"

"He bent over backwards to be nice to you yesterday. I think he's got the hots for you."

"Oh, c'mon. I'm just Luke's kid sister as far as he's concerned."

"Not anymore. You're an attractive woman, and Curtin's noticed that. He wants to look good in your eyes. Give it a try and you'll see I'm right."

CHAPTER 34

". . . the truth is, these savages have an innate sense of delicacy; say what you will; it is marvelous how essentially polite they are. I pay this particular compliment to Queequeg, because he treated me with so much civility and consideration, while I was guilty of great rudeness . . ."

—Moby-Dick

I drove to the Providence airport under an overcast sky. A severe storm was forecast for the evening, or possibly the next day, the fallout from yet another hurricane. I just hoped the heavy rain and strong winds didn't start until after Nate's plane had landed safely.

At the airport, I joined a group of people lined up outside the security check-in. While I waited, I glanced at the local paper I'd picked up on my way out of Spouters Point. A picture of Happy's dead body had made the front page under the headline, "Jaws Killer Strikes Again." This was sure to inflame every animal lover for miles around. I knew some people had a lower tolerance for the killing of animals than they did for the killing of humans. A screenwriter friend had once told me that it was an unspoken rule that while you could knock off all the people you wanted in the movies, you were not allowed to kill a cat or dog.

Curtin was quoted as saying he was ninety-nine percent certain the dog had been killed by the same person who'd viciously murdered a yachtsman at the Spouters Point Museum a few weeks earlier. Based on what evidence? I wondered. There hadn't been time to do a DNA match, even if the police had gotten a sample of Jimmy's DNA during their search of his house.

I continued reading. "The Indians have been known to kill dogs," Curtin told the reporter. He went on to relate a story about a woman living on the Dottaguck reservation years ago who had killed her dogs rather than pay the licensing fees. The incendiary tone of Curtin's remarks alarmed me; they seemed aimed at stirring up a lynch mob mentality.

I turned to a back page for the rest of the story. Another headline caught my eye: "Bald Eagle Sighted in Vicinity of Clambanks." I was about to read the accompanying story when movement around me made me look up. Passengers were starting to come off the plane. I glimpsed Nate. With his trademark dark glasses and his mouth set in a grim line, he looked intimidating. But the moment he saw me, he grinned and quickened his pace. Then his arms were around me, and he held me close. All the tension between us melted in those first few moments of his embrace.

"God, I've missed you!" he murmured.

"I've missed you, too!" I didn't want to let go of him, and he seemed reluctant to separate also. Eventually we did. Nate reached for his duffel bag, which he'd put down to hug me. I'd dropped the newspaper I'd been reading during our embrace, and it had landed on his bag. Nate scanned it.

"Christ!" Gritted teeth replaced his smile. He tore the paper in two and tossed it in a nearby trashcan. I was glad Curtin wasn't there, because Nate might have ripped him apart as well.

"Let's go," he said brusquely.

"Where to?" I asked in the car. "Reba's?"

Nate removed his dark glasses and looked at me. "I'd rather

we went to a motel first."

He stroked my thigh, and I felt a thrill of pleasure. Fortunately, we were still sitting in the parking garage; if I'd been driving, I might've had an accident. He took his hand away with an effort. "But yeah. Reba's."

When we were on the road, Nate said, "Think Higginbotham could've—"

"Killed his own dog? It's hard to say. On the one hand, he seemed genuinely upset by the death. On the other, how could he have known the bites came from a human unless he made them himself?"

"You get any more on him?"

I told Nate about my failed attempt with Happy and the bagel. "Dumb, I know."

"At least you tried," Nate said charitably.

"Yes, but that's the part that's got me stumped. I just can't imagine anyone with a motive to kill Kavanagh attacking him like that."

"Even Jimmy?"

"Jesus, Nate! Don't start that again."

"Sorry. When I saw what Curtin said in the newspaper, it made me so mad. Paranoid, too."

"Okay, but . . . did that woman on the reservation really kill her dogs?"

"Yes, but there's a lot more to the story than what's in the paper. It happened a long time ago, before Clambanks, before the tribe was recognized by the federal government. That woman was elderly. She lived in poverty in a rundown house on the reservation. She complained to the state about her poor housing and lack of medical care, but nothing was done. When the dog officer came to collect state licensing fees, she chased him away. Then she killed her dogs rather than be harassed by a government that wouldn't lift a finger to help her. I know it sounds cruel, but she felt she had to take a stand."

I tried to put myself in her position, but it wasn't easy. Yet admitting this would feed Nate's paranoia. "I guess I understand."

Nate gave me a long look. I felt he wanted to pry a more definitive answer from me. Instead, changing the subject, he said, "What about that private investigator? You speak with him again?"

"I've been trying to reach him without any luck. How about you? Did you find out anything more about Russell's possible role in throwing the dance contest?"

Nate shook his head. "He's holding fast to his story that someone tampered with his dance stick. And with the stick still missing, there's no way of telling whether he's right or wrong."

A gloomy silence settled over us. We drove on, absorbed in thought. After a while I glanced at Nate and saw he'd dozed off. Just as well. He was undoubtedly exhausted, and talking didn't seem to be getting us anywhere.

CHAPTER 35

" 'Your hat, your hat, sir!' suddenly cried the Sicilian seaman, who being posted at the mizzen-mast-head, stood directly behind Ahab. . . . But already the sable wing was before the old man's eyes; the long hooked bill at his head: with a scream, the black hawk darted away with his prize."

—Moby-Dick

"Nate! You didn't have to come all the way back just because—" Reba exclaimed when she opened the door.

"Oh yes, I did. The cops had no business barging in and scaring you and the kids. I'm here to put a stop to that."

Reba looked worried. She bowed her head. "I shouldn't have called you."

"Why not?" Nate gently tipped her chin up, forcing her to look at him.

Tears brimmed in Reba's eyes. She shook her head. "I can't . . ." she began.

"What is it? What's the matter? Have those cops been back?"

"No, but—" In the background, Kyle barked. "Just a minute." Reba left, and we heard her telling Patty to take Kyle to his room and stay with him. When she returned, she invited us to sit down in the living room. We waited in silence, while Reba closed her eyes and clutched the curly fringe of her bangs, apparently gearing up for what she had to tell us. Finally, she opened her eyes and removed her fingers from her hair. "Jim-

212

my's not in Minnesota. He's here."

Nate stared at her with astonishment. His eyes narrowed and his jaw clenched. "You better be kidding!" He strode over to Reba, towering over her in that menacing stance I knew too well.

Reba shrank in her seat, but she met his gaze steadily. "I wish I were."

Nate pounded the fist of his right hand into his left palm. "Then why the hell did you tell me he was out west?"

"Jimmy couldn't bear to face you. When he went into hiding, he had me make up the story about Minnesota."

"Why couldn't he face me?"

Reba was silent. The only sound was the repeated slap of Nate's fist against his palm like a ticking bomb. The ticking stopped, and Nate said, "Because he did what Russell accused him of: rigged the dance contest so he'd win?"

"Yes," Reba said, still meeting his gaze. "I'm really sorry, Nate. When I heard about your accident, I almost broke down and told the truth. But Jimmy said not to."

Nate went back to his seat and slumped into it, shaking his head. "He had so much going for him, and now he's thrown it all away and brought dishonor to himself and his family. And I—" His voice broke, and he buried his face in his hands. When he spoke again, his words were muffled. "Feel like I've failed him as a friend and mentor."

I felt terrible for Nate, but also relief that the suspicions that had been weighing on me like a bunch of heavy bags were revealed to be true. I put a comforting hand on Nate's shoulder. He shook it off, stubborn in his pain as he was in his anger.

"Please don't blame yourself," Reba said. "Jimmy made his choice. It was the wrong choice, and now he's the one who has to live with it."

Nate removed his hands from his face and looked at her.

"But why? Why would he do something like that?"

"The money," Reba replied simply. "He figured that with the couple of thou from the prize, plus what he got from George Kavanagh, we could finally afford to send Kyle to the dolphin therapy program."

"Should've come to me if he wanted money that bad, 'stead of going to that . . ." Nate paused and glanced at me before continuing. "Frigging gambler."

"I know," Reba said.

Nate rose and began to pace. "You said Kavanagh promised him money. Is that what they were arguing about the night of the murder?"

Reba nodded. "Kavanagh tried to short-change him. Said he needed extra money to pay off his debts. They quarreled, then Kavanagh said he heard something. He told Jimmy to go home and promised to bring him the rest of his share the next day. Jimmy didn't trust him, but he felt he had no choice. He was too afraid of being found out."

"Kavanagh was still alive when Jimmy left?" Nate stopped pacing to stare at Reba.

I was glad he'd asked this because I never could've done so without being called racist. I held my breath waiting for Reba's answer.

"That's what he told me."

"You believe him?" Nate pressed.

Reba flinched at the question. "Yes!" she said fiercely. "I know he did something very bad, rigging that contest, but I just can't believe he's capable of murder."

Nate gave her a long look. "I can't either," he said finally.

"Thank God!" Reba got up and collapsed, weeping, into his arms. I blew out the air I'd been holding in a whoosh. Jimmy might still be guilty, but for the moment, I wanted to give him the benefit of the doubt as much as Nate and Reba did.

"Where is Jimmy now?" Nate asked after Reba had calmed down somewhat.

"In Big Otter Swamp."

So I'd been right about the swamp being a good hiding place for someone like Jimmy.

"Jesus," Nate muttered.

"He's all right," Reba assured Nate. "He knows how to survive there. And I've been leaving food and water for him when I can. But now . . ." She shook her head.

"Now the cops are after him," Nate finished. "If you or I go anywhere near the swamp, the police will know he's there. Probably got someone watching the house." He stalked over to the window.

"Do you see anyone?" Reba asked.

"No, but I noticed a car parked down the road a ways when we drove up."

"What'll we do?" Reba flashed him an anxious look.

"I don't know, but I'll think of something." He turned to me. "You got any ideas, Miranda?"

"No, but I guess I could call Erin."

"What good will that do?"

"She's our link to Curtin. I noticed he seemed interested in her, so I told her to ask him to keep her in the loop. She might've learned something by now."

Nate held out his hands, palms upward. "Worth a try."

I made the call from the kitchen.

"I spoke with him like you wanted me to," Erin said.

"And?"

"Good news and bad."

"Start with the good."

"He promised to keep me informed."

"The bad?"

"He got the medical examiner's report on Winston."

I felt a twinge of guilt at having let Winston slip from my mind. Guilt followed by foreboding. I had to force myself to ask: "What did it say?"

Erin made a sound that was half sigh, half moan. "There were signs of a struggle, so it seems he didn't go into the water willingly. I feel so awful for him and his family!"

"I do, too." In my mind's eye, I saw Winston dangling helplessly from the rigging, his mother's anxious face, his brother's angry one, then his grandmother waiting futilely with her dripping umbrella. Poor Winston. Poor all of them. "Does Curtin have any ideas about who he struggled with?"

"Unfortunately, yes. He thinks it's the same person who killed George, that Winston made the mistake of being in the wrong place at the wrong time."

Omigod! This made the situation even worse for Jimmy. I dreaded having to tell Nate.

"There's one more thing," Erin said.

I steeled myself for her answer. "What?"

"Curtin asked me out for coffee tomorrow, but I turned him down. Told him it was too soon, that I'm not ready to—"

"Call him back and say you've changed your mind."

"Miranda!" she protested.

"I know this is hard for you, but if you have coffee with him, you might learn something that can help us."

"All right," Erin agreed reluctantly.

When I went back to the living room, Nate and Reba looked as dispirited as before. "Erin find out anything?" Nate asked with a flicker of hope in his eyes.

"No," I lied, "but Curtin's promised to keep her informed."

Nate opened his mouth to say something, but ended up stifling a yawn. "You must be exhausted," Reba said. "You and Miranda are welcome to spend the night here, unless you'd be more comfortable at a motel."

Nate returned to the window again. "Thanks, Reba, we just might take you up on your offer. But first, Miranda and I need to take a little drive."

"Where are we going?" I asked in the car.

"Just drive and I'll tell you where and when to turn," he said mysteriously.

I drove straight for about a mile. Nate kept glancing into the rear view mirror. "Is someone following us?" I asked.

"Yes."

"Want me to lose him?"

"No, I want him to be able to follow us."

"Why?"

"I'm ready for another wild-goose chase. Only this time it's the cops who'll be led astray, not me. Turn right here."

For the next couple of hours, we meandered along back roads in the vicinity of Jimmy's house and farther afield. When I got too tired to drive, Nate took over. My eyelids fluttered shut and my head drooped. I dozed. I woke up as Nate pulled into the parking lot of a motel.

"Where are we?" I murmured groggily.

"Outside Kingston."

"I thought we were going to spend the night at Reba's."

"Changed my mind. I don't want to give up the game just yet. And this way, we'll have our night in a motel after all. Okay?" He put a hand on my knee.

During the night I awoke to the steady drumming of rain. I thought of Jimmy in the swamp, getting drenched, and shivered. But Reba had said he knew how to survive in there. And he was safe from the police for the time being. Wet, but safe.

The rain made it hard to get up the next morning. Nate and I were snuggling in bed when my cell phone rang. It was Erin. "Curtin called to cancel our get-together for coffee. Said he'd gotten a tip on Jimmy's whereabouts, and they're sending a search party out."

"But who—how?"

"He said a little birdie told him. I got him to admit it wasn't a bird but a bird watcher. The guy spotted a bald eagle hovering over Big Otter Swamp. When he went in for a closer look, he found signs that someone had been camping there and called the police."

"Shit."

"What's the matter?" Nate asked after I hung up.

"The police know where Jimmy is."

CHAPTER 36

"But they cotched him agen an' they chained him
tight,
Kept him in the dark widout any light.
They gave him nuttin' for to eat and drink,
All of his bones began to clink.
An' now his ghost is often seen,
Sittin' on the main-truck—all wet an' green."
—*Alabama,* or *John Cherokee,* Sea Shanty

Rain lashed the windshield. Beside me, Nate resembled Darth Vader in a black hooded slicker. We'd made a brief stop at a sporting goods store in Kingston, where we'd both bought slickers, and Nate had gotten a pair of high rubber boots and other supplies including a Bowie knife. I suspected he'd use it as a weapon if necessary.

"Pull over," Nate said.

I stopped the car and peered out. On the right were dense woods. "I don't see a trail."

"Trust me, there is one." He gripped the door handle.

"Want me to wait?"

"No. It'll attract attention. I'll call on my cell when and if I can."

"Okay," I said doubtfully. "Be careful."

He gave me a quick kiss. Then, seeing my worried expression, he said, "Look on the bright side, Miranda. At least there are no alligators in this swamp."

No, I thought. But there are poisonous snakes and other nasty creatures. Not to mention armed men. In the distance, I heard dogs barking.

"I better go," Nate said.

He vanished into the rain. A cold dread filled me. The barking dogs sounded as if they were getting closer. Moving in for the kill. God, I hoped Nate got to Jimmy before it was too late. Hoped they both made it out alive. But they were two against how many? How many men had been persuaded to join the hunt for the savage believed to have viciously murdered two people and a beloved pet?

During the Dottaguck War, a couple of hundred Indians had taken refuge in the swamp. Most had been chased down and killed. The centers of the wild rhododendrons growing there were supposed to have turned red with the bloodshed. I pictured today's hunters tromping through the rhododendron bushes, through muddy pools, where copperheads lurked, into the very heart of the swamp with their dogs and guns.

I drove to the Spouters Point Museum. It was deserted, the heavy rain having kept visitors away. My shoes and pants below the slicker got soaked walking from the visitor center to the Quarterdeck Cafe. I'd fortify myself with coffee before seeking Erin. I'd just opened the door when a figure cloaked in a sea-green slicker and carrying two large plastic containers of food brushed past me. I recognized Mark. "What's the big hurry?" I called. He continued walking quickly toward the waterfront as if he hadn't heard me. What the devil? This was the second time he'd given me an uncharacteristic brushoff. Mystified, I followed at a distance. Mark stopped and glanced around several times. Obviously, he didn't want to be observed.

Mark arrived at the sail loft building by a roundabout route. I hung back while he entered. He shut the door, but failed to close it all the way. I slid noiselessly inside, eased the door shut, and flattened myself against the wall. Mark approached the bottom of the ladder leading up to the second-story loft. "It's okay, you can come out now," he said softly. "I've brought food."

I detected movement behind a partially furled sail in the loft. A moment later, I caught a glimpse of matted hair and a nut-brown face. The homeless woman emerged from behind the sail, her gaze trained on Mark.

So she was one of his strays. I should have known. He probably saw himself as her protector and wouldn't betray her trust, even to me. Now he spoke gently to her, coaxing her down the ladder as he might, a frightened child. She descended slowly and cautiously. I stood perfectly still at my post near the door, fearful that if I moved a muscle, I'd give myself away and she'd vanish.

When she was near the bottom, Mark held out his hand to her. She hesitated a moment, then to my amazement, she took it and let him help her down. I felt a burst of admiration for the patient way he dealt with her.

A gust of wind blew the door open with a whoosh. It banged shut again, but not before a figure in a blue, hooded rain jacket stepped inside. The woman dropped Mark's hand and backed up against the ladder. He turned around. "Who is it?"

The figure removed his hood. "Tony Venezia. I'm a private investigator looking for Sheila Kavanagh. I have reason to believe this woman's her."

"You followed me!" I blurted.

Venezia, Mark and the woman all stared at me. "Yup," Venezia said, "I figured you'd lead me to her eventually."

"She's really . . . Sheila?"

"Maybe. The old man saw a faint resemblance. Okay, babe, let's see if you are." He started toward her. She went into a crouch and bared her teeth.

Mark stepped between them. "Leave her alone."

Venezia continued advancing. "Outta my way." Mark held his ground. Venezia pulled a gun and waved it at him. "Put your hands up and go over to that wall." Mark did.

I inched toward the door. Venezia spun around. "You, too, Miranda."

I went and stood next to Mark, my heart racing.

"You're making a big mistake," Mark said.

"I'll be the judge of that." Venezia motioned at the woman with the gun. "C'mon, I haven't got all day." He moved closer. She growled. I glanced at Mark. He lowered his hands and thrust his chest forward like an animal straining at the leash.

"Don't," I whispered.

Venezia must've heard me because he pivoted and aimed the gun at Mark. "Uh-uh," he said. The woman lunged, snarling, at Venezia's legs. The gun went off as he fell sideways. Mark slumped. "Get her off me!" Venezia screamed. He thrashed on the ground, struggling to free himself from the teeth sunk into his shins.

I grabbed an oar from a hook on the wall and brandished it over Venezia and his attacker. "Stop it!"

The woman lifted her head. Her eyes locked with mine. The next instant, she let go of her prey and sped past me out the door.

CHAPTER 37

*"Soon all the boats but Starbuck's were dropped; all the boat
sails set—all the paddles plying; with rippling swiftness, shooting
to the leeward; and Ahab heading the onset."*

—Moby-Dick

I left Venezia writhing on the floor and ran to Mark. Propped
against the wall, he was clutching his thigh. "Are you hurt?"

"It's just a flesh wound." He fumbled in his pocket and
removed a walkie-talkie. "I'll call Security."

"Gimme that." Venezia stood next to us with the gun.

Reluctantly, Mark surrendered the walkie-talkie. Venezia
waved the gun at me. "Your cell phone, too, Miranda." I gave it
to him. Keeping the gun trained on us, Venezia backed toward
the door. "You try and follow me, I'll shoot." He slammed the
door. I ran to it.

"No, Miranda!" Mark cried. "Give him room."

"But you're hurt."

"No reason for you to get shot, too." He took a step forward,
but immediately winced with pain.

"I'll wait."

When Mark gave me the high sign, I opened the door slowly
and peered out. The coast looked clear. Keeping an eye out for
Venezia, I took off for the security office at the edge of the village green. I hadn't gone far when I noticed a figure in the sea-
green slicker of a museum staffer approaching. "Help!" I yelled.

The figure dashed over. "Miranda—what . . . ?"

I stared into Erin's rain-splattered face. "Mark's been shot."

"Shot!"

"The private investigator did it. He's after the homeless woman. Call Security on your walkie-talkie."

As she made the call, we ran toward the sail loft building. The security guard caught up with us at the entrance. Erin hugged her brother, then let the guard examine the wound. "Doesn't look too bad." He removed a first-aid kit from his pack and cleaned and bandaged the wound. "You better see a doctor, though." The guard helped Mark up, and the four of us made our way to the door, Mark limping, with an arm slung around the guard's shoulder.

Outside, Erin suddenly stopped and stared at the waterfront. "The *Sheila Anne*'s gone!"

"You're kidding."

"No. Look." Erin pointed toward the dock and I saw the empty berth. She peered out the Spouter River. "I think that's her over there."

"Where?"

"On this side of the drawbridge."

I glimpsed a sloop stopped in front of the drawbridge. The bridge was down, but as we watched, it began to rise.

Erin's eyes shifted from the sailboat to the departing figures of her brother and the security guard and back again. Her expression went through a series of rapid changes, as if she were making up her mind. She grabbed my arm. "Let's go."

"Huh?"

"We can't let whoever it is take the *Sheila Anne* out in weather like this. They'll wreck her."

"But—"

"C'mon. If we hurry, we might be able to catch her before the drawbridge goes up all the way. There's a speedboat over at the boat rental place we can use."

"Wait. I think someone's already going after her." I gestured toward one of the other docks, where a figure was untying the rope of an inflatable boat with a motor. He pushed off and jumped in the boat. I caught a glimpse of a blue rain jacket. Venezia. Damn! If he was after the *Sheila Anne,* then the homeless woman must be on it.

Erin tugged on my arm. "C'mon, we're wasting time."

"No!" I protested. "The homeless woman's on the *Sheila Anne,* and the PI's after her. He's got a gun."

"I don't care." Pivoting, she raced toward the boathouse.

"You're crazy!" Or rather we were both crazy, because in that moment I knew I'd go with her. I ran after her, catching up just as she was getting into the speedboat. I hopped in and Erin started the motor.

We got underway none too soon. Without waiting until the bridge was fully raised, the *Sheila Anne* gilded beneath it, its mast so close to the underside of the bridge I was sure it would splinter. Erin must have been thinking the same thing. Her mouth was agape with surprise and alarm. We'd lost our chance of catching up with the *Sheila Anne* while she was stopped, but so had the PI. The inflatable's engine must have stalled because we saw him struggling to restart it halfway between us and the drawbridge. He got it going and sped toward the bridge.

By the time we reached the drawbridge, it had begun to descend again. *London Bridge is falling down,* I thought nonsensically, as we went under. I knew it was irrational because we had plenty of room, but I still had a vision of the huge, gray monster crushing us.

Once we'd cleared the bridge, I craned forward, peering into the rain after the *Sheila Anne* and the inflatable. The sailboat still had a good lead, but we were gaining on the inflatable. As we closed in on it, Venezia slowed and turned halfway around.

Keeping one hand on the tiller, he fired at us with the other.

"Get down!" Erin cried. I crouched in the bottom of the speedboat.

"You, too!" I said as Venezia aimed at her.

Erin shook her head. "I'm going to try to get past him."

He fired. She ducked at the last minute. I pulled her down the rest of the way and held her there.

"Too dangerous." We huddled in the speedboat while Venezia fired more shots at us. Then, apparently satisfied he'd frightened us off, at least for the moment, he went after the sailboat at full throttle.

"Damn." Erin frowned at his departing wake. "I hoped we'd catch up with the *Sheila Anne* while she's still on the river, before she passes into the Fishers Island Sound, but now it doesn't look like that's gonna happen."

"Why the river rather than the Sound?" I asked.

"It's a lot rougher on the Sound," Erin said.

We started after the inflatable, keeping a safe distance between us. On either side, I could make out the dim outlines of the riverbanks. Eventually, they melted away, and we were in the open waters of the Sound. The wind increased to gale force, and the waves spiked from one foot to five feet and higher. *Bam, bam, bam!* The speedboat pounded through the waves like a truck on a bumpy road. I clung to my seat, teeth rattling, as I was jolted from head to toe. My only consolation was that it would be harder for Venezia to shoot at us here than in the more confined space of the river.

The waves sometimes blocked our view of the inflatable, but we could usually make out the white sail of the *Sheila Anne*. Then, as we dipped into an especially deep trough, the *Sheila Anne* disappeared. When we came out of the trough, the *Sheila Anne*'s sail was no longer there. The bare mast swayed back and forth like a tree in the wind.

"Do you see what I see?" I shouted to Erin.

"Yup. No sail. She must've run into trouble and had to take it down."

"Now that the sailboat's dead in the water, we should be able to get to her."

"Right. If the PI doesn't get there first."

Venezia must have had the same thought. The next thing we knew, we spotted the inflatable coming at us. When Venezia was within range, he started shooting. Erin turned the speedboat around and we fled, increasing the distance between us and the sailboat, but also drawing the pursuing inflatable further away from it. After a while Venezia turned around and headed toward the sloop, which was still without its sail and foundering in the waves. We followed him and he chased us away again. We played this game of advance and retreat until Venezia apparently tired of it and made a beeline for the sailboat.

We followed at a safe distance. As we approached the *Sheila Anne,* we glimpsed a figure moving on deck. The sail began to rise just as the inflatable pulled alongside. A second figure joined the one already on deck. The two figures merged into one, separated, and merged again like dancers in a strange tango. Then they vanished altogether. The sail remained where it was, only four or five feet up the mast.

"I don't like the looks of this," Erin said. She gunned the motor and we rocketed toward the *Sheila Anne.* When we were close, Erin steered the speedboat alongside the sloop and cut the engine. The inflatable was tied to the railing of the *Sheila Anne,* but there was no sign of Venezia or the homeless woman. Erin and I exchanged worried glances. "I'll go first," she volunteered.

With the speedboat's rope in hand, she sprang up onto the deck of the sailboat. The force of her movement pushed the speedboat away from the *Sheila Anne.* A widening gap of water separated the two boats. Panicking, I jumped too soon, grabbing wildly at the safety line that ran around the side of the boat. Erin let go of the rope, and caught first one of my arms, then the other. I clung to her for dear life. She strained over the edge. For a moment it looked like she'd either have to let go or be pulled into the water herself. Then, with a sudden burst of strength, she hauled me on board. We sprawled on deck, breathing hard.

"All that work for nothing," a voice behind us said.

CHAPTER 38

"But suddenly as he peered down and down into its depths, he profoundly saw a white living spot no bigger than a white weasel, with wonderful celerity uprising, and magnifying as it rose, till it turned, and then there were plainly revealed two long crooked rows of white, glistening teeth . . ."

—Moby-Dick

Venezia stood over us with the gun. "Looks like you lost your boat." He gestured toward the speedboat, now drifting away. "Too bad we can't all fit in the inflatable."

"Where's the woman?" I asked.

"Stowed in the forward berth. We got into a fight, and she fell down the companionway, taking me with her. Hit her head and knocked herself out. She's coming with me. You're staying behind. You could try sailing back, but it's gonna be hard with your hands tied. You." He waved the gun at Erin. "Get some rope and tie up your friend."

Erin pointed at a coil of rope on deck. "I'll have to cut a piece of that."

"All right, but no funny business."

Erin removed her rigger's knife from her belt and held it up so he could see.

"Do it!" Venezia cried impatiently. Erin picked up one end of the coil and made as if to cut it. The next instant, she flung the entire coil at Venezia. It looped around him like an octopus. He dropped his gun as he struggled to free himself. Erin spun around and sawed at the line that attached the inflatable to the *Sheila Anne* with her knife. I went for Venezia's gun. My fingers were just about to close on it when Venezia stepped down hard on my hand. I withdrew my fingers with a cry of pain. Venezia grabbed the gun and shook it at me in a threatening way. "Oughta shoot you. Or at the very least pistol whip you."

"I wouldn't do that if I were you," Erin said. "Gonna need all the help you can get if you want to get back to shore."

"Whaddya mean?"

"Looks like you lost your boat, too." She pointed at the inflatable's severed line.

"Bitch!" Venezia shrieked. He lurched to the edge of the *Sheila Anne*. For a moment I thought he'd jump in after the inflatable. It bobbed in the water, a dark, rapidly diminishing shape. Venezia turned back to us. "You'll pay for this. But first you're gonna sail us back to Spouters Point. Take the wheel and get us headed in the right direction."

"We can't go anywhere until we've raised the sail," Erin said. "I need Miranda's help with that."

"Okay, but don't try anything, because this time I'll shoot." Venezia positioned himself by the companionway, keeping his gun trained on us.

Erin and I went to the mast and began pulling on the halyard. The sail rose majestically upward. Rope giving way to wire, Erin wrapped the wire around the winch, while I held the rope. She cranked the winch tight, and I cleated down the halyard. A gust of wind filled the raised sail and the boom swung around. Caught unawares, Venezia didn't get out of the way in time. The boom whacked him in the head. He went down like a bowling pin. His gun flew from his hand, slid across the deck, and disappeared overboard. Venezia lay in a crumpled mass next to the companionway.

"Knocked silly," Erin said when we checked on him. "Better take him below and tie him up before he wakes up and causes more trouble." I dumped Venezia unceremoniously down the companionway and followed, closing the hatch behind me.

"While you're there, get me a safety harness and put one on yourself," Erin called after me.

After I'd tied up Venezia, I got two safety harnesses from a locker. Untangling the nylon straps of the harness, I put it on over the life jacket I already wore. Then I reopened the hatch.

Rain stung my face, and the wind whipped at me with such force I could barely keep my balance. The weather seemed to have gotten worse. Maybe that was because I'd had a brief reprieve. I would've given anything to go below again. Instead, I fought my way to where Erin stood at the wheel, grim-faced, legs apart, balancing herself on the cockpit floor as on a teeter-totter.

"We can't make it back to Spouters Point," she yelled. "We've drifted too far, and the wind's against us."

"What'll we do?" I knew I sounded frantic, but I couldn't help myself; the thought of being swept into the open sea was too terrifying.

"I think we can get to Fishers Island."

"Okay." I felt a tiny spurt of relief. At least we weren't being carried into the void.

"I'll stay at the helm. You go below and warm up." Erin reached for the safety harness. In my fright, I'd forgotten to give it to her.

"Sure?"

"Yes. If I need help, I'll call you."

I held the wheel while Erin put on her safety harness and fastened it to a nearby cleat. Then I scooted down the companionway like an animal returning to the safety of its burrow. Back in the cabin, I swaddled myself in a blanket.

"What about me? I'm cold, too," Venezia, now fully conscious, whined. I got another blanket and wrapped it around him.

The warmth felt wonderful. Soon, though, my sense of well-being gave way to claustrophobia. I felt trapped in a box that someone was violently shaking. I took a deep breath, fighting back the bile rising in my throat. Glancing at Venezia, I saw him watching me. "Untie me, and I'll give you half the million the old man's offering for his daughter's recovery. You could quit working, invest it, and live on the interest."

I pretended to consider his offer. "But if he thinks she's his daughter, why didn't he say so when I showed him the picture?"

"He's paranoid. Thought it was a scam, and hired me to see if you were legit."

"You followed me to the Sea Shanty, into the cattails, and hit me on the head?"

"Must've been her."

"But you were . . . the casino patron at the museum?"

"You gonna untie me or not?"

"What if she isn't Sheila?"

"One way to find out. Untie me and I'll show you."

"I don't know . . ." I stalled, hoping to string him along until I'd found out everything I could. I heard Erin's voice calling me. "I'm needed on deck," I told Venezia. "We'll talk more when I get back."

Bracing herself at the wheel, Erin looked pale and exhausted. "What is it?" I asked.

"I need to go forward to tighten a line. Can you take the helm while I do that?"

I nodded. As we changed places, Erin said, "Keep it as close to a hundred eighty degrees as possible. And watch out for rocks and reefs. The Sound's loaded with them." Erin pointed out a dark, forbidding shape on the GPS's sonar screen.

If I'd been bilious in the cabin, I was even more so now. My stomach flip-flopped every time the boat plummeted into the trough of a wave, and shot upward again. I tried to focus on the GPS screen, but the rain mostly obscured it. Why did I think I could keep nausea at bay when I'd gotten seasick just watching the movie *The Perfect Storm?* It took every ounce of strength I had just to stand there, my insides heaving, gripping the wheel, while the angry seas tossed the thirty-nine-foot sloop around as if it were a plastic toy.

Erin was only gone a minute or two, but it seemed like an eternity. To distract myself, I thought about what Venezia had told me. He'd said there was a way to find out if the homeless woman really was Sheila—a scar or birthmark on a part of her body hidden from view? I had to make him tell me.

Erin returned and we changed places carefully. Then I slid down the rabbit hole again. Venezia's eyes were closed, but they popped open almost immediately. "Gonna untie me?" The woman in the forward berth moaned and shifted her body slightly.

"How do we find out if she's Sheila?"

"Untie me."

"Tell me."

We volleyed these two phrases back and forth several more times. Then, in my best wheedling tone, I said, "Come on. Aren't you dying to know? I would be if I were you. 'Cuz if she's not Sheila, your efforts will've been wasted."

Venezia cocked his head and looked thoughtful. "All right," he said finally. "It's the watch. Sheila had it inscribed to him. Alex what's-his-name."

Nothing to it, I thought as I started toward the forward berth. Or was there? I remembered how she'd bitten Venezia. But he was the enemy, while she might not feel threatened by me.

Sensing my hesitation, Venezia said, "I could check but—" He held up his linked hands.

"No way."

"While you're there, have a look at that thing she's got around her neck and tell me if it's a finger bone."

I drew back with horror. "What're you saying?"

"Don't play dumb. You've seen how she likes to use her teeth."

"But—"

"The watch," he prodded.

Before I could change my mind, I strode to the berth. The woman lay on her side with her arms folded across her chest. The bone on its leather string rested on the cushion near her head. Was it a finger bone? I couldn't be sure. I forced myself not to think about how she might have gotten it if it was. One thing at a time: see if there was an inscription on the watch. I started to unfasten the clasp.

"Look out! She's trying to steal your watch!" Venezia shouted.

The woman sprang into motion, a kicking, clawing, biting fury. I felt a stinging pain in my forearm where her teeth broke the skin. I wrenched my arm away, but she hurled herself after me, knocking me down. We rolled on the cabin floor, each trying to get the upper hand. She got on top, legs straddling me, pinning me down. She wasn't heavy, but she was strong. I twisted beneath her, struggling to fend off her scratching nails, her biting teeth. I slapped at her face and hands. She found an opening in my flailing fingers and butted her head through, teeth aimed at my neck. I caught her chin with the heel of my hand, jerking her head back. She hit and clawed my upraised arm, nails raking the bite wound.

My heart jumped into overdrive. I went crazy with pain. All I could think about was destroying the beast that was hurting me so much. With a supreme effort, I heaved myself out from under the beast, and clambered on top. Grabbing it by the hair, I pounded its head into the floor. Somewhere, faraway, someone was calling to me, but I couldn't make out the words. It was as if the volume had been turned way down. I couldn't even hear the noise the thing in my hands must've made when it struck the floor. Again and again and again.

There was an awful crash. I was thrown off the beast into something hard. Everything went black.

CHAPTER 39

"Retribution, swift vengeance, eternal malice were in his whole aspect, and in spite of all that mortal man could do, the solid white buttress of his forehead smote the ship's starboard bow, till men and timbers reeled."

—*Moby-Dick*

I came to, dazed and aching. The cabin was a shambles. Books had fallen from the shelves. Drawers had emptied, spilling bottles, cans, cups, plates and utensils onto the floor, now a minefield of broken glass and crockery. The homeless woman lay at the foot of the stove. Her eyes were closed and there was a trickle of blood at her lips. Dead or merely unconscious? Venezia was slumped nearby, his eyes also closed. I wondered about him, but not for long.

He groaned and rubbed his eyes. "Feel like I was dumped from a fast-moving car."

His gaze flicked from me to the woman. "Christ Almighty! Is she . . . ?"

"I don't know." I crawled over and was about to feel her pulse when I remembered how she'd attacked me earlier when I thought she was unconscious. Grabbing a shard of crockery with one hand, I checked her pulse with the other. While my finger was pressed to her wrist, I noticed the watch. Quickly unclasping it, I examined the back of the face. "To Alex from

Sheila with love," the inscription read. "She's alive and she *is* Sheila."

"That's a relief. I thought you'd killed her."

"Me?" A horrific memory returned. A memory of the time my brain had shut down to the point that my one thought was to destroy the thing that was causing me such pain.

"Then I'd have to kiss my cool million good-bye," Venezia was saying.

"You really are slime. You're only concerned about her because of the reward."

"Not true. I don't like to see anybody die. But it so happens this one's worth more to me alive than dead when all I'd get is a measly finder's fee."

I shook my head with disgust. Then I remembered Erin. She'd been on deck when disaster struck. I had to see if she was okay. I picked my way through the rubble to the ladder, and opened the hatch.

My heart skipped a beat when I saw she wasn't at the wheel. Oh, dear God, no! Then I spotted her. She'd been thrown from the cockpit, and the tether of her safety harness was tangled in the lifeline that went around the boat.

"What happened?" I asked as I helped her.

"We were caught in the curl of a big wave and knocked down."

"How'd we get up again?"

"The weight of the keel did it."

"Thank heaven!"

"How are the others?"

"Alive, but Sheila was knocked unconscious again."

"She's really Sheila? How do you know?"

I explained.

Erin let this sink in, then she said, "I better call the Coast Guard."

I fought back mounting panic. "It's that bad?"

"Yes. I should've called them a lot sooner, but I thought I could get us out of this. Now I don't know."

"I'll take over while you go below."

I took my position at the wheel and did my best to follow the course Erin had set, while avoiding rocks and reefs and another knockdown. No easy task, because I now ached all over and my forearm, where Sheila had bitten and scratched me, especially hurt. I was thankful when, minutes later, Erin joined me in the cockpit. "Did you reach the Coast Guard?"

"The radio's busted, but I've brought flares." Erin put one into a flare gun and shot it into the air.

It lit up the gray sky like a ray of hope, but as it faded, my heart sank. "Gonna try another?"

"Not yet. I've only got two left."

Omigod. Our situation appeared more and more hopeless. Still, I tried to put on a brave front. "I'm doing okay at the wheel. Why don't you go below and rest?"

Erin shook her head. "Rather stay here than with that creep. Offered me a big chunk of change if I untied him. When I refused, he fed me a crazy story about how you nearly killed Sheila."

"It's true. I did come close to killing her."

"What?" Erin stared at me, wide-eyed.

I explained about the attack and how the pain had driven me wild.

"She actually bit you?" Erin sounded appalled. "Human bites are dangerous. You better take care of it before it gets infected."

"I'll be all right."

"No, you need to . . ." Erin broke off as a cresting wave loomed in front of us. When we were safely over it, she shouted, "Know what I think? Bastard probably killed George. He'll do anything for a price."

"You might be right," I yelled back. "There's one way to find out."

"How?"

"Ask him."

"You really think you can get him to confess?"

"I'm going to try. Can I borrow your knife?"

Erin looked surprised, but gave me the knife, along with the two remaining flares to stash below. "Don't forget about your bite wound," she called after me.

Venezia was back on the couch, huddled in a blanket. "Gonna cut me loose now?" he asked when he saw the knife.

"Did you kill George Kavanagh?" I pointed the blade at him.

"I wasn't even on the job then. My girlfriend can vouch for me."

"The hell she can. You two argued outside the Spouters Point Inne. Then you went to your van, but you never left. I saw you."

"That doesn't mean I killed Kavanagh."

"Tell the truth." I brought the blade close to his face.

Venezia went bug-eyed with fear. "You wouldn't—"

"Why not? You shot Mark, fired at Erin and me, then you sicced Sheila on me. I've got a score to settle." I laid the blade against his cheek.

"Swear to God I didn't kill him! He was already dead when—" Venezia broke off.

"When you got there?" I finished.

Venezia nodded.

"But if Kavanagh was already dead, you must've been the one who stuck the killing lance through him and dumped him in the water. Why would you do that, unless you stood to gain from it?"

Venezia said nothing. He didn't have to. His guilt was written all over his face.

"You tampered with Kavanagh's body so you could claim

239

you killed him and cash in on his death with your employer?"

Venezia looked away. "Let's just say I saw an opportunity and took it. Now will you put that thing down before someone gets hurt?"

"People already have been hurt, thanks to you." I pressed the blade against his cheek in a fresh surge of anger. Then, restraining myself, I withdrew the knife and returned it to its sheath.

Venezia had filled in one piece of the puzzle, but the most important piece was still missing. I was back to square one when it came to the actual killer. Was it Jimmy, Higginbotham, or even Luke? Each had a motive, and each was probably capable of committing such a brutal murder. If I had it in me to kill, as I'd come close to doing with Sheila—albeit in self-defense—the others did, too.

Which of them was the most likely? Or was it someone I hadn't even considered yet? Pondering this, I surveyed the wreckage. I spotted the red cross on the first aid box. Erin had told me to take care of my bite wound. I might as well do that. Opening the box, I found a small bottle of antiseptic, rolled up my sleeve, and applied the medicine to the red gashes on my forearm. The stinging pain made me cry out. But with the pain came a revelation. There had been red gashes like mine on Kavanagh's neck. Human bite marks, according to the medical examiner. And now that I knew my attacker was Kavanagh's second wife, I realized she had probably attacked him, too. I didn't know what had happened on this very boat in the midst of an even worse storm. Perhaps I never would. But whether rightly or wrongly, Sheila might blame her husband for the loss of her lover and the ordeal she must've suffered, adrift on the open sea—blame him so much she'd tracked him down to exact a terrible, twisted revenge.

Some of what I was thinking must have been apparent on my face as I stared at Sheila, because Venezia said, "Scary, isn't she?

She's the one who should be tied up instead of me before she wakes up and—"

The next moment, the boat came to a horrible, crunching halt. I was hurled against Venezia. His eyes rolled in their sockets. "What happened?"

"We hit something. I'm going on deck."

Outside, the scene was nightmarish. The *Sheila Anne* was stuck on a rock. I could just make out part of its jagged shape beneath the swirling water. The rock held the *Sheila Anne* in its grip while the waves battered her mercilessly. Erin was folded over the wheel like a snapped twig. She must have been thrown against it when the boat struck the rock. I fought my way to her. She was alive but unconscious. Unfastening her safety harness from its cleat, I put my arms firmly under her armpits, and dragged her to the companionway. Then I half slid, half carried her down. I laid her on the aft berth and wrapped her tightly in a blanket.

"Omigod! Not her!" Venezia cried. "She was our only hope. Now we'll never get out of this alive!"

Thanks for the vote of confidence, I thought. But the truth was I was petrified, especially when I noticed a pool of water accumulating on the cabin floor.

"We've sprung a leak. Help me bail." I untied his hands, got two buckets, and we set up a relay system. When Venezia had filled a bucket, I took it up, dumped it into the self-bailing cockpit, and returned for another. The water was coming in faster than we could get it out. I felt like Mickey Mouse in *The Sorcerer's Apprentice.* Then I remembered the flares. If ever there was a time to use them, it was now.

On my next trip onto the deck with a full bucket, I took the flares with me. I deposited the water, and was just about to load a flare into the flare gun when I felt Venezia tugging hard on my elbow. "Die, die, we're going to die!" The flare slipped from my hand and disappeared into the foamy water.

"Damn it! You made me drop a flare. Now I've only got one left."

I tried to shake him off but he clung to me, bawling like a baby, demanding my attention. "Listen. Gotta listen. Can't have this on my conscience. Accident. Didn't mean to kill him."

"Kavanagh?" The sudden switch from denial to admission startled me. But terror does strange things to people; in Venezia's case, it loosened his tongue: "No, that Korean kid." He hurried on with his confession, as if afraid he'd run out of his allotted time. "Saw me dump Kavanagh overboard. Thought I'd killed him. Chased the kid and got 'im into my car. Escaped on the bridge. Caught 'im again. Struggled. He fell."

My brain snagged on the image of Winston flailing in the air as he went down. It couldn't have been more than a few seconds before he hit the water, but for him, confronting his worst fear, it must have seemed like forever.

"Didn't mean for him to die." Venezia's words snapped me back to the present. "Believe me, doncha?" He looked at me imploringly, seeking absolution.

"Yes, yes," I said, anxious to get on with the business of firing the last flare.

"Thank you. Thank you so much!" He moved away from me, toward the side of the boat.

"What're you doing?" He didn't answer but stood poised with his arms outspread in diving position. He'd gone mad. Stark, raving mad. "No!" I grabbed one of his arms.

"Leggo! Not staying on this frigging death ship." He shook me off and gave me a shove that sent me into the safety line. I felt like a boxer in the ring just before the final knockdown. I came back, swinging. My first blow missed completely, but the second clipped him on the jaw hard enough to make him reel backward. He lost his balance and fell. His head banged on the base of a winch, knocking him unconscious. I dragged him below and tied him up again.

Back on deck, the reality of my situation hit me with hurricane force. I was on a leaky boat, stuck on a rock, bashed by waves, with three unconscious people. Two of the three, Erin and Sheila, were experienced sailors, but if Erin had doubted her ability to get us safely to port, how could I, a mere novice, expect to? If help didn't come soon, the boat would sink and we'd all drown.

My hand shook as I loaded the gun with the last flare. With a silent prayer, I shot it into the air. A reddish glow illuminated the sky. I basked in its light as in the sun's warmth. But as the glow faded, so did the adrenaline that had carried me this far. I was numb from the cold, and drained of all energy. There was nothing more to do except go below and join the others in a slide toward oblivion that would eventually become permanent.

At the top of the companionway, I hesitated. Was that the roar of an engine? No. I must be hallucinating. Yet there it was again. My ears strained toward the sound, while my eyes sought its source. A wave loomed over the sailboat and blocked my view. A wall of water crashed on me, knocking me down. Luckily, my safety harness held firm. I struggled to my feet, tipping my head from side to side to get the water out of my ears, rubbing my eyes to clear my vision. Squinting into the storm, I could just make out the dim outline of a ship. I shouted and waved my arms wildly to attract the attention of someone on board. It was no use. The ship was too far away. I felt like a castaway on an island, watching her one chance of rescue slip away.

I was stuck where I was. Unless I could get the boat off the rock. This was a possibility I hadn't considered. When my car was stuck in the snow, I shoveled it out as best I could, then got in and jockeyed the vehicle back and forth until it was dislodged.

Could I accomplish a similar feat with the sailboat? It was worth a try.

But to even try, I needed to channel Erin. What would she do in this situation? For a long moment, my mind remained blank. Then, it was as if a flare was fired inside my brain. I studied the position of the boat in relation to the waves. They were hitting it broadside, risking another knockdown. But if I got the boat pointed more into the weather? I turned the wheel as far as it would go in that direction. Then I let out the sail. Nothing happened.

This is crazy; you'll never get off the rock, an inner voice said.

Oh yes, I will, I shot back. I turned the wheel and played with the sail to better utilize the combined force of wind and water. Miraculously, the right wave came at the right moment, lifting the sailboat off its rocky trap.

Now, all I had to do was find the other boat before the *Sheila Anne* became a watery tomb.

CHAPTER 40

"Buoyed up by that coffin, for almost one whole day and night, I floated on a soft and dirge-like main. The unharming sharks, they glided by as if with padlocks on their mouths; the savage sea-hawks sailed with sheathed beaks. On the second day, a sail drew near, nearer, and picked me up at last."

—Moby-Dick

"I still can't believe you got the sailboat off that rock, and made it to the cutter." Mark sat beside my gurney at the hospital in New London.

"I can barely believe it myself," I said. "I wouldn't have even tried if you and Luke hadn't gotten the Coast Guard to search for us. How are the others doing?"

"Erin's got a couple of broken ribs, but she's awake and they've given her something for the pain. The PI's also conscious, and the police are with him."

"What about Sheila?"

"She came to when they were taking her for a CT scan. Became so agitated they had to restrain her and give her a tranquilizer."

"What about the CT scan?"

"They're pretty sure it's just a concussion."

"That's a relief." I would've never forgiven myself if Sheila had suffered serious brain damage at my hands.

"They're contacting her father."

"I need to make a call myself."

Mark gave me his cell phone and tactfully withdrew. I dialed Nate's number. I didn't expect to reach him, but figured I might as well try. To my amazement, he answered.

"Nate! Are you okay?"

He mumbled something, then the line went dead. Damn! At least I'd heard his voice, knew he was still alive. I looked up to see Curtin standing in the doorway. "What're you doing here? You're supposed to be—"

"We called off the search because of the weather. When I got back to the station, there was a message from Luke. By the time I reached him, he was on his way to the hospital. I've seen Erin, but she's in no condition to talk. Told me I should speak with you. Ready to make a statement now, or should we wait?"

"Now."

I'd just about wrapped up my statement when a commotion in the hallway alerted us to Graf-Jones's arrival. Curtin opened the door and went out. I followed. Mark emerged from Erin's room and came and stood beside me.

Flanked by his bodyguard and a team of men in white coats, Graf-Jones strode down the corridor. A doctor came forward to greet him. So did Venezia with a uniform on either side of him. "Boy, am I glad to see you," Venezia said. "Now you can explain to these officers that I was acting on your instructions when—"

"Where is she?" Graf-Jones interrupted, addressing the doctor instead of Venezia.

The doctor pointed at a closed door. Graf-Jones went in. He came out almost immediately, his face livid. "What have you done to her?"

"She was very agitated when she regained consciousness. We had to restrain her to keep her from hurting herself or the staff. She's also been sedated."

"That was hardly necessary," Graf-Jones said. "Remove the

restraints and get her ready to leave. I'm having her transferred to a private facility. The ambulance should be here any minute." He looked at his watch and tapped his foot impatiently.

The doctor glanced from Graf-Jones to his bodyguard and the men in white coats and back again. "All right. But you'll have to sign some forms." He told the nurse to get these, and summoned two strong-looking orderlies to prepare Sheila for another ambulance trip.

"I went to a lot of trouble to find her for you," Venezia said, "so I hope you'll let the police know I was only acting in the line of duty."

"I'll deal with you later," Graf-Jones said brusquely. The nurse brought the forms, he skimmed and signed them, then returned to his foot tapping. "I don't understand what's keeping the ambulance," he complained.

Curtin approached Graf-Jones. "I need to have a word with you."

The bodyguard stepped between them. "What about?" he demanded gruffly.

Graf-Jones waved the bodyguard aside and nodded at Curtin to continue. "It has to do with your daughter," Curtin said. "Charges will be brought against her. I need to know where you're taking her."

"Charges!" Graf-Jones sounded shocked and indignant.

The two men moved down the corridor out of earshot. Curtin spoke in a low voice, every now and then gesturing at Mark and me. When they were finished, Graf-Jones conferred briefly with his bodyguard, then came over to us.

"I apologize for any trouble you may have experienced on account of my daughter. As you are undoubtedly aware, she is not herself, and cannot be held responsible for her actions. However, I wish to make amends. My attorney will be in touch with you shortly."

In other words, he thought he could buy us off. I felt a surge of anger. I opened my mouth to protest, but Graf-Jones had already turned away. The EMTs had arrived and were rolling a gurney into Sheila's room.

As they wheeled her out, Sheila half rose and looked wildly around. She let out a cry that was part groan, part growl. Graf-Jones took her hand and bent over her. "It's all right, my dear."

Sheila snarled and clawed at his face. He recoiled, hand on his scratched cheek. The EMTs tried to hold Sheila down, but she was too much for them. It took the bodyguard and a couple of burly orderlies to control her. "Idiots!" Graf-Jones fumed. "You've given her the wrong medication. It's made her worse, not better."

"What do you want us to do?" the doctor flared. "Give her something that will knock her out completely?"

"She needs a different medication," Graf-Jones snapped. The two men scowled at each other. Mark limped into the breach. "Let me talk to her." At the sound of his voice, Sheila moaned and strained toward him. Graf-Jones signaled to the men around her to step aside. Mark spoke softly to her. We couldn't hear what he said, but his words had a calming effect. Sheila settled back on the gurney.

Graf-Jones looked at Mark with amazement. "Thank you," he said simply. I was stunned. Graf-Jones had such an air of entitlement that, until now, I wouldn't have expected him to thank anyone for anything. I could only imagine what an effort those two words cost him.

"I could ride in the ambulance with her if you think it would help," Mark offered.

"No, Mark," Jane said firmly.

Graf-Jones's lizard-like eyes rested briefly on Mark's very pregnant wife before returning to Mark. "That is very kind of you, but unnecessary." He nodded at the medical personnel who had come with him. One of them jabbed a needle into Sheila's arm, and she lay still. "Perhaps you can visit Sheila when she is feeling better," Graf-Jones told Mark. "Right now, it is important to get her to a place where she can be properly cared for."

At a signal from Graf-Jones, the EMTs began to push Sheila's gurney toward the exit.

"What about me?" Venezia called.

"You're coming with us." Curtin and the two other uniforms closed in on him.

"Why? I haven't done anything wrong," Venezia protested. "I was just doing my job. Ask my employer. He'll vouch for me. Anson, Mr. Jones, Mr. Anson Graf-Jones," he shouted after Graf-Jones's departing figure. "Remember me, Tony Venezia? I'm the guy who brought your daughter back. You gotta talk to these cops."

The procession halted in front of the exit. "See, they're stopping," Venezia said excitedly. "He'll come back and straighten things out for me."

The bodyguard opened the door to let Graf-Jones and the others pass through. "No!" Venezia cried as the door shut behind them.

CHAPTER 41

"For all his tattooings he was on the whole a clean, comely looking cannibal. What's all this fuss I have been making about, thought I to myself—the man's a human being just as I am: he has as much reason to fear me, as I have to be afraid of him."
—Moby-Dick

The Spouters Point Museum hadn't opened yet when I arrived. It was a beautiful fall morning, cool but with clear skies and calm water unlike the torrential rain and rough chop of a few weeks ago. Mark met me at the side entrance behind the Spouters Point Inne. He looked a lot better than he had at the hospital in New London, though I noticed he still limped slightly when he opened the gate and stepped aside to let me in. "How are you?" I asked.

He shrugged. "I can't complain. How about you?"

"I can't complain either. Where's Erin? I thought we were having breakfast together."

"She and Luke went out for an early morning sail in one of the cat boats."

"Whose idea was that?"

"Luke's. I suspect it's his way of trying to clear the air, make peace with her. Let's wait for them at the wharf."

We sat down at the end, dangling our legs over the water like two carefree kids. But my thoughts were anything but carefree. Especially when Mark picked up his mandolin and played the first plaintive measures of "The Maid on the Shore."

"I wonder what happened on the *Sheila Anne* and afterward to make Sheila so . . ." I paused, searching for the right word.

"Savage?" Mark said. "I have an idea, based on things she said at different times. Confused me with another person. Called me Alex."

"After Alex Broussard, her lover?"

"Yes, though I didn't know it then. She said she always believed I'd come back, that what happened to me was simply a bad dream. We were supposed to live, not her husband. It made her furious when she found out he was still alive, while I'd been reduced to skin and bones, and finally just one bone."

Omigod. So Venezia was right; the bone around Sheila's neck was a human bone. "But if that's all that's left of Alex, then . . . ?"

Mark took a deep breath before continuing. "She talked about how I'd sacrificed myself so she could survive. She wasn't happy about it." He paused, tugged on his albatross earring, and shook his head. "No, that's putting it way too mildly. She was tormented by it. Kept saying she would've never done it if I hadn't begged her. Even then, it was wrong. She should've been the one to . . . to let me feed on her."

"So she . . ." I couldn't bring myself to say the word, the taboo against it was so strong.

Mark frowned at the water, a faraway look in his eyes. "It's hard to believe someone could . . . do what she did. But imagine what it must've been like on the life raft out there in the middle of the ocean, as the days stretched on with no help in sight, and they grew weaker and weaker from hunger and thirst."

"I guess none of us know how we'll act in extreme situations," I said. "I certainly didn't."

Mark turned to look at me. "You mean when you got the boat off the rock and went after the Coast Guard cutter?"

"I'm talking about something really awful I did before that."

"You don't have to tell me, if you don't want to," Mark said quickly.

"I want to," I said with a defiant edge in my voice. I'd told Erin and now I might as well tell Mark how in a moment of blind fury I'd banged Sheila's head into the floor over and over again. "The worst part was that she stopped being a human and became an object I needed to destroy."

Mark raked his hand through his hair, causing strands to come loose from his ponytail and fall in a disorderly fashion around his face. "You were fighting for your life, Miranda. I just hope Sheila can find something to quiet her mind, unlike the maid in the song."

"Me, too." I looked out at the river and glimpsed a flutter of white sail. The cat boat glided across the water so effortlessly, it was hard to imagine sailing was anything but easy, that in a storm it could be fraught with peril. As the boat came closer, I saw that Luke held both tiller and sail, while Erin sat motionless in the bow. The breeze feathered her short hair into her face.

When the cat boat came alongside the dock, Mark caught the rope while Luke got out. The boat bumped against the dock and moved away. Luke held out a hand to Erin. She stood poised, arms at her sides, ready to hop out. At the last moment, she took his hand.

CHAPTER 42

"Now, there is this noteworthy difference between savage and civilized; that while a sick, civilized man may be six months convalescing, generally speaking, a sick savage is almost half-well again in a day. So, in good time my Queequeg gained strength . . ."

—Moby-Dick

"I asked each of you here for an important reason," Jimmy said. "Here" was the top of Stargaze Hill, where I'd come with Nate, Jimmy, Reba, Patty, Kyle and Russell Long Knife shortly after leaving Erin and her brothers.

"While I was hiding in the swamp, I had a dream," Jimmy continued. "An eagle first appeared to me on this hill, and he's been following me ever since. In the dream he told me I'd wronged several people. He said I needed to make amends. When I asked him how, he told me to listen to my heart. I tried, but heard only silence. I had this dream several nights in a row, but my heart did not speak until Nate and I had taken refuge in a cave in the swamp. I was wet, exhausted and still very frightened. Eventually I fell asleep. This time, the eagle guided me to a sleeping figure. It was turned away from me, its face in shadow. I lit a match and saw my own face. I put my ear against my twin's heart. It was beating like a tom-tom. Then, as the thumps grew fainter and fainter, my heart spoke to me."

Jimmy took a deep breath, summoning up his courage.

"Please join hands and form a circle." When we were all in place, Reba let go of Nate's hand to make room for Jimmy, who stood in the middle of the circle, the odd man out. Jimmy stayed where he was. "I'm not worthy to join you." He went over to Russell and knelt at his feet, his head bowed.

"Russell Long Knife, I have wronged you. I was foolish to think I could beat you in the fancy dance contest. Greedy, too. When the white man came to me with his betting scheme and offered me a cut of his winnings, I agreed, even though I knew it was a bad thing. Then, when I realized I couldn't win, I rubbed a chemical on your dance stick to make you drop it. I paid a boy to run off with the stick, so my treachery wouldn't be discovered. You lost and I won unfairly." Reaching into a backpack he'd brought with him, Jimmy withdrew an envelope and held it out to Russell. "The prize money belongs to you."

"Damned straight it does," Russell muttered, snatching the envelope from Jimmy's hands.

He took out the bills and made a show of counting them. Nate squeezed my fingers in his, as he might have wrung Russell's neck. Jimmy, meanwhile, was rummaging in the backpack. He produced a dance stick. "This stick is to replace the one I ruined."

Russell grabbed the stick and raised it over Jimmy's head, ready to strike. "I ask for your forgiveness," Jimmy said.

Russell raised the stick higher. Nate strained forward, while Reba and I tried to hold him back, as the stick sped downward. Inches short of Jimmy's head, Russell slowed the motion so that what would have been a blow became a gentle tap on the head. "I forgive you," he said gruffly.

We all heaved a sigh of relief. *The hardest part is over,* I thought, as Jimmy continued around the circle, asking for forgiveness and presenting each person with a small gift. There were emotional moments, but for the most part, the ceremony proceeded smoothly.

Yet watching it, I didn't feel calm. I was absorbing too much tension from Nate. He shifted from one foot to the other, his eyes darted from Jimmy to me and back again, and his hand alternately clasped and unclasped my fingers, all of which suggested conflicted feelings—about the occasion, or me? We'd told each other about our different ordeals—his in the swamp, mine on the sailboat—in exhaustive detail. Still, I sensed Nate was holding something back. I was, too. I had yet to tell Nate about the moment I'd turned into a killing machine.

Nate's toe brushed against mine. Jimmy stood before me. "You don't need to—" I began. But he had already knelt.

"My evil touched your life also," he said. "It was like a pebble thrown into the water, creating ripples that spread outward."

I gazed around the circle. Everyone was staring at me. Russell had a slight smirk on his face. Probably he expected me to make a fool of myself. Nate looked concerned. Perhaps he was worried about how I'd handle things. I was worried myself. I was painfully aware of being the only white woman in the group. I felt self-conscious in the same way I had the evening I'd first met Jimmy and his family.

"Miranda, I have wronged you," Jimmy went on. "You love my brother, and he loves you. But my evil drove you apart. I ask your forgiveness." He looked at me imploringly. Nate clasped my hand tightly.

"I forgive you," I said softly.

Jimmy took what looked like a small wooden salad bowl out of the backpack and handed it to me. I reached for the bowl too quickly and dropped it. Russell suppressed a chortle. A prickly heat spread over my face, as I bent to retrieve the bowl and the small drawstring bag that had fallen out of it. Jimmy picked them up and gave them to me.

"Sorry," I said.

"My fault. I let go too soon."

The drawstring bag that came with the bowl contained several purple-and-white shells. "A hubbub set," I said.

"Nate told me how much you enjoyed the game." Jimmy smiled. My feelings of embarrassment vanished in the warmth emanating from him. I smiled back.

Jimmy knelt before Nate. "My brother, I have wronged you," he said in a voice husky with emotion. I understood now why he'd saved Nate to the last. Nate's forgiveness was the most important to him, and therefore the most difficult to ask for.

"When I was down and out, you helped me get back on my feet. You had faith in me, but I betrayed your trust. I don't deserve your forgiveness, yet—"

Nate's arm swung outward. He looked like a bear about to take a swipe at its cowering victim. Instead, he grabbed Jimmy and held him in a wrestling grip that became an embrace. They clung to each other for a long moment. When they separated, Jimmy pressed a small stone into Nate's hand.

His gaze swept the circle. "Thank you. Thank you all." He went over to Kyle, and was about to lift him up when Russell intervened. "Let me carry him."

They started toward the trail, Kyle holding Jimmy's upraised hand and looking anxious as he rode on Russell's shoulders. The others slowly followed. I turned to join them, but Nate motioned me to stay. When everyone was out of earshot, he drew himself up in a stance that would have been menacing if he hadn't immediately lowered his shoulders and removed his dark glasses.

"Something I've been meaning to say, but couldn't until now. I care a lot about you, Miranda, but you'd never know it the way I acted. Every time you suggested Jimmy might've done something wrong, I jumped on you for being racist. Same with the homeless woman. I told you to leave her alone because I thought she was an innocent victim and you were just making her life more miserable. Turns out you were right, and I was wrong."

"You're not the only one who was misled by her. Mark—"

"That's another place I went wrong," Nate interrupted. "I made helping Jimmy my number one priority and expected you to do the same at the expense of *your* friends. I never considered how you might feel when I asked you to check out Luke's alibi. Or that you might put yourself in danger while I was off chasing Jimmy in the West and later in the woods. When I think of what could have happened to you on the sailboat in the middle of that storm." He shuddered. "You forgave Jimmy, but can you ever forgive me?"

"I can and do! How could you even imagine I wouldn't?"

Nate let out his breath in a rush. He flung his arms around me with such force that we nearly went down together. We steadied ourselves, but continued to sway gently as if slow-dancing. All our differences seemed to vanish, along with our defenses.

"I'm in no hurry to leave this hill." Nate's fingers caressed my cheek.

"Me neither." I kissed his hand.

He took a step back and looked at me expectantly. "Well?"

ABOUT THE AUTHOR

Leslie Wheeler is an award-winning author of biographies and books about American history. *Loving Warriors,* her biography in letters of American feminist Lucy Stone, won the English Speaking Union's Ambassador of Honor award. Leslie now writes the Miranda Lewis mystery series. Previous titles are *Murder at Plimoth Plantation* and *Murder at Gettysburg.* Her crime stories have appeared in the anthologies *Wind Chill, Seasmoke, Still Waters,* and *Dead Fall.* A member of Sisters in Crime and Mystery Writers of America, she lives in Cambridge, Massachusetts, with her son, a cat and a host of fictional characters. In her spare time, she enjoys cooking, gardening and going out on other people's sailboats—provided they do all the work.